First Course

a novel

Jenn Bouchard

Relax. Read. Repeat.

FIRST COURSE
Jenn Bouchard
Published by TouchPoint Press
Brookland, AR 72417
www.touchpointpress.com

Copyright © 2021 Jenn Bouchard
All rights reserved.

ISBN-13: 978-1-952816-49-9

Editor: Jenn Haskin
Cover Design: David Ter-Avanesyan, Ter33Design
Author Photo: Sharona Jacobs
Cover images: Apron by chelovector/Shutterstock.com; Tiles by Vinko93/Shutterstock.com; Utensils by Wichittra Srisunon/Adobe Stock

Visit the author's website at www.jennbouchard.com
@JennBouchardBOS @JennBouchardBOS @jennbouchardbos

First Edition

Printed in the United States of America.

For Betsy A. and Paige S.

1 - Vienna

THE WAY TOO FAMILIAR OPENING bars of Billy Joel's "Pressure" pulsated from Cole's phone, telling him it was time to wake up. His lanky body—clad only in plaid boxers—showed no signs of stirring. Suppressing a groan, I reached over him to shut off the alarm, and I kicked my boss out of bed. He needed to get in the shower and get to work before I did.

"You know that he's been on the phone pacing in his office for twenty minutes," Blair said to me as soon as I walked into my cubicle in our River North office about an hour later on that mid-June morning. He was sitting in my chair when I arrived, thumbing absentmindedly through papers on my desk.

"Really?" I whispered, glancing over at Cole's windowed closed door and swatting Blair's hand off my stuff. Cole was the only person at *Young Chicago* with a door that closed.

"How *was* he this morning?" asked Blair dramatically, in a hushed voice. I raised an eyebrow at him and shrugged my shoulders, feigning a faux innocence. Blair always tried to magnify the forbidden soap opera quality of my relationship, and I tried not to play into it. "Come on, Janie," he continued. "I am assuming that Mr. Emerson got that Northwestern travel mug from you, my love. Maybe you should add a UCLA one to your collection. Frannie the accountant might be getting suspicious."

"It's a local university. He could've gotten it from anyone." But he was right. In my bleary-eyed morning state, I hadn't even thought about the travel mug situation. Maybe Cole would like a mug from his alma mater for Christmas. I never knew quite what to get for him, as you can only buy someone so many live Billy Joel recordings. And then there was the age difference. Cole was 14 years older than me, and despite his relative immaturity, it was tough to figure out what to buy a guy in his late thirties with a trust fund. Nothing really impressed him. A travel mug might be nice.

"Earth to Janie," said Blair. "You look tired. Late night alphabetizing Mr. Hollywood's Billy Joel CDs? People his age still listen to CDs, right?" he asked teasingly. He was lucky that I liked him so much. I looked back over at Cole's office. Cole was now sitting in a chair, gripping his forehead, still on the phone. Things were not looking good.

"Okay, get out of my office. I need to write about these new tattoos that people are getting on their wrists. Apparently, this is all the rage around the city right now," I said, trying to distract myself with work.

Blair chuckled. "Imagine what those are going to look like when these babes are 70 and their skin is wrinkled and saggy. No one is going to know that's a flower or a clover or whatever. It'll look like the grandkids got them with a Sharpie," he said, examining his own unadorned wrists. "God help me if the boys all start getting them, too."

"Ahh, but that's why they will need to go to their dermatologists who can either remove the tattoos or use the latest skin-tightening or smoothing procedure. See, Blair, they need us to tell them where to go and what to do. We provide such a service." I winked at him with false optimism. From the looks of things in Cole's office, something was happening, and it wasn't good. "And we can then change our name to *Old* Chicago. Which sounds way too much like Old Style Beer, and then *your* community won't want to read us anymore, which is like half of our readership. But I digress. Go get something done!" I pushed him out of my cube and pretended to close my nonexistent door behind him.

I tried to push the feeling of dread out of my mind, knowing that Cole was in some sort of distress in his office. With a name like *Young Chicago*, it was probably doomed from the start. No one quite knew what the intended audience of the free print monthly magazine was, given its title. Office managers of pediatric practices assumed it was a periodical geared towards youthful families in the metropolitan area and ordered cases of it for their waiting rooms. They were subsequently not amused to find articles about the newest martini bars on Rush Street and the hottest places to meet singles in the Lakeview neighborhood. Conversely, the "young" adults who might enjoy these vodka-soaked articles weren't sure if *Young Chicago* was actually meant for them. Needless to say, there were issues.

As a complimentary print publication, *Young Chicago* relied heavily on advertising for its survival. From my first day as a twenty-two-year-old employee straight out of Medill School of Journalism at Northwestern University until now, almost two years later, I was very happy not to have the responsibility of securing advertisers to keep our "little engine that could" afloat. In our relatively small office over the cubicle walls, I could feel the stress and frustration from my two co-workers whose sole purpose was to sell blocks of space to tanning salons, bikini waxing estheticians, liquor stores, and whoever else might appeal to Chicago's under-35 crowd. It was a tough job, and it seemed to be getting more challenging as time went on.

Despite the fact that I was worried about my boyfriend *and* boss, I tried to work. I talked to some tattoo artists as well as a few women who had gotten the tattoos. My attempt to write the article was half-hearted and weak as I knew something was wrong with Cole, so I surfed the web for funny clips of people yelling "Baba Booey!" at PGA tournaments to send to my sister. My 30-year-old sister Alyssa lived in our hometown of Concord, Massachusetts in a fairly buttoned-up existence with her husband and two children. She was tall, lean, classically beautiful with long brown hair and smooth, well-cared for skin, and dressed almost exclusively in Lilly Pulitzer. She went to daily exercise classes such as hot power yoga and frequently organized teacher appreciation weeks. Howard Stern was her top-secret guilty pleasure that she listened to in her car whenever she could sneak a few moments to herself. If the PTA moms knew who she really was, they would be horrified. I loved that she had a dark side.

The day slowly ticked on. Blair and I went out to lunch, forgoing our usual takeout sandwich or salad options for a sit-down lunch at nearby Hub 51, complete with a round of stiff cocktails. If the ship was possibly going down, we would sink with slightly less pain. Cole still had not left his office, and occasionally we could hear shouts and the sound of his slammed phone from the other side of his office door. He had not texted me or emailed me any edits on the outline of the tattoo story that I had sent to him mid-morning, which was very much unlike him. By three o'clock, Blair was looking on career websites for anyone seeking freelance journalist work. People worked all around us in our open-concept office, but as we approached the end of the day, tones became more hushed and fewer phones rang. There was a sinking feeling deep in my abdomen, and I don't think I was alone. These were journalists, and they had good instincts. When Cole emerged at 4:15 that afternoon and summoned everyone to gather outside of his office door, no one seemed particularly surprised. We were ready for our sentencing.

"Hi everyone," he mustered, with his voice cracking slightly. He was a tall, fairly handsome guy, and I loved him. I could tell that he was upset but was trying to stay strong for his employees, and I hated the distance that I had to maintain at that moment. "I'm sorry that I haven't been very available to you today, but I have had to deal with some challenging communications from our parent company, Midwest Monthlies. They were purchased by a larger corporation this morning named National Print and Digital, and they are scrapping anything that hasn't been profitable in the past year. As you know, we have struggled lately with finding our niche market and keeping our core advertisement base. This is no one's fault; we are in a tough business as you are fully aware. You will all hear from the HR department at NPD in the next week as they work out severance and COBRA for your healthcare." He paused, looking out over all of us. This was the most serious and flustered I had ever seen him. Cole wasn't always the most mature, the most centered person—he had lived a fairly comfortable and spoiled existence—but at this moment, he noticeably felt the weight of the situation and the lives standing before him. "I am terribly sorry, you guys. I believed in us and what we were doing here. We had a really good run. If anyone needs a reference, give 'em my cell. I'll vouch for all of you." He sighed and shook his head, as if he was still in disbelief by what had transpired in just a few hours. "Now we need to pack up our shit and won't be able to get back in the building tomorrow. I am going to see if maintenance has any empty boxes to help people haul crap out of here. Let me know if you need anything." He lowered his head and walked back into his office, keeping the door open this time.

Like everyone around me, after we digested the confirmation of what we had begun to suspect that afternoon, I started to pack up my things. I had been at the magazine for over two years, starting as an intern during my senior year at Northwestern. As I gathered papers and knick-knacks, folders and pictures, I realized that the laptop and iPad on my desk were no longer mine. I started backing files up on flash drives and on Dropbox, grappling with the awareness that I was not only unemployed, but I also had no technological devices beyond an outdated iPhone. And I would now have to pay for the data charges. Dammit.

By six o'clock, the floor was haphazardly littered with discarded papers and food wrappers and cups, the evidence of once-loyal foot soldiers who were frustrated with their new situation. Everyone was gone, except for me sitting at an empty desk with a laptop wiped clean and a blank iPad. My belongings were in two cardboard boxes and my backpack, ready to go to my apartment. And Cole, who was still sitting in his office, had been drowning out the sounds of his former employees' packing with a stream of Billy Joel songs. For the past twenty minutes though, "Vienna," the song Cole always listened to when he was in an emotional funk, had played on repeat. It was time to intervene.

"Hi," I said, looking at the weary guy sitting back in his desk chair, hands folded behind his head, eyes closed. His dark hair was rumpled, evidence of him running his hands through it all day in frustration. The graying at his temples was more apparent, as the 38-year-old boy who in many ways had not wanted to grow up very much had been forced to age in the last ten hours.

Cole opened his eyes, looked at me, and gave a small smile. "What are you going to do now?" he asked.

Okay, small talk... we are getting back to more normal Cole-Janie relations. "I packed up everything into a couple of boxes and my backpack. I left the electronics on my desk. I think I will call an Uber and drop everything at my apartment. What do you want to do? Say 'fuck it' and book some last-minute outrageous dinner reservation? It doesn't matter who sees us together anymore. That's one bright spot." I tried to brighten my face with a hopeful grin, but it felt forced.

He let out a small chuckle. "No, I mean next. Life. What's next for Janie?" Billy Joel began singing "Vienna" again. It was definitely on a loop.

Oh. "I hadn't gotten that far yet. How about after I drop off my stuff, we at least go get a drink and brainstorm? We can save the outrageous dinner for another time." Perhaps the answer was in the glass of some kind of craft cocktail. In all honesty, I had no idea what a 24-year-old with a journalism degree and experience at only one publication was supposed to do next. Cole had plenty of contacts and could likely help me.

He stood up and started putting papers into his workbag. "I've got a flight to L.A. tomorrow morning."

His mom lived in Los Angeles. I had only met her once briefly, as she wasn't interested in coming to Chicago to visit (too cold and "Midwestern" for her, as she had stated). She was a semi-retired pop star, who had one hit song in the 1980s called "Hot Pink Love." The proceeds were enough that she didn't have to do much with her life to bring in steady income, and Cole was set up with regular financial disbursements. From what he had told me, she spent her days sitting at her pool and occasionally socializing with other aging "artists." She went by the name RoyalE and was very tan and very thin. As a potential mother-in-law, she seemed terrifying, and it was always a bit of a relief when Cole didn't ask me to come along on the flight to the West Coast. The miserable couple of hours I had spent with her over dinner at the Ritz Carlton in Lake Tahoe a few months earlier had been enough.

"When are you coming back?" I thought it was a fair question, but I wasn't sure that I was going to like the answer. It turns out that my instincts were spot-on.

Cole drummed his fingers on the desk, not looking up. "It's a one-way ticket." He opened his arms up, and I climbed into his lap. It felt strange to act this way in his office after hiding our situation from everyone around us for its tenure, but none of that mattered anymore. The magazine was done, and it looked like the relationship was as well. This felt like goodbye.

I tried to squash every biting, sarcastic, snarky comment that was bubbling up in my brain and throat at the moment. *Don't call him a mama's boy. Don't call him a trust fund baby. Don't tell him to grow up. Is this how I really see him???* "What will you do there?" I asked, attempting to keep my voice steady.

He sat up a bit straighter, forcing me to shift my seat on his knees. "No idea. What are you going to do here?" Point taken, but I guess I unrealistically expected more out of someone fourteen years my senior. *Anyway.*

"I guess I don't know either. We only get a month of severance so it's not much time to figure things out."

"Janie, Janie. You've got your life ahead of you. Don't just sit in your apartment making hors d'oeuvres for the next month." There was a distinct possibility that I was going to do that. With cocktails. Aesthetically beautiful and delicious cocktails. "You have so many talents, so many gifts. You need to share them with the world. Remember, *Vienna waits for you.*" I stared at him until he tapped on the framed, autographed picture of Billy Joel that still sat on his desk.

I got off of his lap and stood up. I felt anger building. *Enough.* "I've never understood this. What is Vienna? Am I traveling to Europe? I don't think so. I have thousands of dollars in student loans from Northwestern to pay." He was trying to be metaphoric and poetic, but he spoke from a different place than I did. He had "Hot Pink Love" money.

Cole gave a huge grin, disregarding my response that had bordered on yelling. I wanted to punch him in the face. "You'll find your Vienna. So will I. There's a big future out there for you, Janie. You're going to be great." He closed his eyes, sat back again in his chair, and started singing along with Billy. It was over. I stormed out, ordered an Uber from my phone, and got the hell out of there. Almost a year of my life and all I got was Vienna.

I CAME HOME TO SCARLETT sitting on the couch and Blair curled up on the oversized chair in the living room in a fetal position. He was clutching a Mike's Hard Lemonade like a baby bottle and looked like he was in pain. Scarlett was wearing her glasses and looked like the psychologist that she was in training to be.

I put down my boxes and backpack. "I think in the traditional office scenario, Scarlett would be sitting in the chair and Blair would be on the couch. We had Mike's in the fridge? Where did *that* come from?"

Blair sat up a bit. "I brought my own. I didn't know how late you would be with Mr. Hollywood, and I wasn't going to wait for you to make me one of your creations. Sigmund Freud over here is an excellent therapist, but drinks aren't her specialty."

I went right into the kitchen area and started pulling almost everything out of the refrigerator. "Mr. Hollywood is going to Hollywood. Or Malibu, to be exact. To *Mommy*."

Scarlett grimaced. "Sigmund Freud, it is. Yikes, Janie. It's over?" Scarlett had witnessed the entire evolution of our relationship, from him offering me an internship and hiring me three months later, to him seducing me through sending me very specific Billy Joel songs throughout the day for a week, veiled in his attempt to educate me in classic American rock. On the Friday that I received "She's Got a Way" and "Always a Woman," I texted him that I would

8

be at a bar around the corner after work. He showed up, we drank beer, and he kissed me about two hours later. From that moment on, we spent almost every evening together. This was a major life change, and Scarlett knew it.

I started chopping things. Garlic, onions, zucchini. Olive oil sizzling in a pan. Balsamic vinegar ready to reduce on the stovetop. Sliced baguette toasting in the oven. Prosciutto ready to julienne. "Yeah, I think it is. He's going there with no plans to return. He basically told me to figure out my future, although for him that means lying on a raft in his mom's pool. Is that my phone buzzing or one of yours?"

It was mine, with a text from my sister Alyssa. "On way to Maine with girls. Just us. Will call you tomorrow. Traffic sucks ass." I didn't know that she and my nieces were going up to our family house in Cape Elizabeth, but we hadn't talked in the past week either. I quickly responded, "Catch up then. Lots here. Put headphones on girls so you can listen to Howard." She wrote back, "Done." I would dump all of my shit on her tomorrow. Maybe she or her husband Patrick had an idea as to what I should do with my life. Having a sister and brother-in-law who were six years older—and also incredibly smart—was very helpful when you needed help from someone with life experience and perspective.

Once the ingredients for my impromptu crostini were prepared and everything was assembled on a white IKEA platter, I began pulling out the booze. Blair yelled over to me, "What are we drinking?" I opened the refrigerator looking for fruit—it was summer, after all—and found a hunk of watermelon. "Watermelon margaritas," I responded, and began to dissolve sugar and water for simple syrup. Scarlett asked, "How did we get so lucky to be your best friends?" and went back to consoling Blair. I muddled watermelon, squeezed lime juice, and poured tequila and Cointreau into proportions that seemed reasonable. It was cathartic to create food and drink that would taste good and be enjoyed. I joined Blair and Scarlett with my creations and handed them each an icy glass.

Blair took a generous sip. "Oh my God. This is so fucking good." Scarlett nodded her head in agreement.

I took another sip. "There's something a little off. Hold on." I went back into the kitchen area and cut three lime wedges. I rejoined my friends and squeezed a wedge into each drink and gave another taste. "There it is."

Blair looked confused. "I thought you already put lime juice in these. Why did that make a difference?"

This was one thing I knew about. One of my earliest cooking memories was watching my mother make a pasta salad and just before serving it, she squeezed a small lemon wedge over the entire dish. I learned all about the benefits of "acid at the end" in cooking that day, and I later discovered that it worked for cocktails, too. "It's a little trick that brings out the flavors in the drink. You can thank Corinne for that one."

Scarlett gave a small clap. "All hail Mama Whitman. The things we learn from her. Like the merits of making your own Bloody Mary. I'll never buy them premixed again." It was true; my mom made a killer Bloody Mary. "Janie," she said, shifting the conversation. "I'm so sorry. He's an idiot. He's going to realize quickly what a mistake he made."

Blair nodded vehemently. "He's so in his head over the magazine that he's probably not thinking clearly. I bet he calls tomorrow."

I wasn't so sure, but it was comforting just to sit with my friends, devouring the crostini and the margaritas. Scarlett was supposed to meet up with the guy she had just started seeing and was finalizing plans to join him at bar trivia. Blair was contemplating his options for the evening, and since he wasn't dating anyone at the moment, it was either going to be finding an impromptu "date" via an iPhone app or sitting with me and whatever else I threw together in the kitchen. My bet was on losing out to a muscular guy in Andersonville, although I am sure that I made a better spinach dip.

My phone started buzzing, but this time it was an actual phone call. Cole? Maybe he had second thoughts and wanted to see me before leaving? No, it was my sister. "Alyssa?"

"Janie." She was gasping and crying so hard she could barely say my name.

"What is it? What's wrong?" I wasn't used to *ever* hearing her like this. My sister was the most settled and stable person I knew. And we

Whitmans just weren't criers. Something very bad had happened.

"You need to get here. The plane. The plane they borrowed. I don't know how. I can't believe it. Not them. You need to be here. Please get here." Her voice was desperate and urgent and painful to hear.

"Okay. As fast as I can," I squeaked out. I hung up. I didn't know what else to say.

Scarlett was staring at me. "What's going on? That didn't sound good."

I looked around the room at the apartment. It was spinning slightly. I saw the platter of crumbs where crostini had sat. I saw glasses with half-melted ice cubes. I saw a small framed picture of Cole and me on the counter, his hands on my shoulders, both of us laughing. I cleared my throat and refocused on Scarlett and Blair, who were now sitting next to each other with concerned expressions on their faces. I had to say something. "I think my parents just crashed a plane."

2 - Amville

"A BEAUTIFUL WHITMAN GIRL lying in a hammock." I groaned silently to myself as I felt Lance Ashton standing above me. Lance was the summer neighbor of my youth, my temporary romance for many of those years, and someone who once made my heart beat so loudly in my chest that I swore he could hear it from across the room. Six years had passed since the last time I had kissed him, and that was totally fine with me.

I blinked my eyes open and managed a half-smile at Lance. His grin was enormous as he stood in front of me, sweating through his too-tight Vineyard Vines t-shirt. Just shy of six feet tall, Lance had been a fairly cute teenager, or at least I had thought so. Since college, he had gained roughly thirty pounds, stopped shaving every day, and didn't get regular haircuts. Needless to say, I hadn't felt an attraction to him in a long time.

"Hey there. Do you need anything?" I asked him. *Was that rude?* I wasn't really trying to be awful, but the last two weeks had taken a toll on me. Things had been even harder on my sister Alyssa, who was sitting about ten feet away from me in an Adirondack chair, wearing oversized sunglasses, taking sips out of a very large glass of chardonnay, while pretending to watch her daughters play in the yard. I may have lost my job and my boyfriend, but Alyssa's marriage was on the verge of collapse. Looming over all of this heartache was the loss of our parents, which almost made the other problems seem small. But they weren't, especially not for Alyssa.

After I arrived in Maine on the last flight to Boston the night that everything had happened, Alyssa and I spent many hours dealing with the aftermath of the plane crash as well as her own personal hell. At that point, she had not even called Patrick yet to tell him about the crash; everything was just still too raw for her. The day had started fairly normally for Alyssa, she told me. As it was the beginning of summer, she had her two daughters Trish and Susie enrolled in an art camp program for the morning. She dropped them off and drove to her usual hot yoga class in the center of our hometown of Concord, Massachusetts. She went into the studio and set up her mat and arranged her towel and water bottle alongside it. The usual cast of characters was present, and many of them were Alyssa's friends. She saw Kathy walk into the room and gave her a wave. They were regulars in the class and their older daughters were in preschool together, so they saw each other often. Kathy walked right over to her with a sense of urgency.

"So, she looked at me with big serious eyes, almost crying. She was like 'I can't believe you're here right now' I had no idea what she was talking about, and once Kathy realized this, she said, 'Get your shit. We need to get out of here right now.' I scrambled to grab my mat and stuff. I had never seen Kathy like this, and it made me feel instantly nervous. What was I about to hear? What had happened?" Alyssa was a very dramatic storyteller; she always had been. She could drag anything out, often adding pauses for effect. Normally I would have been annoyed, but this was her story to tell, and I was just too damn tired to care. I just concentrated on keeping my eyes open and my head nodding in acknowledgement.

"Once we were outside on the sidewalk, we sat down on a bench," Alyssa continued. *"Kathy was pretty pissed but not at me. She said something like 'I can't believe I have to tell you this. He should fucking be the one. What a dickhead.' And, of course, I'm like 'What the hell are you talking about?' My heart was racing, and I felt so sick. I couldn't figure it out. I kept thinking who is HE? Who is the dickhead? I was in total denial. So, then Kathy finally asked*

me if I had seen Patrick at all. And I said, yeah, briefly. He had texted me around six last night to say he had a last-minute dinner in the city and was going to be late. And then he texted me around eleven to say it was going pretty long and he would just crash in the guest room because he had to get up really early for a breakfast meeting. I did hear the garage door open and close a couple of times, but I didn't get up. We've had some nights like that lately, so I didn't think anything of it. I think then I knew what she was getting at, but I didn't want to believe any of it."

"So, then she goes on about her date night with her husband Sean, blah blah blah, they went to the movies in Burlington—or maybe it was Waltham? I don't know, anyway, they're having so much fun they end up at the Colonial Inn in Concord—in our town—for a drink. They were sitting at one of the high-top tables in the bar and suddenly Patrick stumbled in and sat at the bar. He was pretty hammered." She paused almost theatrically. "He wasn't alone."

This was a ridiculous amount of atypical content to process at about three in the morning, but I squeaked out a simple, "Who?" Alyssa and Patrick had been married since right after graduating from college and had been together since freshman orientation at Cornell after meeting in some cheesy icebreaker. They always had seemed so together. Sure, his hours had gotten considerably later from what she had recently told me, but there had been no other signs of a problem. And this was mortifying, in the middle of their small town for all to see.

"Lorraine," Alyssa said. I must have looked confused, so Alyssa continued. "The blonde waitress at our favorite restaurant in town, Leonard's. I think you've been there with us." I nodded, vaguely remembering the spot. "She serves us food regularly. She's both hot and slightly trashy, exactly whom a financial advisor would go for if he suddenly lost all sense of reality and morality. And responsibility. For his family. Don't forget that one. Goddammit."

Alyssa took a deep breath and continued. "They were there for about ten minutes, at the bar, according to Kathy. It was dark, and she doesn't think he saw her. They were hanging all over each other. They were drinking martinis, and the vodka or gin or whatever it was, sloshing out of their glasses. They were sloppy."

"Vodka," I said. "His was definitely vodka." Patrick drank vodka almost exclusively when he wasn't having a beer. What the fuck was my almost-brother doing? To my sister, no less? "Go on," I managed to say.

Alyssa yawned and continued. "And then they got up with their drinks, and Kathy managed to covertly follow them into the lobby. Lorraine went up the stairs of the Inn and Patrick was running after her, getting something out of his pocket. I'm guessing a key. And that was it. Kathy left the inn. I can presume what happened next." She was sad and weary-looking, but her face was dry. There was still so much shock.

"So, what did you do?" Too tired to make coffee or open a bottle of wine, I had pulled out a bottle of scotch and two glasses, filled with ice. I felt like I had to do something to help care for Alyssa as she told this painful story.

"I went to see—you know…" Her voice drifted off, and I knew she meant our parents. Alyssa had seen them mere hours before their plane crash.

"What did they say?" I asked, only using pronouns for their names. I couldn't get myself to say Mom or Dad. Even to the investigators that night, we had only referred to them as Michael and Corinne. Formal names made it seem like it hadn't happened to them.

"He was at work," Alyssa said. Our father had been a corporate pilot for the CEO of Sliced Hooks Golf Products – but our mother's hours as an esthetician in a local salon varied, and she often was home. "She was in the herb garden when I got there. As soon as she saw me said, 'I am so sorry,' and I was like 'You know already?'" Concord was small. This was bad.

"She had just gotten her hair cut. The receptionist had been at the inn last night. She said that Patrick was quite the spectacle. She hadn't told Dad yet. She was worried that he might kill him. Although it was kind of bitchy for the receptionist to tell her, don't you think? Some fucking discretion would be nice."

I just nodded. There was nothing to say.

Alyssa drained the rest of her scotch, which she rarely drank. She was clearly exhausted both physically and emotionally. "Dear God. I'm not going to be able to go anywhere in that town," she continued. "This is humiliating. Janie, I haven't even talked to him yet." She sighed. "Anyway, she told me that they were going to fly to Portland tonight—I guess it's technically last night now—whatever—before they went to Quebec for the weekend. They were planning to spend the weekend in Quebec..." Her voice quieted. Everything suddenly felt so temporary, like it wasn't even real. "She told me I could bring the girls to Maine," she said softly. "So, I went to the house— my house—and threw together just the basics for myself and the girls. Plus, I can always go shopping. Racking up a huge American Express bill for Patrick could be incredibly satisfying. And I then drove back to the Concord Arts Center. Just before going in to get the girls, I texted Patrick just one line: YOU FUCKING ASSHOLE. And then shut off my cell phone. Oh, I texted you. And then shut it off."

Two weeks later, after everything that had happened that day and night, Alyssa was dealing with the fallout. Our parents' funeral had been held back in Concord, with all of her friends in attendance. She sat in the church pew with Trish and Susie in between her and her estranged husband. Patrick had apologized, had offered to go to therapy, and had promised never to speak to Blonde Lorraine ever again. It was too much to grapple with so soon, especially in the horrific aftermath of death. She told him to stay home and that she would be in touch when she wanted to talk to him. In the meantime, she had a beautiful house near the coast to live in, our late parents' cars to drive, a wine cellar to work through, and her little sister—me—to cook meals for her and her daughters. This would do for now.

In the yard of our parents' Cape Elizabeth home, Lance looked slightly hurt at my question. "I thought you girls might want some company. Mom sent over some food." Another silent groan. Lance's mother Meredith was overbearing, coddled her son to no end, and was a terrible cook. I needed a lot of things in life, but Meredith Ashton cooking for me was not one of those things. And what *was* it with all of these mama's boys? Were they all like this, or did I just happen to know all of them?

"Sorry, Lance. We just have a lot on our minds these days. The door is unlocked if you want to just leave everything in the kitchen." He nodded and walked off towards the back door of the house.

Alyssa shifted her gaze and watched him walk away. Once he was out of earshot she asked, "Is it just me, or was Lance once a lot cuter?"

I let out a small giggle. It felt good to laugh a bit. "I think so. Or at least I need to tell myself that. Otherwise I wasted a lot of time in my younger years."

Alyssa smiled, clearly remembering me chasing Lance around as a teenager. "It must be weird now, being around him in these circumstances. You don't seem in the least bit interested. It's obvious to me, but I don't think he has a clue."

I sat up in the hammock, watching my nieces blowing bubbles and jumping around. At five and three years old, they were closer in age than Alyssa and I were as kids, but we had played similarly in this very spot. "You were already settled into life in Concord with Patrick the first summer I came home from Northwestern. I was dating Mark—remember him? He spent the summer in New York in an internship for business school and we met up every other weekend. I worked at the catering company during the week and on the weekends we weren't together. It was the first summer that Lance and I didn't hang out in that kind of way. It was so awkward. The next summer Mark and I had broken up because he had moved to Hong Kong for his new job, but Lance was dating that Amville girl. Kristy. She broke up with him just before they graduated. He's been living here with his parents ever since. No steady work, not doing much of anything, for two years." I paused, making a quick inventory of emotions at that moment. They were all over the place those days, but one thing was certain. "I just don't feel a thing for him besides friendship. He was a big part of growing up for me, but that's exactly what it was. I'd rather be alone than revert to something out of nostalgia."

Lance walked back to where we were lounging. "Drinks tonight, ladies? I'm free and you both seem to be." *No kidding.* He had such a hopeful look on his face. If he wanted to hang out with two mourning girls and the Disney Junior set, he must be really desperate.

Be nice, Janie. "We'll be here. Come by whenever." I could mix him a drink. Put out some antipasto. Perhaps take a shower first. We could be friends. We had so much history; we could turn that into a nice, adult, platonic friendship. Fine.

"Great! I'll see you all around five." He really wasn't that bad. It just wasn't, no, it *really* wasn't there. "And your house phone is ringing," he said as he walked back towards his house.

I sprang out of the hammock and ran into the house to grab the call. I had talked on a landline phone more in the past two weeks than I had in the previous two years. Calls from lawyers, aviation investigators, media, old family friends… I never knew who would be on the other end of the line. Alyssa wouldn't answer in case it was Patrick calling from other phones trying to talk to her, so I had phone duty. "Hello?"

"Hi there, my name is Kate Heathcliff. I work in the Development Office at Amville College. Is this Corinne Whitman?" She was bubbly, in a nervous, high-pitched, halting sort of way.

Seriously? "No, it isn't. This is her daughter. Janie."

"Oh, hi. Is Mrs. Whitman available?"

This was getting ridiculous. "No, she's not." I was wondering how far I should take this. How on earth could the Development Office of my parents' alma mater not have heard of their passing? The story had been all over the Maine media, and the school was less than two hours away from Portland where the crash had occurred.

"Oh, okay. Could you tell me when she might be home?"

I had to nip this in the bud. I almost felt sorry for her… *almost.* I tried to keep my voice as neutral as possible. "Unfortunately, she never will be again. Because she's dead. She and my father died in a plane crash two weeks ago." There was silence on the other end of the line, and I felt anger start to well up in my voice. "Speaking of which, how did you guys not hear about this? Don't you have a research department or something? My sister and I have both heard from our colleges about this, and our schools are nowhere near here."

Kate Heathcliff cleared her throat and replied, verbally tripping over herself in the process. "I am so, so sorry. That is so tragic. Yes, we do have a research team, but we have had some turnover this summer and I believe there has been a lapse. Oh my God, I feel terribly about this insensitive oversight."

I began to get past my annoyance with this call. This really wasn't her fault; it was fairly ridiculous, but I didn't want to shoot the messenger in this situation. "Kate, is it? What can I help you with? Why did you call for them today?"

Kate seemed relieved. "Oh, you are too kind. Thank you. Anyway, your mom always helped us at a big college fair in Portland every summer. It's so hard to find people who can do this kind of volunteer work in the summer when everyone is so busy. It's next Tuesday night. I was just calling to see if she wanted to be a part of it this year. But obviously now... Hey, would *you* want to do it instead?"

Who *was* this naïve woman? No one would believe that this phone call had taken place; it fell into the "you can't make this shit up" category. Why did she assume that I was here with nothing to do? That I didn't have a job to go back to? That there wasn't someone waiting for me (besides Scarlett and Blair) in Chicago? How does one even respond to this? "Um, I'm a Northwestern grad. Amville is great and I loved going up to the campus with my family as a kid, but I think you probably want an alum for this."

Kate began to get excited and enthusiastic. "Oh no, it would be fine! You would be paired up with a wonderful young alum named Rocky Macallen who is a guidance counselor at one of the local high schools. So he really knows his stuff and is great at talking to high school students, plus he has worked this college fair before. It would be so fantastic for him to have your help. It's really too much logistically for one person to do alone. What do you think? Could you do it?" She seemed so eager.

It was an incredibly absurd request. I had absolutely no reason to do this. I also had nothing going on besides babysitting my heartbroken older sister, making grilled cheese sandwiches for my nieces who didn't understand why they weren't seeing their daddy, and politely trying to show Lance that our teenage romance had been over six years ago. "Sure, why not." Before hanging up, I gave her my email address so that she could send me the necessary information. Because I picked up the phone that afternoon, I would soon be selling the merits of Amville College to teenagers. I looked over at the portrait of my smiling parents on the wall. "This is because I went to Northwestern instead of Amville, isn't it?" I asked aloud. The twinkle in my dad's eye confirmed my suspicion.

3 - Cheeseball

THE BEAUTY OF ANTIPASTO IS that you really don't have to know how to cook anything in order to make it. My mother was an accomplished cook and taught me how to work magic with just about any ingredients, but I perfected the art of the antipasto in my college summers working for Sensationally Maine, a local catering company. I had assembled countless platters for social events all over southern Maine and loved the creativity and ease of it.

I found my father's favorite Tommy Bahama platter in the dining room cabinet, covered it in big green lettuce leaves, and began to fill it with beautiful things that I had purchased and prepared over the past few days. There was salami and prosciutto nestled with cantaloupe, small mozzarella balls skewered with grape tomatoes and basil leaves, petite bowls of olives and marinated artichoke hearts and roasted red peppers, and crunchy Italian breadsticks and crostini crackers. I added a small wedge of salty Parmesan and a few bunches of juicy red grapes to fill in spaces. This was way too good for Lance Ashton, but Alyssa and I needed to eat, too. Heck, we deserved something downright gorgeous. I shoved the revolting-smelling container of deviled eggs that were sent courtesy of Meredith Ashton that afternoon to the back of the refrigerator, vowing to discard them as soon as Lance left. Onto the most important item of the night... if I was going to spend a couple of hours with Lance, some anesthesia was needed.

My mother's Maine herb garden was still going strong, mostly because my nieces loved watering it every day, with the colorful child-sized watering cans that I found in the garage in the days following the crash. I picked a bunch of mint and muddled it with simple syrup in the bottom of a large pitcher. I rinsed the frozen strawberries that I had found several bags of in the freezer; Mom must have gone picking just before she died, unless these were left over from last summer. I dumped them into the fancy blender that my parents had used for the preparation of countless cocktails, added the mint and simple syrup, squeezed in a few limes' worth of juice, and gave it a healthy glug of white rum. I whirled everything together and put it back in the pitcher, which was now full of ice. I topped it with club soda and gave it a taste. It was summery, a little sweet, and packed a bit of a wallop. Mark, the guy I had dated during much of college, had been a bartender before starting business school at Northwestern's Kellogg School of Management. From him I had learned how to navigate a much more mature relationship than I had experienced with Lance, as well as how to make a great strawberry mojito, among other things. Both had proven to be valuable in my life so far.

I set up the little girls with a kid-friendly version of what we were going to enjoy, complete with raw veggies, cut-up fruits, cheddar cheese, and crackers, as well as a Disney movie and milk with crazy straws. Alyssa watched with awe. "You're doing a much better job as their parent than I am these days. I haven't done jack around here."

We walked back into the kitchen, and I took out appetizer plates and cocktail napkins. "You need to get out of the house tomorrow," I said to her. "You haven't left since the funeral. It's been two weeks. I will deal with the girls and pick up more groceries. What about finding a yoga class? I bet you miss it by now."

Alyssa stretched her arms over her head and let out a yawn. "I guess I should. I think there's a place near the high school. I'll look at their schedule later tonight. Thanks, Janie. Maybe it'll help me feel a little more like myself."

I handed her a mojito. "I am also an enabler. Drink up, little camper. We have a less-than-inspiring guest coming over."

Alyssa broke out of her somber tone and did a silly little sexy dance and said in a sing-song voice, "You're the one who did you-know-what with him." The girls were in earshot, but Alyssa sounded ridiculous.

Ugh. "Twice, about three lifetimes ago. And I'm not sure if one of those times really counts. Don't make me think about it."

Alyssa was about to ask what I meant about one time not counting, but thankfully the front door opened, and Lance walked in unannounced, like he had been accustomed to since he had been old enough to make the short walk from his house to ours. For once that summer, I was glad to see him. "Hey ladies!" he proclaimed, as he came into the kitchen. "Mom sent over a cheeseball." He put the creation on the counter, and Alyssa bit her lip and looked away. It looked like something that a cow threw up. It diminished the quality of my antipasto platter by its mere presence adjacent to it.

I had to move on quickly. That fucking thing wasn't going away. "Lance, would you like a strawberry mojito? Fresh mint from the garden and local strawberries."

He nodded eagerly, and I poured him a glass.

"Hey, question for you," I said, trying not to make eye contact with Alyssa regarding the cheeseball. "Do you know someone who works at Amville named Kate Heathcliff? She's in the Development Office."

"No, but I don't know a lot of the staff. I only go to a few events here and there in Portland, depending on who else is going and if it's going to be an open bar. Why?"

"She called here today. Really long story, but she roped me in to helping out at a college fair. I'm going to be working with some alum named Rocky."

Lance almost choked on an ice cube. "Macallen?"

"You know him?" There was definitely a story here. It could be interesting. I didn't know much about Lance's time at Amville, other than the fact that he had dated Kristy for over two years and that he had barely graduated due to the fallout of their breakup. This was more insight.

"Oh yeah, but not in any deep or meaningful way. He's a fucking asshole."

Alyssa glared at him and pointed to the girls sitting in the living room watching "The Little Mermaid."

"Oops, sorry. I'm not used to, you know, kids… Anyway, I really didn't know him well, but at Amville, you kinda know who everyone is at least a little bit. He was part of this little crew of guys who were musicians and made it their goal to go to as many Ben Folds concerts as possible and played a lot of golf. They all lived together, drank together, were kind of cliquey for Amville. You get the idea. He went out with this chick named Danielle for most of college and they broke up at the very end, similar to me with Kristy. I really had nothing to do with him until a few nights before graduation, when I was at a party and saw Macallen and Kristy dancing and making out in a corner. It was awful." His face looked pained talking about it. His breakup with Kristy was still so raw.

Alyssa seemed more interested in the story now that there was the familiar element of betrayal. "What happened? What did you do?"

Lance straightened his shoulders and puffed out his chest a bit. "I punched him in his fucking face."

I had known Lance since we were three years old, and I had never seen or heard of a single violent tendency or moment. I was shocked. You're kidding. I've never seen you do anything remotely like that before."

He shrugged, trying to play off his brutishness as typical for him. "I was pretty drunk and really pissed. It was one punch, but I had good enough aim considering the circumstances. He hit the ground and I bolted from the party. When campus security showed up, Macallen did—to his credit—try to diffuse the situation by telling them that it was too dark for him to see who did it. I guess Kristy backed him up. They totally knew it was me; I remember Kristy yelling my name right after it happened. But some bitch (another glare from Alyssa) outside the party told security that it was me. That was why I almost didn't graduate with my class."

This was crazy. These were the details that Meredith Ashton had left out when telling my mom about Lance's graduation woes… such as the fact that a young man received his diploma with a giant black eye. If you were Rocky

Macallen's parents, did you frame and display those graduation pictures? So many questions...

"Wow," I said. "Do you know if it was a one-time thing between them or something more?" This guy had definitely gotten under Lance's skin.

"No idea," said Lance. "Last I could tell from some Facebook reconnaissance, Kristy lives in DC and is engaged already to some congressional staffer. So obviously it was short-lived. But it sucked pretty bad. Have fun working with him, Janie. He's a real winner."

"Have you seen him since graduating?" I know that I was focusing on this history between Lance and Rocky Macallen, but it was a side of Lance that I had never seen. Plus, I had to spend several hours with Rocky next week, and I wanted to know what I was getting myself into.

"Only once, when the college president was hosting a big event in Portland and there were over 100 people there. I managed to stay at the opposite end of the room from him the whole time. Before I go to an alumni event, I check the registration to see if he's going to be there." That was some serious dislike.

Alyssa excused herself to go give the girls their baths, leaving us alone. It was the most parenting she had done in a while. I digested all of the information that Lance had just given me, wondering what Rocky was really like. "Well, at least *he* didn't rat you out to security. What was the so-called bitch's issue with you?"

Lance chuckled. "I pissed her off in a class one time. Said something that wasn't perfectly 100% anti-male. It was a women's studies class."

I couldn't help but laugh. "What on earth were you doing enrolling in such a thing? That sounds like your worst nightmare."

"Kristy had told me that I needed to learn how to relate to the female gender better. It was an honest effort. But a miserable experience."

I laughed again. He focused on my face, looking at me in a way that started to make me feel uneasy. It was just the two of us in the downstairs of my family's house, as we had been so many times before.

His voice softened. "Oh, that laugh," he said and smiled, and I could see his mind drift back to a time when we were much younger and without so many issues. "Don't you think this is fate? I mean, I'm not trying to diminish what just happened to your parents. You know I loved them and I miss them, too. But you, me, here, like no time has passed. We've got a second chance now." His eyes were way too hopeful. This was hard. First deviled eggs and a cheeseball, now this with so much history behind it.

"Oh, Lance. I'm here because my life is a mess. My parents aren't just not here; they *died*. Tragically. My sister's life is a total disaster. She's dealing with everything that I'm dealing with but multiply it by ten. We need to get our shit together. That's why we're here." I paused. I needed to do this now. "It wouldn't be fair to drag you down into the rabbit hole with me. What we had as kids was lovely and full of good memories. I don't want to discolor that with pain. I—"

My monologue was not effective enough. He planted a big, sloppy, rum-soaked kiss on my lips. It would probably be easier to go along with him for a bit, but terrible in the long run. I pulled back as tactfully as I could. "Lance, it's not happening. I want to be your friend. You're one of my oldest friends. That's what I need right now. I really need a friend. I'm sorry."

Lance was quiet for a few moments. "I need to figure out my life, too. I've been pretty much paralyzed here since graduating two years ago. Kristy and I were going to move to New York together. I was starting to interview for jobs. I wanted to be a consultant or something. Consulting for what, I have no idea. I just wanted to do the kind of job that you were supposed to do with a liberal arts degree and an econ major. Once she dumped me, I didn't know what to do or how to do it. Coming here seemed like the only thing that made sense."

I could understand that. Our Cape Elizabeth childhood was safe, stable, and secure. While I had only spent my summers and some holidays there, Lance had lived there year-round. For both of us though, it was home, and it was the only place that I could imagine being at that moment, too. "What do your, um, parents think?" I glanced at the cheeseball again, which Lance had partially eaten and I had pretended to sample. What *was* that thing encrusted with? It looked like some kind of grass.

"It's the weirdest thing. My mom seems happy that I'm still at home," he said, and I suppressed a chuckle. "And my dad doesn't say much, as you know. He can't get in too many words with her around." That was an understatement; the woman never stopped talking.

"Okay, so we will brainstorm. We will figure something out. Maybe someone at Amville can help you? Connect you with an alum or something? Isn't that what the whole liberal arts experience is all about? Hey, why don't you call this Kate person? Tell her she owes me one."

Lance slowly nodded. "I'll do it. That's a solid idea. I'll look her up tomorrow and give her a call. Thanks, Janie. I appreciate your help with this. I'm lucky to have you as my friend. And sorry about, you know, the kiss." He looked a little sheepish.

"It's okay. Old habits and all that." My nieces had just come downstairs in their pajamas to say goodnight to us.

Susie pointed at the cheeseball. In her small three-year-old voice she asked, "What's that?"

Trish announced, "It looks like what I saw in the barn on my preschool field trip to Drumlin Farm last year."

Alyssa quickly shut down the dialogue. "You are right, Trish! You saw cows at the farm and cows make milk, which gets turned into cheese. And that is a cheeseball. Okay, say goodnight. I want you to get a good night's sleep before Auntie Janie gets you all to herself tomorrow morning while Mommy goes to yoga."

Trish's eyes lit up. "We're going back to Concord tomorrow so you can go to yoga? Yay!"

Alyssa looked unsteady and without words, so I stepped in. "Mommy is going to try a yoga place here in Cape Elizabeth so that she can go to classes when she's here, too. And I have a special surprise for you both tomorrow morning, but I need you to get lots of sleep tonight so that you can find out what it is, okay?"

Susie said, "I love surpwises. I go to bed now. Come on, Twish." She grabbed her pink blankie off of the edge of the couch and started walking towards the stairs. Trish ran after her.

Alyssa looked at me and said, "thank you," and followed after the girls.

Lance waited until they were all out of earshot. "What's going to happen there?"

I sighed. I had absolutely no idea. "She won't talk to him. He tries to call her, he calls me, he texts me a good portion of the day. I think that with everything that has happened here, she can't process the enormity of it. She has a life in Concord, but it's a small town and the idea of facing these issues while having to run into people who know what happened every time she walks into CVS or at preschool pickup is a nightmare for her. What he did, even if he's truly sorry, is so humiliating. He's not going to let her keep the girls away from him forever though, and he could put a hold on the credit cards if he wanted to as well. I think she knows all of this but isn't ready to deal with it yet. I hope I don't have to really push her to start making some decisions. She really should get there on her own. I do know Patrick well enough to know that he's not going to wait a lot longer. It could get ugly. I hate to see the girls stuck in the middle of this."

Lance nodded. "Everyone's got their shit to deal with. Okay, I'll let you girls have the rest of your evening. Thanks again for the advice. I'll give Kate Heathcliff a call tomorrow. Let's just keep this between you and me for now, all right? I don't need Mom's input on this one."

A mama's boy who didn't need her advice concerning his future plans... maybe I had been a positive influence on *someone's* life today besides just being his bartender. "Good plan. And maybe bring her back the rest of the cheeseball? That plate is so beautiful I would hate for one of the girls to break it by accident." I wanted that dreadful thing out of the house.

"Are you sure? Can I put it in another container for you? Alyssa might want some; I don't think she tried it yet."

"Oh, I think we're both fine. We ate so much antipasto. Maybe your *dad* would like some!"

"Okay, good call. Thanks again. The drinks were great. I'll see you soon. Tell Alyssa I said good night."

It was with great relief and some curiosity that I grabbed my laptop and retired to the couch after Lance left. I was thankful that I had been able to impress upon him that things were over between us and that friendship was a much better option for this point in our lives. The kiss was weird but whatever, it was done. My curiosity stemmed from the comment that Lance had made earlier about Facebook reconnaissance on Kristy. What *was* Cole up to? He wasn't a Facebook user—he preferred Twitter, which I hardly ever looked at—so I hadn't seen anything from him since our breakup. I had barely been online since arriving in Maine, except to look up a few recipes. I quickly went to his Twitter page, where nothing had been posted since he announced to the world that he was going to California: "The mag is done, AND SO IT GOES. Going to CA, hit me up if ur there, u know the digits. #billyjoel #sayHELLOtohollywood." Pretty odd, a bit cheesy, and for a brief moment, I was almost embarrassed for him.

I would have to attempt another route. I googled "Cole Emerson" AND "California." I almost wish I hadn't. I was hit by a barrage of images, stories (Perez Hilton knows who Cole is, apparently), and links to videos on tmz.com and HuffPost Live. Holy shit. There he was, looking tall, thin, handsome, stylishly dressed, and seen just about everywhere in the greater Los Angeles area with a girl named Cari Connors who was from the reality television show *Connors Crew*. The show featured a former supermodel named Star Connors, her wheelchair-bound and paralyzed former racecar driver husband Clark Connors, their alcoholic free-loading son Blake Connors, and finally, their somewhat promiscuous, club-hopping 22-year-old daughter Cari. The show was kind of a joke, a train wreck that people watched just to see what kind of ridiculous trouble the family would get into each week so that we could then talk about them and shake our heads. *She is even younger than me*, I thought. Cole went from running a magazine that served a major metropolitan area to apparently spending his days, according to *People*, with a trashy reality star drinking iced coffee and lounging by his mother's pool, and his nights, according to *US Weekly*, with the same trashy reality star drinking Cristal at "the hottest clubs." I felt sick.

It was at that moment, flipping through online slideshows of the guy who I had spent almost a year of my life with, as if he was a total stranger, that I finally realized the size and scope of my situation. I had no job, and my career training was in an industry that seemed to be going the way of the Tyrannosaurus Rex. I was living in my deceased parents' house with my grieving sister and her two small children. My brother-in-law was a philandering douchebag. I was dealing with lawyers and the NTSB on a daily basis as we tried to settle the details of the crash and my parents' estate. All three of the men from my past—Lance, Mark, and Cole—were enjoyable to be with at the time but in the back of mind, I had probably always known that they weren't significant prospects as life partners. I had made decisions that benefitted the present and immediate future, but I had no long-range vision. This was probably why I liked cooking so much; there was an impending and enjoyable payoff to my work, both in my own satisfaction and in the delight of those who I served. But there had to be more to all of this, and I knew that I didn't want to go back to catering or scrounging around for magazine stories. I was looking for a total life revamp at this point— a second act—but as I tried to look out into what was ahead for me on the horizon, it was so hazy that I ultimately saw nothing. It was too heavy to focus on anymore that night.

I closed my laptop, went into the kitchen, and started cleaning up the night's dishes. I could hear Alyssa chatting with the girls in hushed, sleepy tones, which brought a smile to my lips. She had left her phone downstairs, and it buzzed with a text message. It was from Patrick: "One more week before I call the lawyer. They are my kids, too. Please talk to me. Don't make this so hard. Will do whatever you want. Please. Miss you." I took advantage of her being upstairs and quickly scrolled through her messages from him. There were hundreds of similar texts. No replies from her. He was a shithead, but something had to happen here. She was going to yoga the next morning, even if I had to drive her there and push her out of the car… perhaps there was clarity through downward dog, or something like that.

4 - Yoga Dude

WHEN ALYSSA STUMBLED DOWN the stairs at 8:30 the next morning, the girls were finishing up breakfast and I was taking my last swig of coffee from the Northwestern mug I had bought for my mom one Christmas. Her eyes were red and puffy, and her hair was disheveled. "What on earth was in those drinks last night? And are those homemade waffles that my children are eating? Do I live with Julia Child? They're going to get used to this and will file a complaint when I give them the frozen ones from Trader Joe's."

I handed her a plate. "Saved you one. They're Bobby Flay's recipe. And the Trader Joe's ones are good, too. It's just that Bobby's are better. Eat up. You're going to a 9:15 yoga class. Oh, and you ingested a ton of Dad's Caribbean rum last night. Namaste."

"Namaste," she grumbled, pouring maple syrup and diving into the waffle. "These are delicious. I haven't done yoga in three weeks. My chakras are all out of alignment, and I can barely remember the differences between warrior one and warrior two."

I had no idea what she was talking about. My approach to exercise had always been about convenience and value; I did whatever was close and cheap. In Chicago, Scarlett and I had become very good at finding very inexpensive trial memberships and classes through daily deal websites,

31

and I often was given free passes to gyms through the magazine because places wanted us to feature them. Blair and I even made a disastrous though luckily complimentary attempt at Zumba. I had taken yoga classes here and there when the opportunity presented itself, but Alyssa was speaking a different language.

She changed into the one yoga outfit that she had thrown into her suitcase before leaving Concord, and I got the girls dressed for our hour and a half together. As we drove to the studio, she lamented that she didn't have her mat with her and hated the idea of borrowing one. It was only a five-minute drive to the storefront in a small shopping center near the high school in town, and when I pulled up I said, "See you in ninety minutes. Find your zen." She moaned a bit and got out of the car with her purse and water bottle.

While Alyssa was getting to know a new yoga studio, I took off with the girls to secretly investigate registration information about the local YMCA summer camp. They were very excited about everything they saw, but they knew that it was ultimately up to their mom. I promised that I would do my best to convince her to enroll them. Just as I was about to head back to the studio to pick Alyssa up, I got a text from her that read "Getting coffee with someone from class. Will let you know if I need a ride later. Thanks for taking care of the girls." I definitely didn't expect to hear this from her, but I tried to roll with the situation and decided to take the girls home.

By three o'clock that afternoon, I was starting to get a little worried. I didn't want to bug my sister, but I did have paranoid thoughts of kidnappings and human trafficking in my head as I sat at the kitchen table with my nieces putting together puzzles, drinking lemonade, and eating graham crackers. Every so often one of them would ask, "When is Mommy coming home?" which was a great question. They hadn't seen their father since their grandparents' funeral, and now their mother had disappeared for the day, presumably with a stranger. I felt the urge to crack a beer, but I also wanted to keep my wits about me in case I needed to drive in a high-speed rescue mission or make a split-second decision. I had seen too many *Lifetime* movies.

Finally, the front door opened, and the girls ran to the hallway to thankfully give their mom hugs. I was relieved but a bit pissed. "Welcome home, your highness. I'm so glad that you could join us this afternoon," I said, trying not to roll my eyes.

Alyssa giggled in a giddy way that I don't recall ever seeing or hearing. Maybe when she got her acceptance letter to Cornell, but that was too long ago to remember fully; I had been twelve years old. "You're not going to bring me down today, little sister," she said, in a sing-song voice. "Thank you for watching them." It had been a bit more than that, but whatever. "What did you guys do?" she asked the girls.

Trish said, "Mom, we went to the coolest place. It's a camp. It's at the WMD."

Alyssa raised her eyebrows. "Weapons of mass destruction? And you put them in a camp? What's going on?"

"No!" exclaimed Trish. "Auntie, what's it called?"

I figured since she had abandoned me with her children for much longer than the agreed-upon ninety minutes, I had some capital to spend. "It's a YMCA day camp. And I didn't put them in it. I'm not their parent, so I can't. But you are, and I have all of the forms. It would just be for the next two weeks, and I really think it's a good idea. There's swimming and arts and crafts and soccer. All kinds of good stuff. Do you girls want to do it?" I knew that I had them in my corner. The place was super fun, and it didn't involve being sequestered in a house with two sullen women.

Susie and Trish both were jumping up and down at this point. "YAY!" they yelled.

Alyssa shrugged her shoulders. "Okay, but you need to help me with the transportation. I want to go to yoga every day. And be able to go out to lunch and stuff like that. Maybe get a massage. I can't remember the last massage I had. Anyway, I can't just sit here all day."

Said the woman who had been parked in an Adirondack chair with a goblet of chardonnay for the past several weeks. "Um, great," I said. "Hey girls, how about playing with your ponies for a bit in the other room so I can talk to Mommy for a few minutes?" They happily ran into the next room, thrilled by their victory and WMD camp.

Alyssa poured herself some lemonade and began shuffling through the mail on the counter. None of it was for us, but I had the mail from my parents' primary residence in Concord forwarded to Cape Elizabeth so that I could more easily deal with things as they came in. Alyssa had paid no attention to any of it until this moment, when suddenly it seemed very interesting to her.

"What's his name?" I asked her. I knew that face and that feeling. I had experienced it several times in my life, and much more recently than Alyssa had.

"What are you talking about?" She began flipping through a Pottery Barn catalog.

"I think I know what I'm talking about. As you are aware," I said, gesturing to the platter that Lance's mom's deviled eggs had arrived on that I had just taken out of the dishwasher. "I tend to fall for boys. So, what's his name?"

Alyssa closed the catalog. "Okay. It's Doug. He's forty-six. He's been divorced twice. He has two grown children. Yes, he was a young parent. *I'm* a young parent, so we have that in common. He's an author of two best sellers. He lives less than five minutes away from here. He's very handsome and likes yoga, obviously. And it was a *restorative* yoga class. Do you know about those?"

I shook my head.

She continued, "You use all of these weird props and you feel like you're doing nothing, like you're just lying there. But you're really doing a lot, and it feels so good when you're done. And there's soft music and this instructor Clareesa who was like this total earth mother read us poems. Could you imagine Patrick doing something like that? Mr. Bicycle Road

34

Race who only listens to hip hop?" She was growing more animated and her face and neck were flushed. It was uncharacteristic of her, but so was the entire day she had apparently just experienced. "Anyway, I was super confused by the whole thing and all of my emotions came spilling out and I started crying. Like what the fuck, right? Who does that?" she asked rhetorically.

"I fell asleep at one of the free yoga classes I took in Chicago, started snoring and everything. Blair was with me and reminds me of it regularly," I said, mincing some fresh oregano. "What did Yoga Dude do when you started crying?" What was his name again? Darren?

Alyssa ignored my sarcasm. "Being a committed yogi and author, I think that *Doug* is more in tune to human emotions. He was very nice. We had a nice big cup of coffee together. He asked me questions about *me*. No one has done that in a very long time."

I began chopping cucumbers and tomatoes. The chicken breasts in the oven were almost done roasting. "I ask you about how you are doing every single day. I ask what you are going to do about Patrick. I ask how you are feeling about things. About what you're going to do with the girls. What you feel like having for dinner. I ask you about all kinds of things. What I have noticed is that no one ever asks how *I* am. I totally get that what happened to you sucks. I want to throttle Patrick. I really do want to hurt him physically, mentally, in all ways possible. But I know that's ultimately not for the greater good of anyone. And I lost my parents, too. And I know that it's pretty low on the list of issues around here, but I lost my job, and I lost my boyfriend, even though he's a pathetic mama's boy who is now screwing a reality TV star. I hope that he gets an STD." My tirade was over, and I began whisking together a vinaigrette.

Alyssa stared at me but not with anger; her face looked thoughtful, as if she was trying to process everything I had just said to her. "I hear the clap is back in vogue," she said quietly. "Who on earth is Cole seeing? And what are you making? I am very hopefully watching you prepare this food, but don't want to get too excited."

"Do you know who Cari Connors is? And it's your absolute favorite thing in the world. Greek Chicken Salad Wraps. Of all the things that I could possibly make for you, I have no idea why this is your favorite. But I love you and want you to be happy. So, I'm making them."

Alyssa was clearly thrilled about dinner and let out a little squeal. "You are the best. Cari Connors? Is she the one who had a video supposedly leaked of her and that nightclub owner? And it was a big deal because she had just turned eighteen?"

"Yes. Hence my hopes for an STD transmission. Will the girls eat this? I am just going to give them the chicken and veggies separately. Sound like a good idea?"

"Perfect. Thanks. When did you find out about Cole? Today when you were, um, waiting for me to get home?" She started taking out plates and silverware for dinner, which was the most she had helped me in the kitchen since we had gotten to Maine that summer.

"No, last night after Lance left. It's all over the internet, which honestly I haven't paid much attention to in the past couple of weeks. I texted with Blair earlier today, because he's so on top of celebrity gossip—ugh, I use that term loosely here—and he had heard about it but has been stressing out about whether or not to tell me anything given what we've got going on. But really, what's the big deal? I'm here, and we're through, and there's nothing I can do about any of it."

We were both quiet for a few minutes as I assembled dinner for our little family. Alyssa cleared her throat slightly, as if she was signaling a change of topics. "I know that I have to deal with Patrick. He texts me constantly. I just don't know what the right thing to do is here. I haven't had a chance to even really consider what a life not married to him would look like. That's what today was about. It felt so good to have a genuine conversation with a man who wanted to know about me, about my interests, about what makes me tick. For a few hours, I wasn't defined by Patrick's success or even by my daughters. I haven't had an identity in years. Given what Patrick did to me, I think I deserve at least that much."

She finally was making some degree of sense. "You need to tell him something along those lines. Push him off with a reasonable explanation of why you need a bit more time. It's summer and you have some degree of luxury because of that, but it won't last forever. You're going to have to figure things out before the school year starts. Trish starts kindergarten this fall. That's where the kids really come into play. They will also need to see him at some point. He has legal rights even if he's a total ass." I tried not to reveal anything that I had seen from snooping on her phone.

Alyssa nodded. "You're right. The girls will be in camp for the next two weeks. I will push him off until that's over. That will give me time to figure things out better. I think that's fair."

It was. "Okay, you text him, and I will put these wraps together. I also got those veggie chips you like. Seriously, Alyssa, you've been in the hot yoga suburbs for too long. Have you forgotten the merits of some really indulgent salt and vinegar chips? Or even barbecue?"

She laughed. "Just wait until you have your babies. Everything changes. But I'm glad you didn't have babies with STD-boy."

"We don't *know* for sure that he has an STD. It's just my hope for him. Something itchy." With that, we genuinely laughed together for the first time in what seemed like years, since we were kids sneaking ice cream out of the freezer past our bedtime during our Maine summers, or at least since before adulthood had bogged us down. For a few moments, everything felt good.

5 - Rocky

WE SETTLED INTO A GROOVE. The girls went to camp and Alyssa went to yoga and spent her afternoons presumably getting to know Doug, although she didn't share many details with me. I dealt with our parents' estate and the crash investigation and cooked for the family. The day had finally come for me to volunteer at the college fair on behalf of Amville. I had to be at a private school in Portland at 5 p.m. to meet Rocky Macallen and set up our table for a 6 p.m. start. I was oddly nervous, probably because I had not left my parents' house in several weeks other than to drop the girls at camp or to go to the grocery store. My interactions with people outside of my family had been limited to Lance and the friendly staff at the YMCA. I also didn't know much about Amville beyond the Homecoming games and reunions that I had attended as a child with my parents, so I wasn't sure what exactly to say to teenagers and their parents about the college. And what if Rocky really was a total ass? My conversation with Lance hadn't left me very optimistic.

I followed Kate Heathcliff's emailed instructions and got to the school on time, with nothing other than my purse. She had assured me that Rocky would have all of the supplies that we needed. I checked in at the welcome booth and was told where to find our table. A typically confident person, I felt nerves crawling in my stomach. I didn't know what to expect or really what I was supposed to do over the next few hours. The past month had made me vulnerable and unsure in a way that I had never experienced. I had to snap out of it.

He was cute. Not the lanky hipster attractiveness of Cole, not the future corporate executive handsomeness of Mark, not the boy-next-door look that Lance had possessed when I had initially fell for him as a young adolescent, but cute in a very normal, accessible kind of way. He was preppy and clean-cut with sandy dark blonde hair that was freshly cut, a nice button-down shirt and a tie, and a cleanly-shaved face. He looked like a teacher, which made sense since Kate said that he was a guidance counselor. He was unfolding an Amville banner to hang from the folding table assigned to us.

"Hi," I said as I approached the table. "I'm Janie Whitman."

He smiled and stuck out his hand. "Rocky Macallen. It's so nice to finally meet you. I'm so sorry about your parents. I only met your dad once, but I worked with your mom at a couple of these, and I really enjoyed talking with her. She was terrific."

I wasn't expecting any of this. "You knew my mom? Kate didn't—I hadn't put two and two together that you had done this event with her, but that makes sense. Wow. Well, thank you. They both loved Amville and were pretty disappointed when neither my sister nor I wanted to go there."

Rocky smiled again. "I know. You slummed it at Northwestern from what I recall."

How much did he know about me? Mom was a big talker, so there could be quite a bit. *Too much.* "So, what do we do here?" There were stacks of flyers, bumper stickers, and packets on the table.

He began organizing and straightening the piles of materials. "Basically, at 6 p.m. the doors open to parents and students, and people can come over and talk to us. To be honest, it's not a very widely-attended event. It's summer and a lot of people are on vacation. I have no idea why they continue to host this every summer—early fall would be so much better—but Amville is part of a consortium that is dedicated to participating in this event, so we have to have representation here."

Why on earth then did *I* have to be here? "Okay, so we just sit here and wait for people to come over to us? Sorry to ask so many questions, but I just have never done anything like this before. I don't know much about Amville other than what I saw through a kid's eyes at Homecomings and reunions and of course everything I heard in my parents' stories about their time there. There were a lot of stories, but I don't think that most would be appropriate to tell a prospective student."

Rocky let out a laugh. It was louder and bolder than his normal speaking voice was and took me by surprise, but it was also a little endearing rather than obnoxious. I felt my face flush. "Probably not," he said. "I've got a few of those stories, too. We'll save them until after they're accepted and then we can get them to matriculate by telling them then. That's what the accepted students' reception is for." His eyes were twinkling with a bit of mischief, and I felt my heart sink lower. Maybe no one would come to our table, and I could spend a few hours just talking to Rocky. That would be fine.

It turned out that he was right about the low turnout. Not very many people came over to our table in the two hours that we sat awaiting visitors, or to any other table for that matter. I learned from listening to Rocky talk to the few that graced our booth that Amville was often called one of the "ABC" schools due to its presence in Maine and similarity to Bowdoin, Bates, and Colby College. Amville was considered by some to be too remote due to its location on the outskirts of Camden, and Rocky played up the advantages of being near a beautiful coast and in an area inhabited by artists, writers, and other creative types. There was skiing nearby at the Camden Snow Bowl, and there was excellent proximity to Bar Harbor and Acadia National Park. Rocky was great at explaining the attributes of Amville, answering questions, and talking to both teenagers and their parents. I could understand why he was a valuable alumni volunteer. I also really just enjoyed sitting next to him.

The two hours went quickly, with only a few odd moments. Once, a mother asked Rocky a question and before he could reply to her, she answered her cell phone and had a full five-minute conversation in front us, completely blocking the table. Or the teenage boy who berated Rocky for the fact that Amville did not offer a business major, and when he tried to explain to him that it was a liberal arts school, he replied, "Well, I am a Republican and I am definitely not an artist, so I am not applying there."

I suppressed a laugh and covered my mouth, while Rocky called out, "Best of luck with your college search," as the young man walked away. Once he was out of earshot, we both had a laugh. "Not a good fit," he said.

Just before eight o'clock, we began to pack up all of the materials, of which there were many, due to the small turnout. "What's the advantage for you to do something like this for Amville?" I asked, as I folded up the banner. In the couple of years that I had been out of Northwestern, I had attended one free cocktail party because it was in a restaurant that I couldn't have afforded to go to otherwise, and that was the extent of my alumni involvement.

Rocky dumped a stack of brochures in a box. "Schools like Amville need a lot of volunteers. They are small and just don't have the staffing to go to every single event. If no one shows up on behalf of the College—even at a lame event like this—but Bowdoin, Bates, and Colby are here, we look terrible and people start to discount us as a second-tier school. I guess because I spend my days talking to high school students about their futures, I realize how important these degrees and experiences and connections are, so I don't want to see Amville lose its presence in the conversation. It means too much to me. And I guess I'm just a big sap when it comes to Amville."

I wasn't used to hearing a male speak with such passion about something beyond a sports team or a band or in Cole's case, specifically Billy Joel. It was attractive and unusual in my experience. I couldn't help but want to spend more time around him, but I had no idea what his situation was. Did he have a girlfriend? He could be engaged for all I knew. And was he actually really the ass that Lance had made him out to be? There was so much to discover when it came to Rocky Macallen. I wanted to find out all that I could. How could I continue this evening?

"So," I began to ask slowly, trying to figure out how to proceed as I spoke. "What do we do next?"

Rocky closed up the last box. "I need to bring these boxes to my car so that Kate can pick them up from me when she comes to Portland for her next donor meeting. And that's it. Pretty easy."

"I can help you," I said. I slung my bag onto my shoulder and grabbed one of the two boxes. This would prolong our interaction and allow me to read him a bit better. I needed to figure out if I was all right with setting myself up for potential rejection and embarrassment. Given everything that had happened in the past few weeks, I wasn't sure.

"Great," he said, and we began to walk down the hall of the school towards the parking lot.

Rocky's car was exactly what you would imagine a 24-year-old high school guidance counselor to drive, an older Toyota Corolla that he likely bought used at some point during college. He unlocked the car and we put the boxes in the trunk. He closed the trunk and we were standing in the dark, looking at each other. It was both awkward and nice at the same time. "Do you want to get a beer?" I blurted out. I had never asked a guy out in my life. I never had to. This time I did. Gauging any chance I had to get to know Rocky was worth the possibility of rejection in a private school's parking lot. If it didn't work out, I never had to see him again. There wasn't much to lose.

His face eased into a smile. "Yeah. It's summer and I don't have to get up early for work. Let's go." We exchanged cell phone numbers and he told me where to meet him. I walked a few aisles over to my dad's car and began the quick drive to the Old Port. I tried to keep myself calm and not to hit any curbs while driving. My heart was racing, but it felt pretty good.

The pub that Rocky had chosen was one that I had never been to before, but I also hadn't spent much time in Maine as an adult. When I got there, he was already sitting at a small booth and gestured for me to sit across from him. I couldn't help but compare him to Cole, and the differences were astonishing. If I had been in the same setting with Cole, we would have been nervously looking around to see if anyone from the magazine was there. He would have likely been wearing rumpled clothes that he had picked up off the floor, with hipster facial scruff and a knit wool cap on his head. Rocky had taken off his tie in the car, but he still was incredibly preppy and clean cut, with a smooth face and combed hair. I couldn't imagine him in a knit wool cap.

"You found it," he said with a smile. "Sometimes the teachers come here on Fridays after work." The waitress came over with a pint for him. "What do you want?"

I sat across from him, ordered an IPA, and tried to settle back into the booth a bit. I wasn't sure what conversation to initiate. I didn't know where to begin. We had talked about his job at the college fair; I knew that he had gotten certified as a high school English teacher while in his senior year at Amville and was looking for teaching jobs in the Boston area when he and his girlfriend had broken up. I managed to keep an emotionless face during this interchange, not showing that I knew anything about Danielle, or Kristy and Lance for that matter. Certainly nothing about black eyes at graduation. When the breakup threw a wrench in his plans, at the last minute he enrolled in a one-year master's program to get a counseling certification at the University of Southern Maine so that he could stay in Maine and settle into a life that was different than he had envisioned during his relationship with Danielle. During the end of his program, he got hired at his current school. He loved living in Portland and staying involved with his alma mater.

I had avoided talking much about myself or anything that was currently going on with my family, beyond a bit of the "dead parents" topic. We had chatted a little about that, including how Kate Heathcliff hadn't known about their passing when she had called the house. Rocky said that she had called him right afterwards, and that was the first he had heard about it, too. Amville had completely dropped the ball on the entire situation, and she wanted to repair the relationship with my family. He relayed that while her intentions were often good, her approach was sometimes flighty and somewhat confusing.

At that moment, I had never been more grateful for flighty and somewhat confusing. I was sitting across from a very normal-seeming Rocky Macallen and drinking a beer. It was the best moment I'd had in the past month. I was trying to put off telling him anything of the ridiculous drama of Alyssa and me; I didn't want him suddenly excusing himself from the booth because of a previously-forgotten early morning commitment. I wouldn't blame him for it either; it was enough for anyone to run away from.

I could put off the inevitable for at least a few more minutes. "Where did you grow up?"

He took a sip of his beer. "Seattle. You can imagine how conflicted I am every time the Seahawks play the Patriots."

"Oh, that's cool. I've never been there before. I hear it's beautiful. Does your family still live there?"

"Sort of. My parents divorced when I was five. My mom raised me in the city, and my father moved out to the coast and kind of became a hermit. No, not kind of. That's truly what he is. She had to drag him to court every time she needed more child support. He just didn't want anything to do with us anymore. He never would tell her why he left, but he dropped us cold. I haven't talked to him in years. He got remarried but didn't tell us. Mom found out in court one day when his wife was with him. He has two kids with her now. I guess she makes the money, but they creatively kept it separate so that he didn't have to pay us very much in child support. He works on cars and gets paid mostly under the table. We're not really connected to them at all anymore now that I'm done with school though, so who knows what the situation is currently. He's pretty much a dick." He paused and took another sip of beer. "Sorry, that's a lot to hit you with on the day that I meet you." He gave a small sheepish smile. I instantly felt better about my situation. It was as if we were equals in the fucked-up department.

"Well, he sounds like a really great guy," I said. "We all have our shit to deal with, right? My parents just died in a plane crash and that's only the tip of the iceberg." Given what he just told me, I guessed that he wouldn't run away screaming if I told him the rest and of course, I didn't want the evening to end.

He took the bait. "Yeah, I hate to ask, but what's your plan for the houses and staying up here? I thought you worked for a magazine in

Chicago? And your mom had mentioned the last time that I saw her about some boyfriend but it was top secret. But that was a while ago so…" his voice trailed off. Was it hopeful? I couldn't gauge how much I was projecting. And why on earth had my mother been telling people about my "secret" boyfriend? *Corinne…*

"Well," I began the process of spilling it all when the waitress came over to the table and gave me a small reprieve.

"Hi guys," she said. "We are getting ready to close. Do you mind settling up?" It was only ten o'clock, which seemed early for a pub to close, but it was still a weeknight.

"Sure," Rocky said, and began taking out his wallet. I tried to beat him to it, but he said, "Corinne would have liked us having a drink together. Happy to do it." I felt my stomach drop for probably the fifth time that night.

I wasn't sure how to navigate the next step. "I'd love to tell you the rest of this. I'm surprised they close so early."

He glanced around. "I think there are some bars nearby that are open later if you want to pop into one of those?"

Another drink and me driving back to the house was not the greatest idea. "Have you ever been to Cape Elizabeth? It's only about fifteen minutes from here and we have plenty to drink there." I sounded very forward and probably a little slutty. I was not trying to proposition him. I had to save this. "I just can't really drive if I have another drink. I'm a total lightweight."

He stood up, and I did the same. "I luckily have absolutely no place to be in the morning. What about other people? Is anyone else staying at the house right now? I don't want to disturb anyone with it being so late."

"My sister and her daughters are there, but it's really warm out. We can sit out on the back patio. We've got hammocks and comfy chairs out there. I'll get us drinks and they won't even hear us talking."

"Deal," he said, and we walked out to our cars.

6 - Hammocks

ROCKY LIKED BOURBON. So had Mike Whitman, so there was plenty of it in my parents' liquor cabinet. I left Rocky on the back patio with the materials to try to light the firepit so that I could fetch the drinks and some snacks. Thinking of what would go best with straight bourbon in a glass with a big ice cube, I grabbed the salt and vinegar chips that Alyssa had previously rejected and put them in a big plastic bowl. I put everything on a large tray and had started walking towards the door when Alyssa walked into the room and scared the shit out of me. "What are you doing?" she asked, tired and confused. To her credit, it must have looked really strange. I had barely left the house in weeks and now I was walking outside at almost eleven o'clock at night with a bottle of bourbon and potato chips. I also noticed that Alyssa was missing about seven inches off the bottom of her hair.

"That guy who I worked at the college fair with. You know, the one Lance told us about. Rocky. He's outside right now. What happened to your hair?"

Alyssa gave a wry smile. "I'm guessing he's not the complete fucknut that Lance described him as then. And nothing *happened* to my hair. I needed a change. Doug really likes it. I'm guessing you don't?" *Defensive.* Almost combative. Easy, sister.

I proceeded carefully. "No, that's not what I meant at all. It looks good. I just haven't seen you with hair above your shoulders since you were

46

maybe ten and you got that bob cut so that Mom wouldn't insist on putting your hair in a ponytail in the summer anymore. I just wasn't expecting to see this. What did the girls say? I need to get back outside before he runs away."

"Well, we can't have that," she replied. "Susie cried when I picked her up at camp and said you don't look like Mommy. That was great. Trish said it was beautiful and that I looked like a mom character on one of her TV shows. I know who she's talking about, and I'm trying not to take it personally. I'll go with the split decision." She took one chip out of the bowl and ate it, and her face showed the joy of having just enjoyed some kind of forbidden fruit. I wished she'd lighten up a bit. "OK, have fun, little sister. Just don't get too carried away. You've got two nieces who can look out their windows and see whatever it is you are doing down there."

I felt my face get flushed. "Says the woman who is cavorting with the forty-six-year-old in the afternoons while her daughters make creations out of pipe cleaners at camp."

Alyssa's smile went away. "No cavorting. Not yet. Just talking. Now get out there and get to know this guy so that you can eventually cavort with him, but not in our backyard. I'm going back to bed." She opened the back door for me so that I could get everything outside easily, gave Rocky a small wave, and headed upstairs.

Rocky had lit a nice fire and was sitting back in one of the cushioned chairs. "I'm guessing that's your sister?" He took the glass that I handed him.

"Yes, that's Alyssa," I said as I said down. "Don't worry, she's fine. Susie and Trish are asleep upstairs, and she's going to bed, too. We've all been staying here for the past month."

"And she lives in Concord where you're from, right?"

Corinne had had a big mouth, and Rocky seemed to have a great memory.

"She did. I honestly don't know what she's going to do now." I launched into the story of Patrick, the waitress, Cornell, yoga, Doug, camp, and everything else that I could think of that fit into the story of how Alyssa's life brought her to this moment. When I heard myself telling it to

Rocky, I realized that it was complicated, sad, and not likely to be resolved easily.

He seemed to be processing everything that I had told him. "What do *you* think? Do you want to see Patrick and Alyssa back together?"

It was something that I thought about at least a few times every day. "I'm not sure. I have always gotten along with him. He's a little full of himself, but I think that has helped him to be successful. He's very Type A. I mean, I think everyone in our family is to a certain extent, but he's like Type A+++. My mom loved him because he is handsome and charming, and she knew that he would give Alyssa a really good life. And it's true; they live in a beautiful house in what has become a very expensive town. She hasn't worked outside of the home since graduating from college. Not many thirty-year-olds can say that anymore. My dad didn't agree with everything that Patrick said, but he kept his mouth shut because he wanted Alyssa to be happy. And I think for the most part she was. I just can't imagine what it would be like for her to go back to Concord during a school year and see everyone in town. I mean, he did it *right there*. He could have gone into Boston and likely no one would have known, at least not right away. Which is gross, too, because who knows how long it would have taken for Alyssa to realize what was happening? But this was as if he *wanted* everyone to see him. I don't know why you would do that or if it was subconscious, but I'm not sure how their marriage will recover from this if they stay there. So I just don't know."

Rocky was listening thoughtfully. He spent most of his days attending to teenagers talking about their college application woes, family situations, dating breakups, and friendship dramas. My family's issues were more intricate than many, but he had certainly heard worse. "And where does this Doug guy factor in?"

"And that is a great question and a big unknown to me. I haven't even met him, and I don't know if I want to. I definitely don't want the girls to meet him if it can be avoided, and Alyssa is doing a good job of keeping those two parts of her life separate for now. It's pretty easy for the next week and a half or so; the girls are in camp all day. She meets him at yoga and then hangs out with him in the afternoon. I don't really know what they do. She apparently got a haircut today. She says they're not sleeping together, which is good because it would complicate things even more. But if this keeps going on..." My voice trailed off, as I really didn't have any more to say about the topic. I wasn't sure what Doug's motivations were in this; why would he want to be involved with Alyssa when she wasn't even legally separated, had two very young children, and quite frankly, wasn't yet putting out? Maybe she was giving him inspiration for his next book, or perhaps he just liked hanging out with an attractive, much younger woman. I'm not sure if I wanted the answers to any of these questions.

Rocky took another sip from his glass. "And what about you, Janie? We've talked a lot about me, a bunch about your sister, but there's a lot I don't know about you. Are you taking a leave of absence from work or working remotely while you're here?"

I had managed to put all of this off for about six hours. "I'll give you the condensed version of the story, but feel free to ask me questions. The secret boyfriend that my mom told you about was my boss. His name is Cole. You can see him on *Access Hollywood* or *E! Entertainment News* pretty much any day that you want to. Do you know the '80s song 'Hot Pink Love'?"

Recognition lit up Rocky's face, and he started singing softly in a falsetto, "You gotta give me some of that hot pink love, that hot pink love, ooh ooh. Yeah, it's about as '80s as it gets. You really can't go to a dance party without hearing it. RoyalE, right? Kind of a one-hit wonder."

I nodded. "She's totally a one-hit wonder. Rayna Emerson is her real name. The song was huge and those were in the years when record sales and radio play made a gigantic difference. She made a ton of money from that one song. Well, Cole's her only child. He's thirty-eight years old."

It was a strange story to digest. Our glasses were running low, and Rocky poured a bit more into each. He could stay in my backyard for as long as he wanted. "So he is the editor of your magazine?"

49

"*Was* the editor. Earlier in the day of the plane crash, we got word that the magazine's parent company had been acquired, and that they were getting rid of us because we weren't profitable. He decided to go out to LA to live with his mom as well as break up with me that day. It wasn't even a direct breakup that you could at least respect; he simply said that he was leaving and wasn't coming back. My parents' plane crashed that night. It was also the day that Alyssa found out about Patrick. It was very much a craptastic day. And now here we are."

"Good Lord," Rocky said, swirling his glass around. "And here we are. How long had you dated him?"

"Almost a year. It was both easy and hard. The simple part was that our lives were so intertwined because of work that it was easy to just spend all of our time together. The hard part was that no one really knew about us, except for my friend Blair and my roommate Scarlett. And I guess it was also hard that he was pretty immature, and our relationship wasn't actually going anywhere. I think that was okay for me because I'm still so young, but when I think about it, he's thirty-eight and often acted much younger than me. And now according to several websites and entertainment news shows, he's dating a reality TV star who *is* younger than me."

Rocky was amused by my last comment. "This has to be good. Who *is* it?"

"Have you ever seen the show *Connors Crew*?" I asked. "It's Cari Connors."

Rocky laughed. "Oh, she's trampy. It's a popular show among the high school set. I'm sorry to laugh, but that's kind of ridiculous. How could he go from *you* to *her*?" Was that a compliment or a put-down? I grimaced a bit at him, and luckily, he picked up on it immediately. "That probably came out badly. What I mean is, you are such a wholesome, normal-acting person. I don't really know you well yet, so maybe you're not really wholesome or normal," he said, giving a small laugh. "But come on. It's like going from dating the girl next door to pursuing girls on Craigslist."

I couldn't help but smile at him in the dark. "I'll take it as a compliment."

We continued to talk about my life in Chicago, my time at Northwestern, my previous relationship to Mark the MBA student, and how I had no idea what I was going to do with my future or where I was going to live. I loved cooking but didn't want to go back into catering or work in a restaurant. I wanted to do something that would help people and could potentially get into some kind of philanthropy work once my parents' estate was fully settled, but I didn't know what that would even look like. I was still only twenty-four, and when I thought of women who worked in that field, I thought of older society ladies who wore brooches on their suit jackets. I also had no experience with anything like that. It was all very confusing. It was also about two in the morning, the fire had died out, and we had shifted over to the hammocks that hung adjacent to the deck. The night was still warm, the stars were very bright, we could hear waves crashing in the distance from the nearby shore, and I hadn't had a night quite like this that I could recall. There was one more thing that I had to make sure that Rocky knew about before I could pin hopes on getting to spend more time with him.

"This is a beautiful spot," said Rocky. "Is Two Lights State Park near here? I went there once when my mom came to visit."

"Right around the corner. It's only about a three-minute drive from here." I squirmed slightly in my hammock. "I need to tell you one more thing." This was going to be awkward.

"Let me guess. You enlisted in the Marines yesterday and are taking off to boot camp in a few hours, so you won't be able to join me in chaperoning the high school summer play tomorrow night."

"Ah, no. Good one though. Maybe next week. What's the deal with the play?"

"You're avoiding the thing you want to tell me about. You tell me, then I'll tell you about the play. It'll be worth the wait, too. It's a super exciting possibility for you." It turned out that he could be just as sarcastic as I was, and I loved it.

"Okay. I knew a little about you before tonight. Not from my mom or Kate Heathcliff."

He laughed. "Did you Facebook stalk me? See my pictures with my college buddies playing golf, and our attempts to form really lame bands?

That I'm a terrible guitar player but do it anyway? Or did you learn of my rabid, obsessive devotion to Ben Folds? It's all true, but I can't think of what else you would see. I'm not that interesting."

It was time to just come out with it. "Lance Ashton was my summer boyfriend throughout high school. He lives next door."

Rocky was silent. I wondered if this was a deal breaker for him. Did he really want to be where Lance had been? It sounded crude and it was so long ago, but it could be a consideration. This was the guy who had punched him out right before his college graduation. "I didn't sleep with Kristy," he said simply. "But I get it. He was so in love with her and thought that the rest of his life was going to include her. I had been in the exact same scenario with Danielle during pretty much the same timeframe. The whole thing was so stupid. It was senior week, and everyone was partying. She was there, and I was there, and we had lived in the same dorm during freshman year and had a slight flirtation right before she started dating Lance, so there was a tiny bit of history. It was one of those silly things that you do sometimes in those situations in college. I wish he hadn't punched me, but it happened, and I moved on. What's Lance up to these days? I haven't seen him really. We were at an Amville event together in Portland, but he was clearly avoiding me."

Rocky's maturity was staggering to me. I wasn't used to it. Cole was such a man-child, and Lance, well… "Not a lot, between you and me. He lives with his parents and doesn't work. I encouraged him to reach out to Kate Heathcliff about some alumni connections that might be helpful. I think that everything that happened with Kristy stunted him. He needs to move on. It's been over two years now." I weighed what to say next. He hadn't addressed my relationship with Lance, perhaps on purpose. "Is it strange to you that I dated him?"

"Um, yeah," he said with a laugh. "I just can't imagine you being interested in him. I didn't know him very well at Amville, and I think he was holed up with Kristy a lot of the time, but he always seemed kind of one-dimensional. What was the attraction?"

It was a good question. "As you might have noticed from talking to me, there is a pattern in my life. He was right here. We met when we were three years old. It was just natural for us to hang out together being the same age. As we got older and all the hormones kicked in, we were spending every summer together here in vacationland where everything was pretty perfect. It was bound to happen. Once we started college and he was with Kristy and I met Mark, it fizzled out." I decided to leave out Lance's recent attempt to reignite things. "We were really young. It seems like a lifetime ago at the very least. We're just friends now."

Rocky seemed satisfied with what I told him. "I get it. I think we all have people in our lives from that time period who we would never be with as adults, but they served a purpose at the time. They help us to grow up and we learn from them."

His response was a big relief. "I couldn't agree more." I said. It was very late. My eyelids were finally starting to get heavy, and somewhere around this point in our conversation, I drifted off to sleep in the hammock. I wasn't sure at the time if Rocky had done the same, but I couldn't fight it anymore. I woke up to bright sunlight several hours later and a five-year-old Trish and a three-year-old Susie standing next to the hammock staring at me.

"Why are you in the hammock, Auntie Janie?" Trish asked.

"Who's he?" Susie asked, pointing to a sleeping Rocky in the other hammock. He stayed. I couldn't help smiling.

I sat up. "His name is Rocky," I said, smoothing back Susie's bedhead hair. "I'm going to make him breakfast."

7 - Sweet Potatoes on Ice

I SNAPPED OUT OF THE FOG of only a few hours of sleep and tip-toed past a sleeping Rocky, shushing Susie and Trish along the way, focusing on getting them into the house quickly and quietly. Alyssa hadn't come downstairs yet, which was not surprising given her pattern from the summer of letting me deal with the girls. On a different morning I might have been annoyed by the regularity with which it was happening, but this morning was different. I got to cook for Rocky Macallen, and it was way too important to me that I got this right, but also got it done promptly. Knowing he could wake up at any time, I swiftly got to work.

Given my time constraints, it had to be something that didn't require too much time to prepare. I turned the oven on, set it to 400 degrees, and took out a baking rack and placed it on a large foil-lined sheet pan. I quickly emptied out a package of applewood-smoked bacon and laid the strips on the rack and threw it into the top oven. I gave my mom a silent thank you for insisting that they add the second oven about ten years ago, and I set the bottom oven to 425 degrees. I enlisted the girls to collect the ingredients for their favorite biscuits *carefully*—I didn't want piles of flour and baking powder on the floor if I could help it. They were excited to help and motivated by the promise of their desired breakfast.

Alyssa came into the kitchen as I was taking the buttermilk-scented dough out of the mixer and dumping it onto a floured board. "What's going on here? Bacon smells good," she said.

Trish was slowly carrying the carton of strawberries to the counter just like I had asked her to. "There's a boy sleeping outside," she said.

"Really," said Alyssa. "And Auntie is cooking for him for the first time. I get it now. What can I do?"

My sister had finally snapped out of her own personal universe for a moment. "Bless you. Can you make some coffee? And cut up this fruit and put it in a bowl?"

"As long as he doesn't mind that I have crazy hair from sleeping and am wearing my pajamas when he walks into the house." To Alyssa's credit, she had become less concerned about looking perfect all the time. A month ago, she probably wouldn't have met someone for the first time in her current state. Maybe she was letting some of her suburban mom intensity go. She started measuring out the coffee beans for the grinder.

"Aww, crap," I said. "How terrible do *I* look?" I was so focused on getting breakfast made that I hadn't given any thought to the fact that I hadn't even looked in a mirror. Or brushed my teeth.

Alyssa started the coffeemaker. "Susie, run up to Auntie's bathroom and get her toothbrush and toothpaste, please. Jae Jae, you're good. I caught a glimpse of him last night. Cute boy. I'm sure you told him all about us last night. If he didn't run away screaming, then he's definitely worthy of a good breakfast. Just keep going with this. Once he has one of those biscuits, he'll be hooked on you. You want me to get out some butter to soften for them?" Jae Jae had been her name for me when I was little. Since she was six years older than I was, she often helped to take care of me. The roles had definitely been reversed this summer, but it was nice that she was willing to give me a hand now when I needed her.

"Yes, thank you. Yeah, he's really nice. Totally different from anyone I've ever really been interested in before. He's a great listener. I guess he has to be, since he's a high school guidance counselor. Isn't that cool?"

Alyssa began to take out napkins and plates. "Cool? I guess really admirable more than anything else. I can't imagine spending my days talking to teenagers. What a thankless job. He sounds like a good soul."

The biscuits were baking and starting to fill the house with a delicious aroma. He was worth this rushed full-court press. "I don't know if it's thankless. He's only done it for a year, but he finds it really rewarding. But I agree; I have no idea how anyone chooses that. He had a very different upbringing from us, which I'm sure has something to do with it. His dad left them and ran off to have a second family, leaving his mom—" I was cut off by a sleepy-looking, slightly disheveled Rocky walking into the house. So much for that toothbrush.

"Good morning, ladies," he said. He turned to Alyssa. "Hi, Alyssa, I'm Rocky," and stuck out his hand.

"Nice to meet you, Rocky. If you want coffee, it's all right over there. I need to go intercept a three-year-old who has gotten lost in the house with a tube of toothpaste." She took Trish and went looking for Susie, giving us a moment alone.

"Hi," I said. "Best sleep of your life, I'm guessing."

He laughed. "Not bad. It's a beautiful day out already. If it weren't for the eight months of winter, Maine would really be the perfect place to live." He looked around the kitchen. "So, um, you're making all of this food?"

Comments like this always made me nervous. I cooked with such vigor and enthusiasm that people were either really impressed and excited, or else it made them very uncomfortable because it was so foreign to them. Maybe I was trying too hard. "I thought you might be hungry. And I feed the girls breakfast every morning. These biscuits are their favorite, and I always crave bacon when I haven't gotten much sleep. And strawberries and pineapple. I hope this is okay."

He helped himself to coffee. "Good God, yes. I'm just not used to anyone cooking for me unless I'm in a restaurant. Because of our situation growing up, Mom didn't cook much. Being in Seattle, we had a lot of great takeout options, so that's how we lived most of the time, but this is such a treat. Thank you."

The girls came back into the kitchen, and Alyssa was chasing after Susie, trying to wipe toothpaste off of the back of her pajamas. "I have no idea how she did this to herself. Is the food ready? I'm starving." It was, and we all sat down to the most formal meal I had experienced since arriving in Maine a month ago. Everyone had napkins and silverware and things to drink. It was strange but also very nice. I helped everyone get food onto their plates and felt myself relax slightly.

Within a few minutes of starting breakfast, there was a knock on the door. Alyssa, showing more initiative this morning than I had seen from her in the past four weeks, got up to see who was there. I had a guess who it could be, and I was correct. Meredith Ashton was soon in my kitchen, carrying a murky-looking, unidentifiable orange food item.

"Hello, girls!" she said in her always-loud, busybody manner, as she looked around to see if the house was in the total chaos that she expected given our situation. To our credit, it actually wasn't that bad. Once she saw Rocky sitting at the table, her expression changed. "Oh! A visitor! I'm Meredith. I live next door. I've known Janie since she was only three years old; that's Susie's age. Imagine that! She and my son used to—oh, I'm sure you don't want to hear about any of that. Ha! Anyway, this is a very nice family. How do you—" Her rapid-fire questioning was cut off by her own son, who was now in our kitchen, holding a cell phone. As soon as he had entered the room, he had zeroed in on who had unexpectedly joined us for breakfast.

"WHAT THE FUCK ARE *YOU* DOING HERE?" Lance shouted, staring at Rocky. Lance's face turned from a light summer tan to beet-red in about three seconds, and he was seething.

"Lance!" Alyssa, Meredith, and I yelled back, almost in perfect unison. Trish's eyes were as a big as saucers. Susie looked confused.

Meredith was also puzzled and fairly horrified. She put down the dish on the counter and put her hands on the hips of her khaki Bermuda shorts.

"Lance, the girls! Do you know this young man?" Obviously, she had not made the connection that this was the guy who her son had punched out just a few days shy of college graduation.

Lance ignored the question but shifted his attention briefly towards her. "Mom, you left your phone in the house again. Dad is at Home Depot and doesn't know which faucet you want him to buy for the sink. You need to call him back," he said icily, and returned his glare towards Rocky.

Meredith nodded, for once in her life not knowing the right words. She gingerly took the phone out of Lance's hand. "Okay, let's go back to the house, Lance. I'll call him from there. You come with me. Girls, I've left you some sweet potato casserole. Come on, Lance." She was treating him like he was a child, which was appropriate given the circumstances.

Lance continued to stare at Rocky but replied, "All right." He walked out with her, leaving the rest of us to sit silently and watch them depart from our house.

Alyssa broke the silence. "Um, sweet potato casserole? It's August. What's she thinking?"

We all started to laugh a bit awkwardly, but we were interrupted when Lance came storming back into the house. Rocky stood, sensing that things would be worse the second time around. "Let's call a truce, man. This isn't good for anyone," he said. Again, I sensed Rocky's maturity and calm nature. Lance was now behaving like a fourteen-year-old going through puberty who didn't know how to control his emotions yet.

My assessment was correct. Before anyone could do anything to prevent it from happening, Lance swung his fist directly into Rocky's face, making contact squarely on his left cheekbone. Rocky's head recoiled, the rest of us gasped, and Lance yelled, "AGAIN?! You can't leave my life alone!"

Rocky put his hands out to keep Lance at bay. "I could say the same thing about you, you moron." His face wasn't bleeding, but he would inevitably have a killer bruise. He needed ice, but I needed Lance out of my house first.

Everyone was standing now. "Get the hell out of here, Lance!" I shouted.

Alyssa stood in front of the girls, trying to shield them the best that she could from what had unfolded in front of them. "Seriously, Lance, get some self-control. In front of my kids?!"

Lance walked a few steps backwards and shook his head. "This was once my safe place. This is where I was loved." He was almost pathetic at that moment, practically whimpering. "I just can't move forward with anything." He turned and walked to the front door, leaving the house.

I sprang into action, making Rocky an ice bag. Alyssa brought the girls upstairs to get them dressed for camp and to deal with their bewilderment as to what they just witnessed. Rocky and I moved over to the family room couch, and I sat next to him in stillness as he held the ice to his face. It didn't appear that anything was broken or that he needed urgent medical attention. He finally spoke. "He's not as strong as he was two years ago, luckily. He's gotten soft." I laughed lightly. "So, the best part of this is that I have to chaperone a high school play tonight. We never ended up talking about that last night. Do you want to come with me?"

"Do you really want to show up to your school with a black eye and a girl that no one knows?"

"Well, we have to chaperone one event per school year, but this theatre program play counts towards the requirement and it's so much easier for me to get it done in the summer. I'd love to have some company, and I promise you that the kids are super talented, so it's pretty good. You'll be at least mildly entertained." He adjusted the ice bag. "As for the black eye, I don't know how I'm going to explain that."

I thought about it for a moment. "I don't think you're going to have to. Alyssa is very talented with makeup. I had a glaring zit for my senior prom and you couldn't even see it. If you come over first, I'll make you dinner and she'll make the black eye go away. What's your favorite thing to eat for dinner?"

He smiled at me. We were sitting fairly close to each other on the couch, and I was angled towards him, with my legs curled under me. I had known him for approximately fifteen hours. I resisted all urges to touch the parts of his face that weren't aching. "A meatball sub," he said.

I laughed. "Seriously. I'll make you anything you want. A killer steak, you name it. You've suffered enough today and it's not even eight-thirty in the morning."

"I mean it. It's my favorite thing in the world. There's a great place in Portland that I get them from, but I bet yours are better."

He was correct. I make fantastic meatballs. "Okay, deal. What time do you have to be there for the play?"

"We have to collect tickets, so six-thirty."

"Okay, come over about four-thirty. Bring whatever you want to change into for tonight, because the food will be saucy. And I'll make sure that Alyssa is here to work her magic." I paused, not sure what to say about what had happened that morning. "I'm really sorry about Lance. There is no excuse for what he did here today."

Rocky adjusted the ice bag. "I think he's still in love with you, Janie. Not that I blame him; you're spectacular. But why else would he do something like that?"

I fidgeted. "I don't think I've ever been described in that way before."

He shifted the ice bag to his left hand and reached over to somewhat awkwardly touch my hair with his right hand. It was a moment that could have turned into something else, had it not been for Trish running through the room yelling, "Where are my sneakers? I can't find my sneakers! And where is my sunscreen?" We both laughed, and he put his hand down and stood up.

"See you later this afternoon, Janie. That was the best biscuit I've ever had in my life. I'm going to keep the ice bag, if you don't mind." He grabbed his keys from the kitchen counter and walked out, leaving me sitting on the couch in a sleepy daze.

Trish had found her sneakers and sat next to me on the couch to put them on. "Is he your boyfriend?" she asked, affixing the Velcro straps.

I thought about her question, knowing that anything that I replied with could easily be repeated later that day over meatballs. "I don't know. I just know that I like him."

Trish seemed satisfied with my answer. "I like him, too. But I wish he had hit Lance back."

"Trish! Hitting someone is never nice."

Trish nodded. "I know that. It's a very bad choice. But Lance still deserves it. He needs to get a life."

"Where did you hear that expression? Did Mommy say that?"

"Yes, and I agree with her." She handed me her sunscreen so that I could apply it for her. "What does 'get a life' mean, anyway?"

"It means that you need to move on, that you need to find new interests and things to do. Lance is having a hard time doing that. Does that make sense?" Putting things into words understandable for a five-year-old actually helped to simplify the situation and make it even clearer. Lance needed to move on, and we couldn't help him much more than we already had. It was up to him now.

"Yeah, it does. Does Daddy need to get a life, too?"

I didn't sign up for this question. "I don't know, sweetie. Let's go find Susie. We are already late for camp and I really need for you to make me something there today. Maybe you can make something for Rocky, too. He had a bad morning and I bet it would make him feel better."

"Okay, sure. I can do that. What are you going to do today, Auntie Janie?"

"I'm going to take a nap, somewhere other than a hammock. And then I am going to make meatballs."

8 - Makeup and Meatballs

AFTER DROPPING THE GIRLS AT camp, I drove into Portland to Whole Foods to get the ingredients for what I envisioned to be the best meatball subs imaginable. I bought rolls that had just come out of the oven, organic ground beef, and fresh mozzarella. I had a can of San Marzano crushed tomatoes, onions, garlic, and a beautiful chunk of Parmesan. I grabbed a can of dry bread crumbs and after mentally inventorying the needed ingredients, I knew that everything else could be found in my mother's herb garden. I paid for my groceries and headed home to start the process.

I absolutely love to make meatballs. Everyone thinks that they are doing it right, that theirs are the best, but that's the beauty of the meatball. You can impart it with any combination of flavors and textures and come up with something different every time. I finely chopped the onion and garlic and added it to the bowl where I had already put the ground beef. I added some lightly-beaten egg and the bread crumbs. I minced the parsley and basil from the garden and threw those in with some kosher salt and freshly-ground pepper. Finally, I grated the Parmesan and added it to the mix. I rolled the mixture into small spheres and set them on a parchment paper-lined sheet pan and put into the oven. They would smell incredible within a few minutes.

As I put the stainless-steel pan on the stovetop to begin making the sauce, I realized how excited I was to make something for Rocky that he obviously liked so much. I was completely aware that it seemed so anti-feminist of me, and it wasn't the first time that I had dealt with feelings like this. A former employee at *Young Chicago* (who didn't last very long there, as the job wasn't "fun enough" for her) once had told me that it wasn't progressive for women to cook, as it kept them in the antiquated roles of the 1950s. When I responded to her that I liked it and it was the only creative thing that I was somewhat good at, she retorted that just because I was a woman, I didn't necessarily need to be creative.

At that moment, I had realized she was an idiot and I would never win an argument with her, so I bit my tongue and didn't proceed to take things further down the path to insulting her writing ability. It was a ridiculous interchange, but it always reentered my mind when I was cooking for a guy. Corinne Whitman had grown up as an only child with a mother who rarely cooked, which prompted her to teach herself as she got older. My mother was artistic and imaginative in every aspect of her life, and this was the one thing that she passed along to me. I brushed aside the feelings of inadequacy; this was her gift and I was proud to have it.

With renewed vigor, I sautéed the rest of the chopped onions in olive oil and then added the garlic. I included a mix of fresh chopped herbs and stirred them in the pan to release their delicious perfume. In went the tomatoes with some salt and pepper, and I had the beginnings of a delectably simple sauce that would hopefully meld perfectly with the meatballs. I took them out of the oven and turned the stove to the lowest setting, set my alarm on my phone for an hour, and collapsed on the couch for a catnap. I needed the rest, but it was hard to shut off my mind given everything that had happened in the last day. I kept thinking of what it would be like to kiss Rocky, of what his face must feel like after Lance punched him again, and how part of me just wanted to run off somewhere with him and leave Alyssa to deal with her daughters, and troubled marriage, and Yoga Dude, on her own. Somewhere in those thoughts, I finally drifted off to sleep.

I was still tired in the afternoon but had enough of a recharge to get everything prepped for our early dinner. I showered and spent about an hour trying to figure out an outfit that would be appropriate to chaperone a high school play. I really had no idea what I was doing, but I knew that I had to avoid too much cleavage or something that was too short. I also didn't have much of my wardrobe with me, prompting me to realize that if I was actually going to stay in Maine, I would at some point have to stop paying my half of the rent in Chicago and help Scarlett to find a new roommate. And get the rest of my stuff, too. I finally settled on a very simple black sundress that hit just above the knee. It was totally conservative and not in the least bit controversial. Showing up with Rocky would likely be provocative enough.

The girls had had a great day at camp and were excited to eat meatballs with Rocky and to put makeup on him. They had both made him artwork and seemed energized with the idea of someone else coming into their lives. I wasn't sure where any of this was going; I really hoped that he was going to spend much more time with us, but after only knowing him for a day, there was no way to truly tell. The girls were vulnerable and so was I. We loved the idea of Rocky and the notion of him as a more constant presence, but time would tell. I hoped that a good sub and an effective makeup session would encourage him to stick around.

Alyssa had promised me that she would get home by four o'clock; with Rocky coming to the house for four-thirty, I wanted a time buffer. I got the girls cleaned up and changed into decent clothes, the rolls were wrapped in foil and in the oven on low, the mozzarella was thinly sliced, and the sauce and meatballs were on the stove on a low simmer. I was wearing the non-scandalous dress, my hair and makeup were refreshed, and I had found a Pandora station of seventies folk rock that seemed fairly innocuous. I remembered Lance as well as Rocky mentioning Ben Folds, but I thought that might be a bit too stalkerish—as if I was hanging on his every word—plus I wasn't sure that I actually knew who Ben Folds was. This seemed safer. Everything was set, and it was four-twenty-five. The door finally opened.

"You said you would be here at four!" I yelled, annoyed but not surprised at Alyssa's tardiness.

"Oops, and here I thought I was early," Rocky said with a smile, as he walked into the kitchen.

"Oh! It's you! Hi," I said. "I may kill my sister, but I'm glad you're here."

"Me, too," he said. "I mean, not about the sister part, but your house smells so good. I can't wait for this. See, I wore an old nasty t-shirt and gym shorts. I've got my respectable clothes here," he said, gesturing to the clothes that he just draped over the back of the couch.

"Perfect," I said. "I'm totally wearing this apron when I eat. Am I dressed okay for tonight?"

"Yes, especially the apron. You should definitely wear the apron tonight."

"That's what I thought, too. Okay, Alyssa is obviously *busy*, so I'm going to start putting the food together. Want to learn how to assemble the best meatball sub of your life?"

"Absolutely," he replied. "Where are the little girls?"

"Oh, this is the best. They are setting up the master bathroom like a beauty salon so that we can put makeup on you in there. How's your eye? It looks painful."

"Nice, I can't wait for that. It's alright. I've been icing it for most of the day. My roommate Max knows Lance from Amville and wanted to come over to his house today and kick his ass. I luckily talked him off of that ledge, but it wasn't easy. Jim Croce! I haven't heard this in forever. What kind of music do you usually listen to?"

I felt my face flush a bit. "This sort of thing. My dad was really into folk rock like this and some of the yacht rock stuff, too. I've been to Christopher Cross concerts. Jimmy Buffett, too. My parents were pretty much Parrotheads, except they flew around in planes instead of sailing on boats. You're probably horrified. You seem much cooler than that."

Rocky laughed. "No, I get it. That stuff has its merits, for sure. It's much more optimistic music than what I tend to listen to. Okay, so what are we doing here?"

I had laid out a large foil-covered sheet pan with a rack in it, the plate of sliced mozzarella, the pan of sauce and meatballs, and the lightly-heated rolls. I put the broiler on and began showing him the steps. "I'll let you assemble your own, so you can control the ratios and quantities that you like. I've boiled some pasta for the girls, because this will be a little tough for them to eat. Anyway, take a roll and put it on the rack. Put as much of the sauce and meatballs as you want in the roll, and then put some of the cheese on it. I'll broil them and that's it."

He started to follow my lead. "I can't believe you made all of this. It's really amazing."

"I didn't make the rolls. I don't do that." We both gave a small laugh, and then heard the front door fly open. Alyssa ran into the kitchen. She was fairly disheveled, and with her hair much shorter, it looked wild and out of place.

"Hi," she said. "Sorry I'm late. We were doing, um, hip-openers in yoga today."

Rocky bit his lip in an attempt not to laugh, and I asked, "Hip-openers? I mean, what the fuck, Alyssa. You look like you've been rolling around in a barn. Which maybe is what you have been doing while also doing hip-openers, but seriously? The girls are upstairs turning Mom and Dad's, um, the master bathroom into a Red Door Spa. I take no responsibility for what might be going on up there. Dinner will be ready in about ten minutes, and then we need to fix Rocky's eye. Can you still help us with that, please?"

Alyssa seemed to be trying to snap out of whatever far-away place she was in and replied, "Yeah, of course. I'm going to go upstairs and change and see them. Be down in a few." About thirty seconds later we heard the girls cheer, "Mommy!"

"Sorry about that," I said to Rocky once Alyssa was upstairs. "I don't know what she's doing. Well, I think I may know now what she's doing, but I'm not sure where it's going at this point. Summer will be over soon, and she's got decisions to make. But I'm sorry you're seeing all of this family stuff."

Rocky shrugged. "It's life. You should see the parade of asses that my mom has brought home. Luckily, she hasn't married any of them, but they've been really awesome, let me assure you. So, what can I do here to help you now?"

"I think we're all set. I'm going to check on these now." I opened the oven and saw perfectly browned sandwiches. *Yessss...* "Okay, we're good to go here!" I took them out and set the sheet pan on the stovetop. "Just grab your plate and help yourself. Hey, girls!" I yelled. "Come have some dinner!"

We all enjoyed our food, and Rocky assured me that it was indeed the best meatball sub that he had ever had. I have to admit that they came out even better than I could have imagined, so the effort had been worth it. Alyssa, obviously feeling guilty about her afternoon and lateness, tried her best to be very complimentary of me, turning to Rocky and saying, "This is nothing. If this was a proper Janie dinner, this would just be the first course. Her talent is extraordinary." I felt myself redden, but I was appreciative.

After eating, we all went upstairs and got everything ready to remove Rocky's black eye from existence, at least for the next few hours. He went into the walk-in closet to quickly change into his nicer clothes, and Alyssa gathered her makeup, sponges, and brushes. The little girls took turns painting each other's faces with whatever Alyssa would let them use.

Rocky sat on my mother's beautifully upholstered stool that had once belonged to my grandmother in her much more formal Wellesley house. Alyssa applied some eye cream very carefully so that the surface would be smooth and supple enough to accept the makeup without it flaking or creasing. She then dotted some concealer around the bruised area and gingerly blended it with a sponge. There was already tremendous progress. Rocky sat patiently as she then layered on a light powder to his entire face, blending the concealed areas gently so that it all looked as natural as possible. Although there was sort of a strange shadow by his eye, you couldn't necessarily tell that he had been assaulted with someone's fist.

Alyssa stepped back and critically looked at her work. "What do you think? You can still sort of see something. I can put on more makeup and probably cover it completely, but you will need to wear liquid base makeup all over your entire face. It's up to you."

Rocky examined himself in the mirror. "Nah, it'll be dark in there anyway. Wow, this feels so weird. Um, anyway, thanks so much. This is much better. I know where to go whenever I need makeup. Janie, you ready to roll? I know you can't wait to spend the evening at a high school."

"I'm super psyched. Let's go. Bye, girls." I kissed each of my nieces on top of their heads. "Thanks, Alyssa. He looks much more socially acceptable now."

ONE OF THE TECH PRODUCTION students was waiting for Rocky with the cash box when we arrived. "Mr. Macallen! I haven't seen you since school got out! You look sort of different..." His voice trailed off, and he looked back and forth between Rocky and me, as if he was trying to figure out why Rocky's eye looked strange and who on earth I was.

Rocky took the cash box from the boy. "Teachers always look different in the summer, Andy. It's all the extra sleep we get. This is Ms. Whitman. She's going to help me tonight since it's a big job for just one person."

"Oh, okay! All right, enjoy the show. It's really good. We've worked really hard on it."

"Will do," said Rocky. "Break a leg!"

I laughed once the boy walked away. "I can't believe that you talk to teenagers all day. You must be the most patient person in the world."

Indeed he was, and also one of the nicest. We spent the next half hour collecting tickets and money from students and parents, and I witnessed Rocky's easy banter with them and ability to let just about everything roll off his shoulders. A few of the girls were bold enough to ask him, "Is this your *girlfriend*, Mr. Macallen?" I felt my face turn about twenty shades of red, while Rocky answered them effortlessly with replies such as, "if only I was that lucky" or "she's much too intelligent for that." One adult, presumably a father of one of the students in the play, patted Rocky on the shoulder as he walked by and said, "smart man." It was a strange experience for me, but it didn't seem to faze Rocky at all.

Once the show had started, we closed up the cash box and snuck into the back of the auditorium, where the last row was completely empty. We took the two seats on the aisle. It was a student-written production, and it was obvious how much work the kids had put into it. It was light-hearted and funny, which was perfect after the bizarre events of the morning. I loved listening to Rocky's laugh, and at one point I felt myself glancing over at him. I could barely see him, but I could tell that he was smiling at me in the dark, and then he reached over for my hand.

It felt so simple and nice and comfortable to sit in the shadows of the theatre, holding Rocky's hand, watching a high school play. It was the complete opposite of my life from just over a month ago, when I would have been hanging out in some bar in Chicago, stroking the ego of Cole over some feeling of inadequacy that he was experiencing at that moment. My mind began to drift in different directions, and I closed my eyes, feeling exhaustion from the lack of sleep from the night before and the emotional stress of the morning. Suddenly, everyone clapped, and the lights came up. "Is it over?" I asked Rocky, blinking my eyes open.

"No, it's just the end of the first act. It's intermission, sleepy."

I had definitely dozed off. "Oh, I didn't realize there's a second act."

Rocky picked up my hand, which he still had interlaced in his own, and gave it a squeeze. "There's absolutely a second act." And for the first time in the past month, I believed it.

9 - Chris and Anne

ROCKY NEEDED A NEW BACKPACK. The play was over and his responsibilities at school were done, and we were driving north on I-295 towards Freeport, where the L.L. Bean headquarters and flagship store is located. As everyone who lives in Maine for at least part of the year knows, L.L. Bean is open twenty-four hours a day, 365 days a year. I had never been there outside of fairly normal shopping hours, but Rocky told me that it was a common thing for college students at various Maine institutions to go to L.L. Bean at all hours of the night. When we pulled up to the parking lot at nine-thirty under an almost pitch-black sky, it felt a little odd. Most of the rest of the shops in the charming little village had closed for the evening, and a few restaurants still were open but winding down for the night. L.L. Bean was alive and humming.

"So, what exactly are you looking for?" I asked as we walked towards the entrance of the massive building.

"I need a new backpack for school. I went with a different brand last year, but it didn't last, and this stuff is great quality."

It was cute. "You're like a little kid getting ready for a new school year. We should buy you some new pencils and erasers, too." I followed his lead past a fish pond over to the luggage area.

He began to examine different bags. "Totally. Make sure they're number two pencils. I fill out a lot of forms that require them." He flipped through some racks. "I tried a messenger bag for a month and just about destroyed my shoulder. I work in a school anyway, so why not?" He picked up a dark gray bag. "I like this one, but I think they have more in the camping section. Let's go look there and we can compare." He took a bag with him and we continued on our search.

We walked to a different section of the colossal store that was full of tents, sleeping bags, and various kinds of hiking equipment. There were backpacks, but they were large and technical; not exactly ideal for dragging a laptop, books, and college promotional materials to and from school each day. Rocky decided on his original choice, and we continued to peruse the items for sale in that corner of the store. The Rocky that I had gotten to know over the past day or so was very calm, easygoing, and measured. Being in L.L. Bean brought out a different side to him that was more fun, more playful. Within a few minutes, we were both wearing headlamps and trying out weather radios. I was examining a cook stove and some frightening-looking dehydrated food when I turned around and couldn't find him.

"Where are you?" No one else was in the area of the store, but I found myself alone with water filtration systems and fire starters that doubled as whistles.

"In here, testing out my headlamp." Rocky's voice came from inside a tent. I stopped myself from leaping into it as quickly as I could but made myself count to three before crawling into it with him. He would still be in there, and I had to calm down. *You've known him for one day.* I wasn't sure why it had seemed so much longer—perhaps a lack of sleep—but it happily had. *Happy.* I realize that I was actually momentarily happy. My parents were still gone, Cole was still a man-child, Patrick was still a douchebag, Lance was still a bully, and Alyssa was still opening her hips with Yoga Dude. But right then, I was happy. I went with that feeling.

Rocky was lying down on his back, tossing a glow-in-the-dark Frisbee towards the ceiling of the tent. The tent was on the bigger side, and I could easily lie down next to him. We took turns with the Frisbee, until he missed catching it and it clocked him in the face, luckily away from his tender eye. We laughed and reached for each other's hands and were silent for a moment. Rocky rolled onto his side and leaned over and kissed me very softly but quietly, and it felt so different to experience a first kiss that wasn't fueled by a party or drinks at a bar, but instead just by the circumstances of two people being in the right moment, at the right time, who were genuinely and soberly enjoying getting to know each other. I rolled onto my side so that I was facing him, and this time I initiated a kiss. Our headlamps crashed against each other, we laughed again, took them off, and went back to what we were doing. There were voices in the camping area now as a few shoppers had come to that corner of the store, but I was only minimally aware of them initially.

A deep male voice got louder as it approached the tent. "I think this would be big enough. Tell me what you think," he said, and he opened up the tent flap to find two twenty-four-year-olds making out. "Um, wow, I'm so sorry! I only expect to see this during the academic year!"

Rocky sat up very quickly, recognizing a familiar voice. "Professor Manfried?"

The older man laughed. "Rocky Macallen. Why am I not surprised? Good to see you, my friend!"

Red-faced and mortified, I got out of the tent as soon as the professor backed out of its entrance. Rocky followed. We were standing in front of the man and who was presumably his wife in the middle of the camping section of L.L. Bean. I felt like I was a kid in trouble, despite the fact that the professor and his wife were chuckling.

Rocky broke the ice. "So, um, Janie, this is my college advisor, Professor Chris Manfried. And his wife. Anne, I believe?"

Professor Manfried shook my hand. "Yes, good memory, Rocky. This is Anne. We came down from Camden to look at tents for a camping trip we are taking over Labor Day weekend. We figured we would come down here tonight when it was likely to be pretty empty and we could try out the equipment, but it looks like you beat us to it!"

My face turned almost purple as I choked out, "It's nice to meet you both. My parents were Amville grads."

Rocky interjected, "Oh, that's right, they are from around the same era. Professor, when did you graduate?"

"Please, both of you, call me Chris. 1980. Almost forty years ago. Wow. Anne, too. Who were your parents, Janie?"

"Oh my God, they were the same year," I answered. "Mike and Corinne Whitman. Well, she was Corinne Olson while she was there. They got married soon after graduation. Did you know them?"

Anne laughed and patted Chris on the shoulder. "He knew them well."

Chris put his arm around his wife's shoulder. "Now, that's a story. Screw the tent. Do you two care to go have a glass of wine with us? The Harraseeket Inn is a block away, and they have a lovely patio. I'll save the story until then."

WE SAT IN CHAIRS BY THE firepit outside the inn and ordered our drinks. The summer night was warm but not too humid, with bright stars and a gentle breeze. I had known the Manfrieds for about ten minutes, but they seemed very familiar and welcoming. I could tell that Rocky respected Chris and had learned a great deal from him, and it was also evident that Chris had enjoyed working with Rocky at Amville. Although my experience at Northwestern had been positive and had taken me in the direction that I had wanted to go, it was apparent that the small liberal arts college experience was different and special. I was about to discover in greater depth why that was the case.

"So," Chris said, taking a sip of his Malbec. "I apologize for not saying this earlier in L.L. Bean, but you caught me off guard. I did hear about what happened, Janie. I am so sorry. We wanted to come to the services so very much, but we were visiting our new granddaughter in California at the time. We truly wanted to be there. Are you and your sister doing all right?"

He seemed so sincere. It was nice to engage with someone who knew my parents and cared about my family's well-being. "Yes, we are staying in their house in Cape Elizabeth right now, and we have their house in

Massachusetts on the market. Once it sells, we're going to clear everything out of there and will keep this place here in Maine. It's been in the family since my grandparents built it. But thank you. There were a few people from their Amville days who were able to come, which was nice."

"I'm glad to hear that. They were both so well-liked. Such good people. Anyway, I owe you a good story. Anne knows about all of this, so I am not talking out of turn here." He took another sip of wine and stroked his white and gray beard thoughtfully. "I had the biggest crush on your mother. I hope I'm not embarrassing you, but she was a catch. She was ahead of her time, as I'm sure you know. She would grow herbs—and I'm not talking about the seventies kind, but real herbs like basil and thyme—in little window boxes in her dorm room. She would find any kitchen space she could and throw these crazy dinner parties wherever she could find chairs and tables. We would often just enjoy these insanely good meals on paper plates in our laps. We were eating things that no one knew about in those years—I'm talking fennel, Morel mushrooms, you name it! - and everyone clamored to get invites. She would give the girls facials in the dorm bathrooms, and that was before anyone really knew what a facial was. She had this long hair that she would swing around or sometimes tie up in this elaborate knot. She smelled like sunflowers. She—"

Anne cut in. "I am here with you today because Corinne Olson decided to become Corinne Whitman. But I think there were a lot of guys who felt the same way that Chris did."

Chris nodded eagerly in the light of the fire. "I have no doubt. Anyway, I tried, but I got absolutely nowhere. I did get to go to a few dinner parties, but she really didn't give me the time of day. So, as Rocky likely knows, I was an English major. But you had to take a certain number of science classes to graduate, just like today, Rocky. So, I signed up for this Geology class, thinking it might be a little easier. You know, the old 'rocks for jocks' reputation, but I certainly wasn't a jock." He laughed heartily. "It really wasn't easy at all, but luckily my friend Mike Whitman was also in the class. As you probably know, Janie, your dad was a Chem major, but he decided to take a

Geo class for fun. Who the hell does that? Nevertheless, on the first day of the lab, we were told that we had to form lab groups of three. Mike graciously agreed to work with me and to save my sorry English major ass, but we needed a third. Sure enough, Corinne was late to class and hadn't even spoken to anyone yet when this announcement was made. I asked her if she wanted to join us and she agreed. The rest is history. I watched them fall in love. They really were perfect for each other."

We all sat quietly, sipping our drinks, staring at the fire. It was so odd yet so wonderful to hear people who knew my parents in their younger years talk about what made them who they were, who they became, what made them our parents. I had heard some version of the Geo lab story years ago but hearing it from Chris' perspective gave it so much more meaning. "So, Anne, when did you enter the picture?" I figured that I would include the lovely woman who had just listened to her husband lament the loss of his college crush.

Anne chuckled. "I barely knew Chris in school. I actually was friendly with your mom and was lucky enough to get one of those facials once. She really was incredible. Anyway, Chris and I actually started talking at our five-year reunion, and since we were both still single, we decided that we should go on a date. The problem was that he was in graduate school in New York City, and I was working in Boston. So, he got a ride with me back to Boston and took me out to a proper dinner on that Sunday after the reunion. The next day he applied to transfer to Boston University." She took a sip of her drink, satisfied with the way it had all turned out.

"The power of Amville women. And their offspring," Rocky said.

"Indeed," said Chris. "You know, Janie, I feel like we need to somehow honor your parents' legacy. I'm not sure what that looks like, but I feel like we need to do something. Have you thought about anything that seems fitting?"

I really hadn't gotten that far yet. The NTSB investigation had wound down, showing a plane malfunction and no fault on my dad's part as the pilot, and we were waiting on the sale of the house before we could further settle the estate. "Not really, but I don't know how any of that works. To be perfectly honest with you, the Development Office really dropped the ball and didn't realize that they had passed away until they called the house looking for my mom to volunteer at a college fair." That was *last night*. This really had been the longest twenty-eight hours or so. With the exception of Rocky's black eye, they had been delicious.

"Well, that's unfortunate. I wish those things wouldn't happen, but mistakes are sometimes made. As for what to do with Amville, it's probably a bit soon for you and your sister. It's only been about a month or so," acknowledged Chris. "Just please let me know if there is anything that I can do. I've been there for a long time now, and I know the politics and how things do and don't get done. It helps that I knew both of them so well, too. I know what they were about and what they weren't. Just know that I'm here. Now that I'm thinking about it, how on earth do you two know each other?"

I didn't know what the right thing to do was, concerning the things that Chris was talking about, but I was comforted in knowing that I had his support and that he would help in whatever I endeavored to do. "That Development Office snafu that I just told you about? I ended up working at the college fair with Rocky. Um, last night. We've known each other for almost a day and a half." Listening to myself speak, I realized that I must have looked like a total floozy in that tent.

Rocky sensed my unease and interjected, "I dragged her along to help me chaperone a school play tonight. As you can see, I'm all about showing a girl a great time. College fairs, school plays, and L.L. Bean. Maybe tomorrow I'll step it up and buy her a cup of coffee."

Chris laughed. "I have no doubt, Macallen. Bring her up to Amville and get a drink in Rockland. Pop into one of the galleries. We can give you some pointers."

It was getting late, and the Manfrieds had an hour and a half drive back to Camden. We said goodbye and thanked them for the wine and headed back to Rocky's car. On the car ride back to Cape Elizabeth, we held hands whenever it was safe for Rocky to do so while driving. We didn't talk much, but there were a couple of quick kisses at stoplights. Everything seemed so new and exciting, yet he seemed more and more familiar, especially after hearing so much about my parents from his advisor. Our lives had been connected in many ways without us yet knowing each other. It was mystifying and reassuring at the same time.

As he turned onto my street, Rocky asked suddenly, "Do you want to drive up to Amville with me tomorrow?"

There was no doubt. I had no idea what we were going to do up there, but it didn't matter. "Yes. I'll drop off the girls at camp and then meet you at your apartment? I'll make Alyssa pick them up in the afternoon. She can do it. I've been picking them up most days."

I got his address and made plans for the morning. I got out of the car and so did he. It was such a gorgeous summer night on the Maine coast, with salt in the air and the faint sound of the ocean around the corner. There was no one outside of our tent this time and no headlamps in our way, and we shared a perfect, quiet, uninterrupted kiss. It wasn't easy to leave him to go inside.

ALYSSA WAS STILL AWAKE in the living room when I got home, and we worked out a compromise for the next couple of days. I would bring the girls to camp the next day, and she would pick them up. We would follow the opposite schedule for the day after. I was about to go upstairs to bed when she called after me, "I really like Rocky, Jae Jae."

I turned around and joined her for a moment more. "Me, too. He's completely different from anyone I've ever been involved with. Very normal and balanced. I'm not used to that."

Alyssa nodded. "I used to think that Patrick was like that. Maybe he was. His ego got in the way. I think he became too successful at too young of an age. I know that sounds ridiculous, as I benefitted from that success, but it certainly didn't help his personality or his behavior, as we have seen."

For the first time since we got to Maine, Alyssa was opening up. "What do you want to do? You've only got a few more weeks until school starts." I asked, hopeful that I hadn't overstepped in my questioning. I had to figure out what I was going to do as well, but there was less urgency since I was ultimately only responsible for myself. Alyssa's situation was much more pressing.

She was pensive and looked less sad than she had, but still serious. There was no doubt that Patrick had taken significant joy away from my sister. "I'm getting closer to a decision. I need a few more days. I know that I need to talk to him, but I think things will become more apparent soon. Thanks for your patience with this ... and with me. I've needed this time with you in this house. When I'm here, I'm just me." She sighed. "And you cook for me. Mom used to come over to the house with delicious things for us, and that won't happen anymore. What you've been able to do for the girls during this time can't be replicated. I don't know what the next step is, but somehow, we need to be together, at least some of the time. I'm not sure what that looks like and even what you want, but I think we can figure it out soon. Just a little more patience, Jae, okay?"

It was okay. I needed to go to sleep, but I felt like I had so much to tell her. "I need to tell you about these people I met at L.L. Bean tonight. I heard the greatest story about Mom and Dad..."

10 - Jane

I DEFINITELY DIDN'T GET ENOUGH sleep after the play and our L.L. Bean adventure, but Rocky was going to drive the ninety minutes or so up to Camden, so I just had to manage to drop the girls off and to get to his Portland apartment. It was small and basic but decent, not too messy, with a few framed Ben Folds concert posters and golf-themed items on the walls. His roommate Max was dressed in full golf gear, getting ready for his job as a pro at a local country club. Max and Rocky, along with their four friends Kyle, Dylan, Jake, and Rich, met while living on the same floor of their freshman year dorm at Amville. The six of them managed to live together in some combination of rooms for the remaining three years, and now as young adults in their mid-twenties, were still very close and saw each other as often as they could.

Max shook my hand and said, "It's nice to meet you. It's about time that Rocky hangs out with someone else. We're all getting sick of him."

I laughed. "Glad to help out." I checked out a few pictures haphazardly stuck on the refrigerator of a slightly younger Rocky and his friends in various places presumably around Amville, on the golf course, and at the beach. There was so much to know, so much to ask, and hopefully plenty of time ahead to do that.

Rocky lifted up the box of admissions materials from the college fair. "I figured we could return these while we're there and you can meet the

79

famous Kate Heathcliff. My guess is that she'll be delightfully awkward and remorseful about all the ways she has wronged you."

I couldn't wait.

Within a few minutes, we were in Rocky's little car and heading towards I-295 North. It was a beautiful summer day in Maine, and the drive out of Portland was particularly stunning. We quickly passed Freeport, where we had been the previous evening, and then hopped onto Route 1 North through the town of Brunswick, home of Bowdoin College. "I didn't get in there," Rocky said with a laugh. "I always knew it was a long shot, but I was banking on the geographical diversity that I could offer them. I mean, I wasn't from Concord, Massachusetts or something like that." I smirked, knowing that many of the small colleges of the Northeast had been full of my high school classmates; Rocky even knew a few people who I had grown up with in Concord.

On our drive, he told me numerous stories about the rivalries among the Maine liberal arts schools and how those would play out on sports fields, courts, and courses. Rocky and Max played golf on the Amville team for all four years, which helped Rocky to afford his equipment and greens fees. "I'm not the greatest golfer, but I did get a lot better playing there," he said. "It was a ridiculously expensive sport for a kid with a single mom and a deadbeat dad, but somehow my mom figured out ways for me to play when I was younger. Amville was a great opportunity for me to get to play more and for cheap. It's a lot harder now that I have to pay for everything, but Max can sometimes get me on his course. You should take lessons there. You might really like it."

We passed through the town of Bath and over a bridge into Georgetown, spotting large naval ships being built at Bath Iron Works. Our conversation shifted to the topic of the time that I had spent in Maine as a child, about the history of our Cape Elizabeth house and my mother's parents who had built it, how they now lived in fairly poor health in South Carolina and were unable to travel, and how Alyssa and I would now be responsible for making decisions about their health and care as well. As my father had a pilot's license and often had access to planes, we had spent time throughout our summers based in Cape Elizabeth exploring northern New England and Quebec through small airport gateways. The drive to Amville had been a great idea of Rocky's; it was fantastic to have a long stretch of time to get to know each other's histories.

"Here's a question," he asked. "Why Janie? Is your real name Jane?"

I had been asked that question more times than I could count. "It is. My family has called me Janie since I was a baby, and when my kindergarten teacher tried to call me Jane, I kept correcting her. She called home, and my mom backed me up. 'She's Janie,' she told her, and from that point on, everyone has called me that. What do you think? Too childish for an adult? Now that I have to think about another job at some point, I do wonder."

"No, not at all. Names with good stories are the best ones."

It was my turn. "So why 'Rocky'?"

He grumbled. "My weird father and his obsession with the Rocky movies. No joke."

I tried to suppress a chuckle, but it snuck out.

"And the irony is that I don't even talk to the bastard anymore. Oh well, I'm Rocky," he said with resignation.

I also got a thorough introduction to Rocky's favorite musician, Ben Folds. "I've got a playlist for you," he said. "This is just an overview of his catalog, but I think it's an adequate beginning." I listened to songs ranging from "The Best Imitation of Myself" ("what I listen to after a long day at work," he explained), to "Song for the Dumped" ("my favorite song from the miserable end of my senior year at Amville"), and his favorite at the moment, "Alice Childress" ("there's a lot of wisdom in these words if you really listen"). Finally, the song "Jane" came on. "This actually might be my favorite right now," he said, and I sat back and listened with a flushed face, taking in the lyrics. I remembered the time during my adolescence when Lance was trying to escalate our relationship and played "Sweet Jane" from the Velvet Underground for me, but I liked this song much better.

We approached Wiscasset and crossed an even larger bridge. There were numerous stores and stands along the road, selling antiques, kayaks, and sacks of Maine-grown potatoes. There were still more bridges, and we soon passed through Newcastle and Damariscotta. I lost track of towns and bridges as we eventually exited onto Maine Route 90, and Rocky pointed out various locations and sites to me as we approached the Amville College campus. I had spent a decent amount of time there as a kid, often accompanying my parents to Homecoming and Reunion weekends, but seeing it with Rocky and as an adult was like I was viewing it with new eyes. It was compact but featured sprawling green lawns and lovely summer flowers, with tall handsome trees and stately brick buildings. It looked much like any other nice, small college campus in New England, but it was where people I cared about grew up, learned, fell in love, had their hearts broken, and made lasting friendships. It was beautiful.

We parked the car near the main administrative building and found the clusters of offices where the Development staff worked. Kate's office was small but well-located, with a nice view of the campus quad. Rocky knocked on her open door and then walked in carrying the box of materials, with me following.

"Oh! Rocky! What a nice surprise." Kate was most likely in her late twenties and was slightly disheveled; I spotted a coffee stain on her cream-colored jacket and that she had missed a button on her blouse. Her hair was reddish-brown like mine but was curly and bordered on untamed. She wore glasses that were a little too big for her face. She was exactly how I imagined her. She abruptly stood up and knocked over a cup of pens on her desk.

Rocky seemed unfazed; he knew her and knew what to expect. "Good to see you, Kate. I want to introduce you to Janie Whitman. I believe you've spoken on the phone." He was still holding the box of admissions materials, but I could tell that he couldn't wait to make this introduction and to see Kate's reaction.

Indeed, it was good. Kate's face turned red and she appeared even more flustered. "Oh! Janie! Oh my goodness, it's great to meet you." She stuck out of hand clumsily. "I, um, I think I really owe you an apology for how we handled everything concerning your parents. We are working with the Communications Department now and want to make sure we put a tribute to your parents in the next issue of the alumni magazine, and there's much more that we would like to do. My director and I would like to meet with you and your sister sometime soon if that's possible. We can come down to Cape Elizabeth, no problem. Would next Monday work? And what time of day? We can be very flexible."

It was a similar approach to how she had bombarded me over the phone but allowing myself to be talked into the college fair had brought me to Rocky; I doubt I would have ever crossed paths with him under any other circumstances. I couldn't really say no to her now. "Okay, yeah, I am sure that will be fine. I'll talk to Alyssa, but her daughters are in day camp, so maybe one in the afternoon?"

Kate was so eager that she almost started jumping up and down when I agreed to meet with them. "That would be great. Let's do that," she replied breathlessly. "Yay! And how was the college fair? I'm so glad you were both able to be there."

Rocky chuckled. "As you will see from the variety of materials in that box, we didn't have many takers. But we were in the number one spot because of alphabetical order so we had great visibility and we were right next to Bates, and neither of us got much traffic. There seemed to be fewer people there than last year, for what it's worth."

Kate nodded vigorously. "Summer college fairs tend to have lower turnout. It's a really important consortium for us, so we really appreciate *both* of your involvement. Thank you. So, what else brings you to campus today?"

Rocky responded, "I wanted to drop these with you but mostly was just looking for an excuse to show Amville to Janie in the summer when it's quiet and everything's green. I'm taking her over to Rockland for lunch and maybe look at some art or something. I'll pretend to be super cultured to impress her. What do you think?"

I felt myself redden.

Kate had seemed very confused as to why I was there with Rocky and why we were spending time together, but she did—to her credit—try to roll with it. "Oh, okay! Well, have fun. It's a really nice day. It's hard to believe that we were under two feet of snow just six months ago. And we'll likely be under another two feet of snow six months from now! Ha! Um, yeah, so Janie, I'll confirm with you, but we will plan to see you next Monday. Thanks again. It's very nice to meet you."

"You, too, Kate. I'll see you then."

Rocky and I left the office and walked out of the building onto the quad. He led me around the small campus, pointing out where he had lived, where he had taken classes, and where he had attended parties. "This," he said, pointing to one brick building, "is the infamous location where Lance Ashton first punched me. Your house is the second such place. I am hoping that this particular action will not happen in threes." Rocky had opted for an Amville baseball cap that day, which cast just enough of a shadow on his face that his latest injury wasn't obvious.

I shook my head. "Knowing Lance, he won't come back to the house anytime soon. I'm probably going to have to reach out to him at some point and initiate a conversation, but I'm still too pissed to do that. Maybe next week. I don't know. He's such a baby and needs for someone to give *him* a dose of reality, not the other way around. Not that I'm advocating violence, but he's acted so childishly. I think—" I was cut off by my cell phone ringing in my pocket. I saw that it was the realtor working on our house sale in Concord. I looked at Rocky and put one finger up. "Hello?"

I mostly listened to what the realtor told me, asked a few questions, and made plans to address what she needed from me. I ended the call. "The Concord house is under contract," I told Rocky. I started walking ahead on a path that circled around a small pond. He had told me earlier that it was jokingly called "The Outdoor Pool," and that upperclassmen would ask freshmen if they had been there yet. Once they figured out that it was a tiny marshy body of water, they were quite disappointed.

He picked up his pace and walked alongside me. "Is that a good thing?" he asked.

"Yeah, I think so. I mean, it has to be. No one is going to use it. I mean, I guess Alyssa could, if she decides to leave Patrick and stay there. But I can't really see her staying in Concord if they split up. It's too small and she's too embarrassed. Ugh. Yeah, we need to sell it. We want to be able to keep the Maine house, which is paid off, but we still have property taxes and maintenance costs and utilities to think about. Concord was paid off, so it's a good amount of cash for us. It's the only thing that makes any sense. Now I just need to decide what I want to keep from there. The realtor arranged for a U-Haul to be delivered in the morning, so I'm going to go down there. Alyssa is bringing the girls to camp in the morning, but she has already said that she's not going back to Concord right now, so I'm dealing with all of it. Hey, have you ever been to Concord, Massachusetts before? It's lovely this time of year."

Rocky stopped, as did I. We sat on a small bench. "Danielle is from Lexington. Didn't I tell you that? Yes, I've been there. I liked it more than Lexington. But I couldn't tell her that." He turned towards me and put his hand on my knee. I realized that after a lot of hand-holding and kissing the previous night, we really hadn't had any physical contact today. It felt nice to sit with him like that.

"So, that means I could have played sports as a kid against *Danielle*?" I asked. "Did she play soccer?"

"Of course," he said. "Doesn't every upper middle-class kid in New England play soccer?"

"Ugh. I hope we kicked their asses," I said, and gave Rocky a light kiss on the lips. I was quite sure that he had kissed Danielle in this very spot on campus before, but I was happy to add to his Amville associations.

Rocky smiled at me and brushed the hair away from my face. "Do you want me to come to Concord with you to help pack things into a U-Haul? Is that all I am to you? Brute force?"

"You read my mind. I am using you for your body. Nothing more. You figured me out. You are named after Rocky Balboa, after all."

He laughed. "You must have very low standards. I got punched in your kitchen and didn't attempt to strike back. But yes, I'll come to help you tomorrow. You're lucky I don't have to go back to work for two more weeks. You're catching me at a good time. You'll only get nights and weekends once school starts. That is, if you'll still be in Maine. Do you think you're staying?"

"I can't imagine going back to Chicago now," I said. "Alyssa and I talked last night, and she's still figuring things out, but I think that she wants some kind of situation where we're all together at least some of the time. Honestly, other than my friends, there's no reason for me to go back. I need to talk to Scarlett so that she can find a roommate and I can stop paying rent, so that's on the list for me to deal with after tomorrow. I wouldn't mind staying in the Maine house, but I need to figure out what that looks like. I don't know what I would do with my days or how I'd make any kind of income. I don't even know if I need to make money or how much. I need to talk to an accountant and my parents' lawyer again. Ugh."

"Well," said Rocky. "I'm happy to have a steady stream of meatball subs and biscuits, but I know that you will figure something else out, too. There's something good out there for you, Janie, but it just hasn't become apparent yet. We'll figure it out." I noticed that he said *we*. Not *you*. "But the thing that I want to say, and I know it's really strange because I've only known you for a couple of days, but I'm really glad that you want to stay in Maine. I'd be really sad if you left. You're, well, you're really everything that your mom told me you were."

It was incredibly sweet, but it was odd that he brought Mom up just then. "What did she tell you about me?"

He sat a little closer and slipped his arm around my waist. "She told me that she wished that you lived closer, because she would have loved to introduce you to me."

My mom had never mentioned Rocky to me. It was so perplexing yet comforting at the same time. I felt my eyes fill with tears, and I rarely cried. "Why didn't she ever say anything to me? I could have met you. I did come back East sometimes. I could have met you."

Rocky kissed my forehead. "Secret boyfriend. I never could have competed with the son of RoyalE."

"But that's not true. He was *not* a good boyfriend. I just didn't know any better. I wish she had said something."

"But ultimately, it doesn't matter. Here we are right now. And strangely enough, we have the bumbling yet persistent Kate Heathcliff to thank, but I think your mom is happy." She was. I knew that she was.

11 - Concord

THIS TIME, IT WAS MY TURN to drive. Rocky met me at the Cape Elizabeth house at seven in the morning. I had asked him on the drive back from Amville what his favorite breakfast item was, and after much resistance to answering since he knew that I would insist on making whatever it was, he finally admitted that it was cinnamon coffee cake. To make something that would work for the drive, I turned my favorite coffee cake recipe into muffins, and he was over the moon when I handed one to him as soon as we sat in the car. "I'm so glad you're staying in Maine," he said, taking a big bite. "Okay, as much as I didn't want you to go to so much effort, this is delicious." He took another bite. "What's for lunch?"

"Ha! I'm off duty for that one. We're going to my favorite bakery in West Concord, where they make great sandwiches. But you owe me a few hours of work first." We headed towards 95 South and embarked on the trip to my childhood home. "The deal is that I have to watch the girls tonight, and we need to be back in Cape Elizabeth by five o'clock. Alyssa has to go out, and she said she might be late. I'm really hoping that she dumps Yoga Dude tonight, but I really don't know what's going to happen. She made these plans sound urgent. Anyway, you're welcome to hang out with us. I'm going to make pizzas for the girls. I'm talking the real deal, with homemade dough and everything."

Rocky answered, "Well, it's that, or I sit on the couch watching Golf Channel highlights with Max. We need to find him a girlfriend. I think you've presented me with a much better option."

We hit pockets of commuter traffic on I-495 South as we made our way to Route 2 East, but once we exited in Concord, it was a typical summer weekday. Tourists were pulling into town and stopping for breakfast at the eateries in Concord Center. I pointed out my favorite spots and my alma mater Concord-Carlisle High School before we turned onto the street where I had spent my youth when we weren't in Maine. The sign in front of the house read "Under Contract," but everything else looked as it always had. The wooden siding was still yellow, and the lawn and flowers were maintained by a service that I had hired. I hadn't been there since the funeral. A small U-Haul truck was parked in the driveway with the key waiting for me under the front mat as the realtor had promised.

Walking in with Rocky, I saw the house with fresh eyes, almost the eyes of a stranger seeing it for the first time. The realtor had brought in a staging company, so the family pictures were off of the walls and the shelves and had been packed away into boxes stored in closets that we needed to move into the U-Haul and bring back to Maine. Alyssa and I had decided to donate the furniture, and I had a Salvation Army pick-up arranged with the realtor for Monday. Today, Rocky and I were tasked with collecting all of the personal items and getting them to Cape Elizabeth, so that Alyssa and I could decide what to do with them.

I took Rocky on a quick tour, showing him the rooms and various spaces of the house, as well as the locations of the boxes of things that had to be relocated to the truck. The work was fairly simple, as the realtor and staging company had literally done the heavy lifting. The boxes that they had used were small and manageable, and we made quick work of our chores. Our goal was to finish by noon and grab lunch before heading back north, and we were right on track until my cell phone rang as I was loading a box of old photo albums into the U-Haul.

The Caller ID displayed a name and number that I had not seen in almost five weeks. I sat on the back bumper of the truck and took a deep breath. Rocky looked at me with concern and asked, "Who?"

"I'm sorry," I said. "It's Cole. I don't know what this is about." I pressed the "answer" button on the touchscreen of my iPhone. "Hello?"

"Oh my God, it's you. It's your voice." Was he serious? And why was he being so dramatic?

"Hi, Cole. Yes, it's me. Can I help you with anything?" I had not spoken with him since I had left the *Young Chicago* office. Not once had he checked on me. He didn't know that my parents were gone or that I was in Maine. I had deactivated my Facebook account and had only been in touch with a few people since leaving Illinois. What did he want?

"Oh, baby, I'm a mess." He sighed heavily into the phone. "Mom's gone. Overdose. Last night. You didn't see the news?"

I hadn't looked at anything in days, so this information was brand-new. "Oh, Cole, I'm so sorry. I had no idea. That's truly awful."

"Yeah, I didn't know that she was into some of the stuff I guess she's been into. I hadn't seen her in a few days and I was off doing my own thing, ya know, but man, I just didn't believe it was this bad. Ugh. I literally have no one from my old life in Chicago to talk to about this except for you." This was both awful and beyond bizarre. "I'm so glad that you answered the phone," he said. "How's Chicago, babe? What are you doing now?"

Rocky realized that I was going to be on the phone for a while and put another box into the truck. He kissed my forehead and went back into the house to get more things. There was so much to say. "I'm in Maine now, Cole. My parents died in a small plane crash the night that the magazine closed down." There was no easy or sugary way to say any of this, so I didn't even try to make it more palatable. It had been bad, and it still was.

He quickly responded, "You've got to be kidding me. I mean, why didn't you call me? I could've come out there. This is awful. Both of us now, babe. We're orphans. I mean, my dad is still alive but he's a piece of shit as you know. I guess I need to tell him this now, too. That's going to suck. Oh, I'm sorry, you've got stuff going on, too. I need to stop just thinking about myself. That's what Cari says. Oh, that's probably rude, too. Sorry. I've got this girlfriend now."

I tried not to snort into the phone. "I know. That, I've seen. Congratulations," I said dryly.

Cole was increasingly apologetic. "Oh yeah, no, I'm not trying to be rude about things, I promise. Anyway. I literally have no one else to call. You're it, babe. We are having a memorial service on Saturday late afternoon. Over at Northstar in Tahoe. The Ritz. You went there with me, right? You know where that is?"

Yes, Cole, I've been there with you. We spent three days there. I had a remarkably painful dinner with your mother there. I bit my tongue. "Yeah, of course, Cole. I know where it is."

"Right, right, okay, good. Will you come? You can totally bring someone. Scarlett, Blair, whoever. I know it's going to be a weird scene. Hell, it's going to be weird as fuck for me, too. Paparazzi and shit. I'm supposed to plan this thing and speak at it, too. Jesus, this just isn't something you prepare for at our age." I swear I managed not to laugh when he referenced "our age." Given the circumstances, it would have been wrong. "So, how about it? Will you be here?"

"Um, okay, Cole, I need to think about it. I have a lot going on here with my nieces and my sister. That's another story for another day. But I promise I will think about it. Can you text me all of the times and locations?" I had no idea what to do with any of this. It was too much to process.

He seemed relieved, which put more pressure on me. "Oh, yeah, sure, of course! It would be *so* good to have you here. I really have no one to call. Everyone else from Chicago, you know, they just aren't the kinds of friends you call for something like this. You're the one who gets it. You get me, Janie. You're the only one who really has gotten me."

"Okay, Cole. I'll let you know. You take care of yourself, all right? You need to stay strong for, um, yourself. And for everyone who cared about your mom and wants to celebrate her life." Rocky had walked back over to where I was sitting on the back bumper of the truck. "I need to go now. Bye." I ended the call and stared at the screen of my phone.

Rocky sat next to me. "Are you okay?"

"Yeah, I think so. His mom overdosed last night and he's alone. I mean, the girlfriend seemed to be in the background, but he really has no other family or any true friends. Only child with a deadbeat dad like you, but he's not good at making real friendships like you are. I guess I never really thought about how shallow his life really was or is." How had I become the closest person to him in his entire universe? And why had he tossed me aside so easily? "Anyway, he asked me to do something, and I don't know what to do about it. Are we done with packing the truck?"

"I think so. I got the last few boxes in while you were on the phone. What does he want you to do?"

"Thanks for that. Let's go get lunch. This is definitely a conversation that has to be had over food."

NASHOBA BROOK BAKERY was bustling at lunchtime per usual, and Rocky and I ordered our sandwiches and sat on a bench outside by the small stream. It was a clear day, with the sun shining and ducks swimming by us. Small children were milling around and there was a happy summer vibe surrounding us, contradicting my present scenario of having to deal with a request to be at a funeral in California from my ex-boyfriend. I filled Rocky in.

He sat in silence as I told him everything, chewing his sandwich and listening to what I told him. When I was done, he put his sandwich back onto the paper wrapper on his lap. He paused, fully thinking everything through before speaking. He spoke carefully. "He sounds a lot younger than thirty-eight, but if he managed to run an entire magazine, then there's a side that I'm missing from what you've told me so far. Does he really have no one? What about friends from growing up? College?"

These were all good questions. "I think that he's very good at having 'friends' in the moment," I said, making air quotes. "Occasionally, someone from LA would come into town and get in touch with him and they'd have a great time, but I think that would be it. I think they were fairly superficial friendships, and because Cole made the choice to go to Chicago and not stay in LA, he was removed from everything that he knew for so long. Actually, when I think about it with more perspective, it is kind of strange that he wanted to live there and work in journalism. We talked about it from time to time, but I didn't meet him until he was pretty well ensconced into that world. It wasn't like I was going through it with him as he was getting established in the job and in Chicago. By the time that I met him, he was very work-focused and didn't have much of a social life beyond a very casual softball team that he played on. Once we met, I became his social life. That's why it was so strange that he discarded me so quickly and what seemed to be so easily. What he has dived into in LA is very different from his life in Chicago, but it's almost what people would have expected from him given his upbringing. Does this make any sense?"

"Absolutely," replied Rocky. "This food is really good. You could open a place like this in Maine."

"Ugh. I mean, thank you. It *is* good, and I could do something like this, but I don't think that it's what I want to do. Believe me, I've thought about it. Everyone says that I should open a restaurant or café or catering business or something. It's not the right thing, though. There's something else, but I don't know what it is yet. Anyway, there's one additional part of my conversation that I need to tell you about."

Rocky took the cookie out of the brown bag that sat between us and took a bite after offering it to me first. "He realizes that he made a huge mistake. He wants you to come out to LA and live in his mother's mansion on the beach with him. You'll never have to work again, and you can float in the pool all day. As much as I want you to stay in Maine and teach me how to make pizza dough, if you went, I would understand. I would be

heartbroken and probably would never recover, but I would understand."
He gave me a quick kiss on the side of my forehead. He was adorable.

"If you've set it up in your head to be that bad, then this part of our conversation will be easy. He wants me to come out there for the memorial service."

"To LA? See, that's part of the plan. He'll show you the average January temperatures of Maine and LA, and you'll never come back here. Alyssa is great, but she can't cook worth shit. And she's going to end up with Yoga Dude or her silly husband most likely anyway, so she'd probably get sick of me just hanging around the house all the time."

"The girls would still like it," I replied, sipping my iced tea. I loved that he had figured us out so quickly.

"Oh, of course. They would put lipstick on me and make me the subject of their puppet shows. Anyway, are you going out there?"

"Here's the other part, which I would have told you if you hadn't started speculating about Cole's plans to kidnap me and subject me to a life of margaritas and Hollywood's c-list. Pushing all of that aside, he told me that I could bring a friend. He mentioned Scarlett or Blair but given the fact that I could hear his girlfriend in the background, I think that anything is fair game. Do you want to go with me? And it's in Lake Tahoe, not LA. It's less seductive in terms of weather and more, uh, mountainy. But truly beautiful. And he doesn't even live there."

Rocky put his arm around me and squeezed me to him. "Do I want to fly out to a beautiful place and stay in a hotel with a hot woman, and go to a memorial service for a has-been celebrity who I've never met, and stay in a hotel with a hot woman? Of course I do. Whether it's the right thing to do is another question, and I have no idea what the correct answer is."

"You mentioned the hotel twice."

"And the hot woman. I can mention it again if you want. It's a pretty attractive offer."

"So, how do we decide this?" I knew that the topic was fairly loaded. Cole was likely to be a little put-off by me showing up with a sort-of boyfriend-type, but all evidence pointed to his girlfriend also being there. The hotel aspect of it was a little forward, given the fact that we had only known each other for a few days, but I decided not to focus on this facet of the issue. Rocky was fixated on it, but I wrote it off to testosterone.

"We need an impartial voice in this decision," he said, and I agreed. I quickly texted the person who I trusted most when facing a dilemma. Luckily, I heard back within thirty seconds, and I began to initiate a FaceTime call.

Rocky was confused, "Who are you calling?"

I put my fingers to my lips and positioned myself closed to him on the bench, putting the phone in front of us. Soon, Scarlett's smiling face was in front of us. "Hi!!" she yelled and laughed. I had missed her, too.

"Scarlett, this is Rocky. We've been hanging out this week. I won't embarrass him anymore than that right now, so I can fill you in more later."

Rocky was slightly red and simply said, "Hi, Scarlett. Good to meet you."

Scarlett was trying to contain her excitement. "Ooh, hi Rocky! This is fun. Okay, I'll try not to be embarrassing. I'll put on my professional psychological cap now. How can I help you?" She laughed some more, and I realized that Rocky and I must have looked fairly silly sitting on this bench, asking my friend on a video chat for advice.

I gave her the thirty-second condensed version of the Cole story. Scarlett contemplated it for a moment and asked a few clarifying questions. "All right, here's what I think. Cole is feeling alone and vulnerable even though he's surrounded by a bunch of people. They aren't genuine or haven't been a part of his life for long enough. Janie, you represent something in his life that was separate from all of that and from a time when he perhaps was who he really is."

"Although he's probably enjoying his time with the Connors chick, he also likely regrets casting you aside. But let's not focus on that. You're trying to move on—" She winked at her own comment and gave a big smile. "—and he doesn't know that. In his mind, your life is frozen from the night that he broke up with you. That's why hearing that you're in Maine or about your parents was particularly unsettling to him. So, it's up to you and only you if you want to go out there. As for bringing Rocky with you, you have that right. He's going to have his girlfriend there. Although it'll be weird for him to see you with someone else since he only knows you with him, he was the one who ended things with you. You have every right to move on. You're not bringing Rocky to rub anything in his face—at least I don't think you are, because that's not how you are—but you would be showing up because he asked you and because you care about his well-being. There. What do you think? Does that work? It's ultimately up to you, but whatever you decide is justifiable."

Rocky was visibly impressed. "You're good. How much do we owe you?"

Scarlett seemed satisfied. "It's pro bono," she said, adjusting her glasses. "I'll just count it towards my practicum hours," she teased.

She had given me good advice, as I had assumed she would. "Okay, I know you've got class, but thank you. This was really helpful. I'll let you know what we decide to do. Talk to you soon." I blew her a kiss and ended the call.

Rocky collected all of our lunch trash and stood up. "We've got to beat the traffic out of town and hang with the girls, and I can't wait to drive that truck. What do you think?"

I stood up in front of him and put my hands on either side of his face and gave him a quick kiss. "I've only been to Lake Tahoe once in the summer, and this time I won't have to experience a painfully awkward dinner with RoyalE. We'll have to make it quick so that I don't saddle Alyssa with everything for too long, but if you'd like to come with me, it would make this much more tolerable. I feel badly for Cole, but I also don't want to be miserable. I can't be miserable with you." I kissed him again.

Rocky was noticeably trying to contain his excitement. "I can't turn the hot woman down." It wasn't easy to separate ourselves for the drive up to Maine, but we managed to get into two vehicles. And talked on the phone to each other for the entire drive to Cape Elizabeth.

12 - Patrick

MAKING SAUCE IS FAIRLY straightforward; there is plenty of room for error, and there aren't many variables beyond your own personal preferences. Making pizza dough is a different story. Every batch is different, as it is affected by the humidity and heat of the room, the temperature of the water and the bowl that it's in, the exact measurements of flour and salt, and the freshness of the yeast and how well it's fed by sugars, among other things. I had just begun mixing the dough slowly in the KitchenAid stand mixer with the dough hook attached when Alyssa made a hasty departure from the house, looking and smelling incredibly good. Her heels were high, her chestnut hair was blown straight, and she had definitely dipped into our mom's Chanel. She didn't look like a woman about to break up with someone, despite my hopes for her evening out. I did manage to make her pause for thirty seconds to give her the even shorter version of the Cole story and to ask if she was okay with me leaving for two days. She was exceptionally distracted but managed to say, "All right, I'll make it work." I couldn't believe she didn't question me for going out to Tahoe but considering everything that she was involved with at that moment, maybe she didn't feel like she could judge. Or perhaps she didn't care.

The girls worked on building a fort in the living room with couch cushions, and I gave Rocky a pizza lesson. As the dough was rising, I showed him how to make the same sauce that I had made for him a few days earlier for the meatball subs. I then put him to work on chopping vegetables. As we worked side-by-side in the kitchen and the girls played in the next room, it was apparent that if things went well, we could maybe start to build a life together. In some slightly fucked-up family commune sort of way; with Yoga Dude, who I had never met, and Lance Ashton next door, who could never come into the house again for fear that he would feel compelled to hit someone. Maybe it would eventually look differently from this. Or maybe I was jumping way too far ahead and needed to step back and take a deep breath, and just make pizza with Rocky.

They turned out delicious and after enjoying them, we got the girls ready for bed, read them stories, and shut off the lights. They had become so accustomed to me taking care of them that they didn't even ask for their mom. Although I appreciated the ease of their bedtime, I wasn't sure if their lack of expectations for their mom was ultimately a good thing. Regardless, it was fun to "play house" with Rocky and when both girls insisted on giving him a hug goodnight, too, I couldn't help but smile.

It was the first time that Rocky and I actually had a "normal" evening together that didn't involve going somewhere else. We opened a bottle of red wine as well as the windows so that we could hear the waves crashing in the distance, and I set the Pandora station to Ben Folds so that I could further my musical education. Rocky looked content and relaxed on the couch, and I grabbed my glass of wine and curled up next to him. After chatting for a few minutes, I grabbed my laptop and we began making our plane reservations for our trip west. It was cozy and normal, and it validated every decision I had made in the last few days. I was able to tune out whatever Alyssa was doing and enjoyed being in the moment with Rocky.

We both eventually dozed off but were awakened by my cell phone buzzing in my lap. The Caller ID read "York County Corrections." What the hell? Was this a wrong number? I answered hesitantly, "Hello?"

A familiar male voice responded on the other end of the line. *"You only get one phone call.* Hi, Janie."

IT ALSO HAD TO BE A very quick call. Patrick had been arrested at the White Barn Inn in Kennebunkport that evening. The very abbreviated version of the story was that he had alerts set on his American Express card so that whenever Alyssa used the card, he got an instant text message. Since she had left him, there had been very few charges. We had money from our parents, our expenses had been minimal, and as far as I knew, Alyssa had only charged a couple of things for the girls such as camp tuition and bathing suits to the card. Tonight, however, Patrick got an alert for a preauthorization for an expensive hotel stay at the very high-end inn that he had stayed with Alyssa on their wedding night. There was no doubt in his mind that Alyssa had decided to seek retribution for his actions by taking someone else to the inn that had meant so much to both of them, so he quickly abandoned his desk in the Financial District of Boston, hopped in his car that was parked in the garage floors below him, and headed north. Talking a mile a minute, he managed to add, "It's amazing that I'm in here for this instead of reckless driving. Anyway—" He continued to launch into the rest of the story, despite a deep male voice in the background barking, "You have thirty seconds left and then I'm hanging up the phone, sir."

The shortened remainder of the tale involved Patrick getting to the White Barn Inn and in a state of anger and near-delirium, insisting that the front desk staff give him Alyssa's room number. They checked the room registry and told him that no one by that name was listed, which meant that someone else (Patrick knew nothing about Yoga Dude, but by this point, he assumed someone else was in the picture) had checked into the room, but Alyssa had paid with the American Express. Alyssa's actions made her virtually untraceable to him but also issued an incredibly loud "fuck you" to Patrick, furthering his rage. He bolted from the reception area and headed towards the guest rooms. Once the staff realized what he was doing, they quickly tried to stop him. Patrick began pounding on doors and yelling, "Alyssa! I know you're here! Alyssa! Come out here!" When employees couldn't stop him, one ran to get the manager while frightened guests began to call the police from inside their bolted hotel rooms. Patrick never found Alyssa, but the Kennebunkport police definitely found him.

"So, she doesn't know you're there?" I asked. Patrick had graduated *summa cum laude* from Cornell and had an MBA from Boston College. At thirty, he was on the fast track to tremendous professional and financial success. His behavior over the last couple of months was a complete one-eighty from everything that I had known of him over the past twelve years.

"No, she doesn't. Here's the situation. I don't care how you deal with her, but I need to get out of here. I need for someone to bail me out. It's only five hundred dollars, but I need someone to post it, and if you can find a lawyer and get them to drop the charges, even better. Please, Janie, help me. We'll figure everything else out soon. Okay, I need to go. Thanks."

I ended the call and placed my phone in my lap. Rocky was fully awake now and looked at me with confusion. "Who's in jail?"

I turned towards him and placed my hands on his knees. "You've been wondering about Patrick. You're going to get to meet him tonight. And I need to find a lawyer at ten o'clock at night."

"Patrick was arrested? Do you know a lawyer nearby?"

"Yeah, one, and he's really close by. He would do just about anything for me, but this is not going to be pretty." I picked up phone again and selected a number that was in my contacts but that I probably had never called. "Hi, William? It's Janie. I'm so sorry to call you this late…Yes, I am all right, but we have a bit of a problem with Patrick… No, they're still separated, but he came up here tonight… No, we don't need a restraining order, but he's being held at the Kennebunkport police station… Five hundred dollars, which he is fine with, but he also wants to try to get the charges dropped… I'm taking care of the little girls, but I'm going to send someone else with you, my, um, he's, well, his name is Rocky, but he probably shouldn't come over to your house right now. Can you come here and take him with you? Yes, I know it sounds strange, but I think this will cause the least disruption tonight… You're the best. Thank you. He'll be looking for your car. I'll get the cash out of the safe. Thanks, William." I ended the call and looked at Rocky.

"So," he asked. "Who's William?"

I kissed him lightly on the lips and tried to look convincing. "William Ashton, Attorney-at-Law. My next-door neighbor."

"And Lance's dad."

"Precisely."

"And I get to ride in a car with him and bail out your brother-in-law, who I have never met before. While you sit on the couch and drink wine. It's a really good thing that I'm so crazy about you."

It was not a great situation, no matter how you looked at it. "I'm going to be here in case the girls wake up, and I also have the fantastic task of getting in touch with my sister, who has most likely been practicing *virparita karani* with Yoga Dude all night while being oblivious to the ruckus that was happening in the guest rooms off of the hotel lobby."

"Practicing what?"

"*Viparita karani.* It's a restorative yoga pose that she showed me. You put your legs like, oh, never mind. It doesn't matter right now. Anyway, she needs to know what's going on, and the fact that when she gets here, Patrick will be here. Of all things that could force the issue with them, this one is beyond anything I could have imagined. I also think that you could be a great buffer on the car ride. Patrick will probably be super agitated, and you're so good at talking to people. I am really grateful for you and that you're here. I mean it. I'll make it up to you. I need to go get the cash. Could you look out for William?"

I ran into the office off of the living room and quickly dug out the cash. My parents had always left five hundred dollars in emergency cash in their safe, and I had never given it a second thought until then. Between meeting Rocky earlier in the week and now having the exact amount of cash on hand that I needed, I was starting to see signs of them in my life. If this could keep happening, then that could be very comforting, as well as helpful. I just didn't need for these moments to coincide with the arrests of family members.

Rocky was waiting by the door, looking out the window. I handed him the cash. He asked, "Just so I know what to expect, is big Willie Ashton more like wife or son? I want to be mentally prepared for the next couple of hours."

It was a great question. "Lucky for you, neither. He is a very sweet, modest, quiet man. With Meredith as his wife, he can't get a word in edgewise anyway. She's always been the dominant one in that marriage, and Lance is really nothing like either one of them. You'll be fine. Thank you." I kissed him, he kissed me back, and pretty soon we were engaged in one of those fantastic kisses that were synonymous with the beginning of a relationship, when you are still getting to know everything you can about the other person and when everything is exciting and unexpected. It was bliss, but it was soon interrupted by the bright lights of a Mercedes in the driveway. I gave him another quick kiss and watched as he walked out towards William Ashton's car. I could see his shadow as he got into the passenger seat and shook William's hand.

I retired back to the couch and stared at my phone, trying to decide what to type to Alyssa. I put Pandora back on, but more softly this time, and listened to the sea sounds from the nearby shoreline. This situation had to be resolved, and this was the place where it had to happen. Whether they stayed together or dissolved their union, anything would be better than this. I texted Alyssa a simple message, deciding that brevity was best: "Patrick arrested in Kennebunkport for disorderly conduct. Rocky and William Ashton bailing him out now. He will be here in next couple of hours. Girls will see him when they wake up. I'm awake on couch if you need me." I pressed "send" and watched for her read receipt. It took about thirty seconds to see, but it felt like a year. I wanted to believe that she would be a good and responsible parent in this situation and realize that leaving her kids to wake up to their dad—who they hadn't seen in over a month—in the house, would be extremely confusing, especially without her there.

About ten excruciatingly long minutes later, my phone rang, with Alyssa on the other line. "Janie, I'm coming home. I can't drive because I've been drinking champagne for hours and I know you can't come get me, because you're with the girls and Rocky isn't there either. The hotel—I'm at a hotel, which I know sounds terrible, I know, I know—is working on getting me a cab right now. I'm so sorry about all of this, Jae Jae. I've put you through way too much over the past month and asked you to pretty much raise my kids for me. I've been way too selfish and I'm so sorry. It's just been so hard. But I'm so glad you've met Rocky. He's so good and solid and seems to like us even in our fucked-up state of being, and he's cute, too! You would have such nice babies with him." She had definitely been drinking.

I interrupted her. "I know you're in a hotel, Alyssa. That's why Patrick's been arrested. He saw the AMEX charge."

Alyssa started crying, almost letting out a wail. The Whitman sisters rarely cried, so I knew that she was hurting. And more than just a bit intoxicated. "I knew what I was doing but I didn't know what I wanted by doing that. I can't even explain myself right now. I'm so sorry. He's been arrested. This is bad for his career. I hope that William can help him. Janie, this—"

I interrupted her. "Alyssa, he's still an ass. You just need to decide what you're willing to get over and get past and work on. I'll never defend what he did to you. It was awful. And I think that a lot of women in your place would have done something far worse than charge something to his credit card."

"Thanks, Janie. It wasn't just something though. It was a hotel room so that I could drink and screw another guy. At the place where Patrick and I went on our wedding night. Let's be real here."

She had a point, but Patrick was far from blameless. "He was caught in your small town, drinking and cavorting and *also* going into a hotel room. With a waitress. A waitress who had served you food together as a married couple. He is not innocent. Stop beating yourself up, Alyssa. Come home, take a shower, and I'll make breakfast. Is the cab there yet?"

"I think it's pulling up now. Hold on." I listened to her clumsily get into the cab and give the driver the address. At least she got that right. "Okay, I'm in. On my way home. Can you make French toast? Do you have challah in the freezer? I know that sometimes you freeze it. You know that one you make with the fruit? Oh, Janie. I don't know what I would do without you. The girls, too. I just don't want this to end. All of us together."

"We'll figure it out," I said. "Yep, we've got challah, and fruit, and coffee. We'll figure it out."

THE CHALLAH WAS THAWING on the counter, the strawberries were rinsed and draining in the colander, and I was mixing the custard ingredients when the front door opened. Rocky and Patrick walked into the kitchen, looking tired. It was so strange to see them together; two men who had not known each other a couple of hours earlier and had now experienced something as strange as a jail bailout. Patrick walked over to me and threw his arms around me. We had always gotten along well, but I could sense his relief and appreciation as he hugged me. "Janie, I love you so much. Thank you." He pulled back and glanced over at Rocky. "This guy is great, Janie. We need to keep him around. If we haven't scared him off yet, then maybe we can."

I was a little surprised by Patrick's use of "we," and I was worried that he was being a little too hopeful. I didn't know what Alyssa was ultimately going to decide. "Alyssa's on her way home right now. She should be here any minute. I don't really have any sense of how she will be towards you, so please proceed carefully. I know that you've been through a lot, but so has she. I'm making breakfast now that can be thrown in the fridge and baked in the morning, but whatever you want to do is fine. Take a shower, have a snack, take a nap, whatever. I would just recommend the guest room."

"No problem, Janie. I'm going to make some coffee—oh, I see you already have—and sit here and watch you cook for a bit if you don't mind. I've always liked watching you and your mom cook, especially in this house. Is that okay?"

"Oh sure, whatever. Rocky, do you want to take a nap? You can use my room." Rocky had never actually been in my bedroom before. The events of this night had changed everyone's situation with each other.

"Yes, that is a great idea. Don't stay up all night," he said, giving me quick kiss on the cheek. He turned towards Patrick and gave him a goofy little salute. "My work here is done," he said, and headed up the stairs.

Once he was out of earshot, Patrick said, "Janie, seriously, he's a good dude. He just stood there and talked to me about random shit while William was working things out with the police. We talked about the Patriots, the Red Sox, about golf; he really got my mind off of things. I'm really happy for you. You deserve someone like this. I only met that Cole guy once and I don't know what happened there, but Rocky seems like a better fit for you." He was rambling a bit and looked exhausted, and likely not just from this one hellish night. His face looked drawn, he had dark circles under his eyes, and he really needed a haircut.

I began cutting up the challah in a large dice. I didn't feel like getting into the Cole story right now, especially with Alyssa getting home momentarily. "Rocky and I have only known each other since Tuesday. I feel very good about things, but I truly don't know ultimately what will happen. I know that I really like him, but I have no idea if he'll bolt at some point. I've been dropped unexpectedly before, so I just don't know. But for right now, I'm enjoying getting to know him. I'm glad he was here tonight."

Patrick took a swig of coffee. "Is she going to divorce me?"

I poured the custard over the challah in the baking dish as steadily as I could, focusing my eyes on the bread and not looking at him. "I have no idea. She's never indicated to me one way or another. I honestly don't think she knows."

I knew he was going to ask the next question, but I hadn't prepared for answering it. "Who is he?"

I started placing sliced strawberries into the nooks and crannies of the challah pieces in the dish. "I've never met him. The girls haven't either, so you don't need to worry about that right now. They don't even know that he exists. She met him in a yoga class, he's older, and he's been divorced a couple of times. He's a writer. That's really all that I know. I haven't pushed her much on the topic, and she hasn't offered much." I covered my creation with plastic wrap and put it in the refrigerator. "What do *you* want out of all of this?" I knew what I assumed by his actions, but I didn't know for certain.

Patrick rubbed his stubbly face. "I want my family back. I want my wife back. Of course, I want them all back in our house and for everything to pick up where we left off, but I am also realistic and know that I can't just expect that. If she's willing to stay with me, I know there will have to be some changes. I'm willing to make them, but I don't know if she's agreeable to having anything else to do with me. She won't talk to me. I wouldn't blame her if she walked away, but it would be incredibly hard in so many ways and also very sad. But I don't know anything." He looked despondent and hung his head in his hands.

It was likely the most sensitive, introspective thing that I had ever heard Patrick say. He was usually a bit arrogant, often overly confident, and habitually self-centered. "Wow, Patrick, that was a very perceptive and profound statement. I'm impressed." I poured myself a cup of coffee and leaned on the counter opposite from him. It was midnight, which made caffeine consumption fairly stupid, but I needed to see the next segment of the evening play out.

He seemed slightly proud of himself, but still somewhat humble for him. "I had a lot of time to think tonight, both on the car ride to Maine and while sitting in that jail cell. That kind of sucked, by the way. Never want to do that again. I'm so glad that you guys could get me out of there."

The front door opened again, and this time Alyssa appeared. I had expected to see a disheveled mess of a woman, but somehow, my sister even in her woozy state had managed in the cab to pull herself together. I shook my head when I saw her, always in awe of how she was able to look amazing in even the worst of circumstances. Her hair—now much shorter than Patrick had ever seen it—was brushed and shiny. Her makeup was cleaned up and retouched. For someone who had most likely spent several hours earlier that night in a hotel room with a man, drinking multiple bottles of Veuve Cliquot, followed by crying and lamenting her life situation, she looked pretty damn good.

Patrick stood up behind the barstool, almost using it as a barricade for protection. "Lyss. Your hair. Wow, I didn't know you cut it." Of all things to say after not seeing his wife for five weeks, it was a bit strange, but maybe this was all he could manage to say, which was understandable given the circumstances.

Alyssa touched the back of her hair, almost self-consciously. "Do you like it?"

Patrick's face softened a bit, as if he was letting his defenses down slightly. "Oh, yeah. It looks really great. You look awesome."

"Thanks." She turned to me. "Janie. Superwoman. Are the girls still in bed through all of this?"

"Yes, luckily. There's coffee made, and I have that French toast thing in the fridge, but I can bake it whenever you want. Are you hungry?"

"Thanks, Jae. I think I just want coffee right now. You can go get some rest. Is Rocky still here?"

"Yeah, he's taking a nap upstairs. Are you sure it's okay for me to go?" I glanced at Patrick and back at Alyssa. I wasn't sure if she wanted me to leave them alone together. Patrick was just standing quietly, as if he was afraid that anything he would say at this moment could ruin his chances. He might have been right.

Alyssa walked over to the cabinet to get a coffee mug. "It's fine. Go cuddle with Rocky. You've been through enough tonight, too."

If Alyssa was indeed ready to talk to Patrick, then that was my cue to leave. I nodded and walked up the stairs to my bedroom. Rocky looked very cute asleep in the queen-size bed that had been mine since I was a young teenager. I was still in my yoga capris and tank top from earlier, but I was too exhausted to change. I crawled into the bed carefully as to not wake him, but he almost immediately rolled over.

"Is everything okay?" he asked.

"I think so. For now, anyway. Thank you."

"He's better than I thought he would be," Rocky said.

"He's been completely demoralized and beaten down," I whispered. "It might have been the best thing for him." I snuggled up to him, he wrapped his arms around me, and I fell asleep in approximately ten seconds.

13 - Reunion

"DADDY! DADDY'S HERE!" I could hear the ecstatic screams of Trish and Susie from upstairs as they saw their dad for the first time in many weeks. It made me smile yet feel sad at the same time. Our little mostly-girls-only party was likely over for now, but it had always been inevitable that things would eventually change. It was six in the morning, and I had no idea if Patrick and Alyssa had both stayed downstairs for this whole time. Alyssa had seemed ready to talk to him at least a little bit, so hopefully some communication had transpired.

Rocky opened his eyes and turned towards me when he saw that I was awake and sitting up. "Hey," he said. "You're cozy to sleep next to. Any doubts that I had about going to California with you are out the window now."

I turned towards him and brushed the hair off of his forehead. "There were doubts?" I asked jokingly. "I'm glad. Because I spent a shitload of money on those tickets last night. I can't believe we're leaving tomorrow morning. And I also wonder what the hell we are leaving behind here in our absence." I nestled back beside him momentarily, knowing that I would need to get up in the next few minutes to get breakfast in the oven.

"Yeah, how were they when they saw each other? That must have been bizarre."

"It was. They haven't seen each other since the funeral, and she refused to speak to him there other than about simple logistics. So much has gone on since then. They looked at each other almost like acquaintances who hadn't seen each other in years. Her hair. He couldn't get over her hair. He always loved her long hair but the way that he looked at her when he saw her shorter haircut was really amazing. He was almost stunned by her." I thought about all of the major life events that I had experienced with Alyssa and Patrick together as a couple; their engagement, their wedding, the births of the girls. So much of my life had centered on their partnership. To see them together yet apart was strange. "Hey, I never asked you. How were things with William Ashton?"

"Oh, right! You and I really didn't talk last night. He was super nice. He had heard of me from Meredith, which probably doesn't surprise you, but he didn't make any mention of any controversy. I don't think he has any clue that I'm the one who Lance hit before graduation, which is totally fine. I certainly wasn't going to tell him. Anyway, he just told me a bunch of stories about you and Alyssa as kids. I know all kinds of things about you now, Janie. Including how you used to insist on being naked at the beach."

I swatted at Rocky's shoulder. "I was a baby!"

He grabbed my hand and held onto it. "I heard that this went on well into elementary school."

"Liar. Well, I'm glad it went okay. Did he manage to get the charges dropped?"

"Yeah, it turns out that he knows the sergeant from Rotary or something. He wouldn't even take the bail money. I left the five hundred on the dresser over there," he said, gesturing across the room. "The cop just made Patrick assure him that nothing like this would ever happen again, at least in York County. Luckily, Patrick was very contrite and respectful, lots of 'yes, sirs' and stuff like that. It's done now. I'm just guessing that he shouldn't return to the White Barn Inn anytime soon."

"Oh, that's so good. Thank you so much for going." I sat up. "And as much as I want to just lie in the bed with you for the rest of the day, I need to get breakfast started. The girls are going to be hungry. And I'll probably end up bringing them to camp today. I want to give Alyssa and Patrick the chance to talk as much as they want to."

As I walked downstairs, the smell of bacon hit me, as well as the more subtle and sweet fragrance of baked French toast. "What's going on?" I asked.

Susie ran over to me and jumped into my arms. "Daddy's here!"

"Yes, I can see that! So exciting! I was wondering who took over the kitchen duties."

Patrick waved at me from in front of the sink. "I took care of it. Sorry if I stole your thunder, but you get all of the credit for making it, believe me. I can't wait to eat it."

This was shocking. I had never seen Patrick make himself a turkey sandwich, let alone put something in an oven. "I just didn't know this was in your wheelhouse," I said as tactfully as I could.

"Well," he said. "I have watched you and your mom quite a bit over the years, and I've had some time over the past few weeks to get better acquainted with my kitchen appliances. It turns out that they're not as intimidating as I once thought."

It was almost endearing. I had to keep reminding myself of his fairly recent bad behavior. "That's great with me. Given the fact that I have served three meals a day to this crew for over a month, I'm very cool with someone sharing the effort."

The timer went off, and Patrick grabbed hot mitts and took the bacon and the baking dish out of the oven. Alyssa actually got up off the kitchen barstool and poured juice for the girls, and I helped myself to a cup of coffee. Rocky came downstairs and settled himself into a chair at the table across from the girls. They began making silly faces at each other, while the rest of us put food on everyone's plates. When we were all sitting at the big table, I paused to look around at everyone. For better or for worse, for this moment at least, this was my family.

ROCKY WENT HOME TO shower and pack for the next morning, and I dropped the girls off at camp. It felt strange to leave Alyssa and Patrick alone in the house together, but even though they weren't directly speaking to each other in front of the rest of us, things seemed civil enough to be safe. With Rocky and I leaving for two days, they would be forced to co-parent the kids and take on at least the basic functions of managing the house together, provided she didn't kick him out or run off with Yoga Dude again. I was a little anxious about leaving things under these circumstances, but I realized that this might be the kick in the pants that they needed to get their shit together. Or maybe they would implode, and the house would burn down. I had to bet on the more favorable odds.

When I got home, Alyssa was sitting on the floor of the living room cross-legged, staring straight ahead at the floor in front of her and remaining very still. I couldn't tell if she was meditating or asleep with her eyes open. Patrick was sitting in the large comfortable chair that had always been my favorite reading nook, seemingly getting work done on his laptop. Neither was talking, and I had a hard time judging the mood in the room. "Is everything okay here?" I asked.

Alyssa moved her gaze up to me. "We are practicing something called 'respectful co-existence with mutual aspirations.'"

I suppressed a laugh. "Is that in the same vein as conscious uncoupling?" I couldn't resist, thinking of the recent demise of several celebrity partnerships and the rhetoric surrounding them.

Patrick stopped typing and looked up. "We read about it last night, or this morning, or whenever that was. We were looking at different methods of resolving differences while maintaining our individuality and additionally taking into account our future goals. Or something like that. Did I get that right, Alyssa?"

She uncrossed her legs and stood up to stretch. "Yes, that's it. We recognize that we need professional help, but we want to go into counseling with an idea of what we want. We still aren't sure what that looks like, but we know that we have to work on respecting each other's differences and interests and making sure that they are integrated into our future relationship, no matter what that ends up being. I think that's what the website said, anyway." She yawned, obviously tired after apparently not sleeping. She likely had a horrendous hangover, as well.

It was also a very Alyssa-type of plan and approach, and it seemed very different from anything that I would have expected from Patrick. That said, he was a man anxious to salvage what he could of his marriage, and I guessed that he would have agreed to a marriage retreat on Mars if she had suggested it.

"All right, sounds good. I'm going upstairs to pack. What do you think one wears to a memorial service for a has-been celebrity at a luxury hotel in the mountains that's being hosted by your ex-boyfriend?"

Alyssa descended into downward dog. "Something black to be respectful of her passing, and something stunning to make him feel remorse for unexpectedly dumping you. Look in my closet. I went shopping last week. You'll know which one I'm talking about when you see it."

This was news to me. "You went shopping? When did you go shopping? I had no idea."

She stood and dropped into a forward fold. "Like I said, last week. I know. I went shopping while you took care of my kids. I'm not proud. I'm making different decisions now. Please try on the dress."

"Hey, kiddo," said Patrick, easing back into the big brother role that he had played in my life for so many years. "Can I ask why you're even going to this thing? If you wanted a couple of days away with my new BFF Rocky, we could've swung that without you guys having to go to a funeral. Do you really want to see Cole right now?"

I felt a headache lurking behind my temples. Hearing it repeated back to me admittedly made it seem irrational and odd. "I know that it sounds really strange. Hell, I think it's super weird that we're going. I just can't help but feel a twinge of compassion for him. He really has no family left and very few true friends. Everyone in his life exists on a very cursory level. I still think that our breakup was incredibly messed up and he handled it terribly, but we were together for long enough that I have to still consider him to be a friend. And I'm really lucky that Rocky understands this and is willing to go with me."

Patrick laughed. "No, I actually understand his willingness to go with you. If you go alone or have Scarlett meet you out there, he risks Cole begging for your forgiveness and trying to lure you back. So if he's there, that's much less likely. Smart guy. And there's also another bonus for him to go along."

I felt myself redden. "And what is that, Patrick?"

He closed his laptop. "One word. Hotel. Sounds like it's a really nice one, too."

Alyssa looked up from her cobra pose. "Just because Janie is staying in a hotel room with Rocky doesn't mean she has to sleep with him. I mean, she can if she wants to, but she's a contemporary woman in a modern-day relationship. She can call the shots."

Patrick hastily responded. "No, no, I wasn't implying that—oh damn, I won't win this no matter what I say here. Being the protective older brother type to you, Jae, obviously we like him very much, but is there *anything* wrong with him that we've determined yet? I've only known him since about midnight. He seems great, but I'm looking out for you."

Alyssa had now glided into child's pose. I was getting more and more tired watching her float through her routine. "The boy is pretty perfect," she said in a muffled voice, with her face resting on her hands that were palm-down on the floor. "He can't cook anything, but neither can I. He's got a steady job, he has friends, and he's great with Susie and Tricia. His family situation is a bit on the fucked-up side, but they're in Washington State so probably aren't very involved in his life on a regular basis anyway. Oh, and Lance Ashton hates him. Which could be good or bad, depending on how you look at it."

Patrick looked intrigued. "Hates him? That seems kind of harsh. Lance is always so… benign. Is he just jealous because of his relentless love and admiration of our Janie?" he asked, winking at me.

I yawned, wondering if I could pack quickly and squeeze in a nap before picking up the girls at camp that afternoon. It had been a long night. "There is jealousy, but it's a much more complicated story. I'll let Alyssa tell you, but I'll leave you with this teaser: a punch was thrown in our kitchen."

"What?!" Patrick exclaimed, putting his laptop on the floor. "Okay, Lyss, tell me the goods."

I walked towards the stairs, listening to Alyssa beginning to tell the story. "So, do you remember how Lance had that girlfriend at Amville? Her name was Kristy…" I turned around for a moment and smiled slightly at the sight of Alyssa and Patrick turned towards each other and engaged in conversation. I hoped that the dress fit.

14 - Tahoe

ROCKY WAS A SEASONED VETERAN at flying cross-country, as he had made countless trips between Seattle and Maine during his time at Amville. As soon as we boarded the plane in Boston just before six in the morning and sat down, he handed me an old iPod and earbuds. "The greatest hits of one Benjamin Folds. Just promise me you'll listen to it once all the way through over the next seven or so hours we have on planes. I know that you've listened with me in the car, but that was always interrupted by conversation or a stop or the need to look at some bridge or body of water. This will help you to understand me better."

I laughed. "Does that mean that you don't want to talk to me at all today?" Rocky laughed and furiously shook his head.

"I should have made you a playlist of yacht rock," I continued. "I know that you would love some Hall and Oates today."

He nodded with a grin. "Next time, for sure. Okay, I also loaded the movie 'Airplane' on my iPad. I'm hoping you've seen it at some point in your life?"

"Of course! But it's been years. I love the idea of watching that on a plane. So fun. What else, Mary Poppins?"

He continued to pull things out of his backpack. "I saved the *Boston Globe* Sunday magazine from your house this week. I don't think you guys noticed since it was left blank, but they have a killer crossword. We can work on that. I also brought a *Rolling Stone* and a *Time* magazine, figuring that would catch us up on a cross-section of news, because to be really honest here, I haven't paid much attention to the outside world since I met you." He gave me a quick kiss, which sent a jolt of happiness down to my toes. After six weeks of taking care of everyone else, it was so nice to be treated well. And as much as I loved them, to be *away* from them. "I've got snacks, too. That should get us at least to Denver, and then the second flight looks pretty short. What about you, Janie? Anything good in your bag?"

I was woefully unprepared, but most of my flying experience was on two-hour flights between Chicago and either Boston or Portland, Maine. "I have the newest Jennifer Weiner book. And gum. But enough gum to share with you."

"Then we're all set," he said, and soon we were taxiing to the runway and taking off on the four-and-a-half-hour flight to Denver.

THE EXCITEMENT OF TRAVELING with Rocky wore off slightly as the morning went on, and I managed to catch a couple of hours of sleep. After connecting to another flight in Denver, we eventually landed in Reno and rented a car for the forty-minute drive to Northstar. I felt a combination of tiredness from the early morning and long flying day, nervousness for having to see Cole in a couple of hours, and happiness for sitting next to a really nice person throughout the journey. I really needed some coffee.

The Ritz Carlton was even more beautiful than I remembered, nestled into the mountains adjacent to the Northstar ski resort. Rocky, used to the majesty and beauty of the Pacific Northwest, was even impressed by the setting. "This is really incredible. So, she had a house here?

"She actually had a penthouse condo within this hotel. I saw it very briefly, and then we just went to the hotel's main restaurant for dinner. It was all very fancy and luxurious, and she was fairly terrible to me. So there's that," I said with a slight smile.

Rocky nodded, as he pulled up to the valet waiting at the hotel's curb. "So it's Cole's now. He gets the condo. He's her only kid, right?"

I hadn't even thought of that. Alyssa and I had inherited the Concord and Cape Elizabeth houses, but they were nowhere near the scope of residences in Malibu and Lake Tahoe, in a Ritz no less. "Yeah, he is. I guess so. I can't imagine him dealing with any of this."

We both got out of the car and grabbed our bags. "You've been dealing with the two places since everything happened," Rocky said. "From what I can tell, Alyssa has done next to nothing. I'm not trying to be petty or mean, but you've done virtually everything. Isn't Cole like 40?"

"38," I replied. "But you will understand when you meet him. He's good at certain things. I'm still surprised at how good he was at running the magazine. But this kind of thing, I don't know. Maybe I'm wrong."

I could tell that Rocky had many thoughts swirling around in his head, and he was carefully choosing what to say and what to keep to himself. He must have been nervous, too. We checked in at the beautiful reception area and were given the information about the location of the memorial service. We quickly purchased coffees from the café in the lobby to help compensate for getting up at three in the morning. As we walked towards our room, Rocky said, "I've never heard of a funeral in a function space of a hotel before. This is going to be fascinating."

"I know, right? I don't even know how this got put together. I doubt that she had any sort of last wishes determined, since she wasn't exactly expecting to die. I don't think anyone really anticipates an overdose. Cole sounded terribly overwhelmed when I talked to him. I do know that this was the place that she felt happiest and could escape from the scene that she felt LA was, so I guess this makes sense. It'll be likely much smaller and more manageable here compared to anything that he could host in LA, so maybe that was some of the reasoning."

Our room was gorgeous and had views of the mountains from its large windows. It had a gas fireplace and a large soaking tub. I saw the king-size bed and wanted to take a nap, but the memorial was starting in thirty minutes.

I started opening my bag when Rocky grabbed me and pulled me onto the bed with him. I laughed as he began to tickle my sides. "No one needs you to drive them to camp, pick them up from camp, make them a meal, or talk to a lawyer on the phone about anything," he said, and kissed me.

"I'm so tired," I said, and I meant that literally and figuratively. It had been a long stretch of taking care of everyone. "I wonder if Alyssa and Patrick have killed each other yet?"

Rocky began kissing my neck. "You leaving the house was the best thing for them. They need to figure this out. I just get the bonus of being here with you."

I sat up. "I want to stay here, but we have to be at this thing in like twenty-five minutes. I need to get all gussied-up. You know there will be cameras there."

"At a funeral? Like paparazzi? Was she that big of a deal?"

"You read the same *Time* magazine on the plane as me. It's been a slow news week. Okay, we need to get changed. Sorry. To be continued," I said, kissing him quickly on the lips and jumping out of the bed before he could pull me back in.

THERE WAS A LARGE, HEAVY sign on an easel greeting guests to the service that read "Celebrating the Life and Love of Rayna Emerson—Our RoyalE." Her one smash hit—"Hot Pink Love"—was playing on a loop from overhead speakers in the function room. I was wearing Alyssa's pretty fabulous black dress that mercifully fit me, and Rocky was wearing the one suit that he owned. I held his hand as we walked into the large room, trying to ignore the snaps and flashes behind us from the reporters and bloggers who were sequestered to the hallway behind the reserved room. The function area was fairly large but not quite a ballroom, and it opened out onto a patio that overlooked the Sierra Nevada. Chairs were set up outside, as well as a small podium and microphone. There was a piano to the side, and a man was playing Billy Joel songs.

As we made our way to seats in the back row, Rocky started quietly singing to me from the song "Summer, Highland Falls."

I turned towards him. "You, too? I thought you were all Ben Folds, all the time?"

He winked. "There's some crossover on my Pandora station. I can appreciate his work. But I think this answers your question about Cole's involvement in the service from everything you've told me."

"Apparently," I replied. We watched quietly as guests started taking their seats around us. It was a strange mix of people, many who looked vaguely familiar from eighties musical fame, but there were really no heavy-hitters.

Rocky whispered to me, "I feel like I'm watching one of those retrospective shows about the 1980s."

Soon I heard the murmurs from the crowd get slightly louder, and everyone turned towards the doors. Cole and Cari Connors walked out onto the patio. He looked a bit older than when I had last seen him six weeks ago, and more gray hair was starting to creep up from beyond just the sides of his dark brown hair. His charcoal suit was impeccable and had likely been tailored precisely for him. Cari held onto his arm and wore large dark sunglasses. Like most of us, she was wearing black clothing, but hers took the form of a skintight dress with large cutouts on the sides. We could smell her perfume as they walked past our row. She took the seat that was reserved for her in the front row, and Cole took his place at the podium.

"Good afternoon," he said, his voice crackling slightly. I could tell by looking at him how uncomfortable he felt in this moment, speaking to a group of people who he barely knew. "Thank you for joining me today to celebrate the life of my mother, Rayna Emerson. Known to the rest of the world as RoyalE, she entertained us publicly through her music. For those of us who knew her beyond that outward persona, we knew her heart, her love, and commitment to many important causes. Although she spent most of her time in Malibu, this was her favorite place, where she could escape to the quiet and peace of the mountains. As we sit here today and enjoy the beauty of this place, we can feel her radiance and warmth." I couldn't help but shift uncomfortably in my seat. Warm was not the way I would have described Rayna Emerson, but it *was* her memorial. Cole had a tough task.

"Thank you for making the effort to travel to this beautiful spot so that we can properly remember her," he continued. "As Rayna's only child, I appreciate all of the support that you have given me in the past few days, and I am thankful for your presence here." He had found me in the back of the crowd by now, and I felt him staring directly at me as he said this. He was likely wondering who was sitting next to me. I felt a pang of conflicted guilt, especially as I felt Rocky squeeze my hand. "I now invite the friends of Rayna Emerson to come forward and share a memory or two."

The next forty-five minutes or so were filled with anecdotes and musings from friends and associates in the entertainment industry. There were laughs, there were tears, and there was even a sing-a-long at the end with the hired musician playing the piano and the crowd clumsily singing the words to what was apparently Rayna Emerson's favorite song, "Jessie's Girl" by Rick Springfield. Finally, waiters brought everyone glasses of champagne at their seats, and Cole led everyone in a toast with the crowd lifting their glasses towards the mountains. "To Rayna!" The whole thing was very unusual, somewhat endearing, at times awkward, and altogether quite fitting.

The reception that followed took place both on the patio and in the function room. There were two large bars with seating set up at either end of the room, as well as tables sprinkled in between. Waiters offered sushi and various other California-themed hors d'oeuvres constantly, and the piano was wheeled inside to join a classical guitarist for entertainment. It was classy and appropriate and for whatever role that Cole played in the planning, he did an excellent and impressive job. He could rise to the occasion when he wanted to, but it was also so sporadic and unreliable.

Although it didn't seem planned, everyone wanted to talk to Cole, as he was the only relative of Rayna present. A de facto receiving line began to form, and I took Rocky's hand and joined it. "I think we need to do this.

And then I'll have to talk to him again at some point tonight, but that should be it. Thanks for being a good sport."

Rocky lifted his glass of bourbon on the rocks. "I'm all set. And if you see the waiter with that avocado thing again, maybe flag him over," he said with a wink.

It was eventually our turn to talk to Cole, and his facial expression when he saw me in front of him was one of relief. I gave him a hug and as he squeezed me, he said quietly, "Thank you. You have no idea. I have nothing to say to any of these people."

Suddenly, Cari Connors appeared at his side, holding a Corona bottle. I quickly released from the hug and turned towards her, putting out my hand. "I'm Janie Whitman. It's nice to meet you."

Cari handed the beer to Cole, who gratefully took a swig. She shook my hand and simply said, "Cari. And who's this?" she asked, nodding towards Rocky.

"Oh, yes, my apologies." I touched Rocky's back, trying to figure out how to navigate this situation. "This is Rocky Macallen. Rocky, this is Cole. And Cari." He shook both of their hands, and we all stood awkwardly until I said, "It looks like there is a line behind us, so we will talk to you later. It was a beautiful service."

As we walked away from them, I wasn't sure what to say to Rocky. I felt both slightly ill and confused by the circumstances. I just kept walking until we were back out on the patio and I reached the railing. I put my drink down on a small table next to it and finally looked up at Rocky.

"Hi," I said, not really knowing what was right or appropriate or smart. For someone who had spent the last five years of her life either writing professionally or learning how to communicate effectively from some of the brightest minds in journalism, I was at a loss for words.

Rocky, usually so cheerful and easygoing, seemed a little bit rattled by the situation as well. "This is weird, right?" he asked.

Just hearing him acknowledge the peculiarity of the circumstances was reassuring. "Ya think? I felt like coming here was the right thing to do. He has no family or close friends. Everything in his life is superficial. But that was so awkward."

Rocky kissed my forehead. "I'm sure his current relationship is stable and has tremendous staying power," he said quietly with a laugh, just loud enough for me to hear him.

"Yeah, how bizarre is that? She's a reality TV star. Seeing her in person like this adds so much to the complexity of the situation." I sighed and looked around. There were people milling around, talking, laughing, eating, and drinking, while the musicians again played Billy Joel's greatest hits; it seemed more like a cocktail party than a memorial service. I thought of the reception in Concord after my parents' service just five short weeks ago, and how the tone was more hushed, more muted, sadder than this. I wondered how many of these people actually knew Rayna Emerson well and how many of them were just looking for an excuse to go to Lake Tahoe for the weekend. Regardless, it didn't matter. I just wasn't totally sure what I was supposed to do.

"I think I'm going to have to talk to him," I said. "I mean, I know that I just talked to him, but for more than thirty seconds this time. Is that okay with you?"

Rocky nodded. "I totally expect you to. You didn't travel this far to say hi to him for fifteen seconds in a receiving line. I'm just putting my faith into the belief that you aren't going to escape out that side door over there with him and hop into a waiting private jet back to Malibu," he said, gesturing to the other end of the room. "Because I really don't think that I'll be able to console Cari. She'll be heartbroken. I mean, look at her." I looked to my left and saw her very cozily chatting with an older man.

"Who is that guy? He looks vaguely familiar." I could have sworn I had seen him before.

"You, my friend, need to catch up on your *Connors Crew* episodes. That is her mom's step-brother. He's at the house all the time."

I shuddered. "So, he's like, her uncle?"

Rocky nodded. "Sort of. Not technically, so it wouldn't actually be breaking any laws. But the creepy factor is totally there."

It definitely was. "I didn't realize that you watched so much reality TV. This is a different side of you," I said, trying to keep the mood light.

"Oh, it's totally Max. I just catch bits here and there. He DVRs it. He has a thing for Cari, which I can't really relate to. I prefer women with more classic looks who listen to somewhat cheesy '70s folk rock and who like to chaperone high school plays. Much more appealing to me."

"Funny. I guess I'll return the cutout dress I just picked up last week then and stick to J. Crew."

Joking with Rocky helped to take the edge off of the strangeness of the situation momentarily, but I knew that I had to go talk to Cole, who was finished dealing with the receiving line. I promised Rocky that I would be back soon, and I made my way across the room to where Cole was sitting at a barstool with his back to the rest of the room. As I approached, I saw him looking at his phone. Not one for much social media, I was surprised to see him scrolling through Twitter. "Anything good?" I asked.

He looked up and patted the empty barstool next to him, gesturing for me to join him. "I'm thinking of making a big purchase, and I'm trying to get a sense of what the company is pushing out these days. Actually, you'll be a good person to talk to about this. I'm considering buying National Print and Digital."

"The company that made us go out of business? Why?"

Cole took a swig of Corona. "Because fuck them. You guys all lost your jobs because of those assholes. I want to bring *Young Chicago* back. Maybe in a different form and definitely with some major changes, but I still can't get past what happened. I think of you and Blair and everyone else and I still feel so much guilt. I know that there wasn't anything that I could do about it at the time, but there is now. I'm in an entirely different financial situation than I used to be. What do you think, Janie? Come back to Chicago and be the editor-in-chief? I'll have to run the whole company, so I won't be able to manage the paper anymore. You'd be so good at it."

Good Lord. It had been my dream since I was the editor of my high school newspaper to actually run a publication in the adult market. I was twenty-four, which was ridiculously young for such a job, but I knew enough from the time that I had spent with Cole that I could probably handle it. It was everything that I had wanted until a few weeks ago. And now… "I don't know, Cole. A lot has changed for me. There's so much to think about."

He seemed perplexed by my hesitation. "Janie, this is your chance. I *know* this is what you've always wanted. Is it this guy? Who *is* he, anyway? What's his name, Stone or something? I'm guessing you've known him for about five minutes."

I couldn't argue with his last statement, so I ignored it. "His name is Rocky. I sort of met him through my mom." Cole looked confused, and rightfully so. "Long story. Anyway, it's not just him. I only told you a fraction of what's going on in Maine right now. I'm not sure how much you want to hear, but Patrick cheated on my sister and it's caused a real mess. I've been taking care of the little girls and helping to provide some stability for them. He's back in the picture now to whatever extent she's allowing him, and we left them this weekend to try to figure things out and to be parents together. I have no idea what that situation ultimately looks like. I've coordinated my parents' funeral and the sale of their Massachusetts home, as well as worked with lawyers and the NTSB to determine that they luckily weren't at fault for the plane crash." I gestured to the bartender for a beer. "As for me, I have no idea what I want anymore."

Cole looked a bit dumbfounded by everything that he just heard. I had always acted in a supporting role to him, cheering him on, acting as a sounding board. This was likely the only time in the almost-year that we had consistently spent time together, that I had ever laid out a series of issues that pertained to me and not to him. As he attempted to process everything that I told him, he came back to the issue that was obviously bugging him. "So, are you sleeping with this guy?"

"Cole, seriously. What would that have to do with anything?"

"I think it would probably determine if you would move back to Chicago or not. What does he do for work? Or is he still in college? He looks a little young."

Compared to Cole, Rocky certainly did, although he didn't act it. "He's a high school guidance counselor. He comes from no family money whatsoever, which is probably hard for you to understand, so he can't just pick up and move a thousand miles without a job. And let's face it, you probably won't pay me all that much. It's a free print publication completely supported by ads. It's a dinosaur. A sweet and friendly dinosaur like a triceratops, but a dinosaur no less."

"Feisty Janie. I rarely see this side of you, but it's so fun and cute." I rolled my eyes, but he didn't seem to notice or care. "Anyway, I get it, you have shit to deal with. You know, you can leave Stone in Maine. I don't exactly think that my move back to Chicago will be accompanied by anyone, either." He gestured over at Cari, who was now flirting with a man with long gray hair who had to be around seventy years old. "We could pick up where we left off. I really do miss you."

"I don't think I could do all of that again," I whispered. I very rarely cried, but I could feel tears well up in my eyes.

Cole noticed and tipped my chin up with his finger. "It wouldn't be all secretive this time. Fuck it. Who cares? We'll just ignore what people say and live our lives. How about it, Janie? We were good."

We *were* good. But it was too one-sided and focused on Cole, and I needed more than that. I deserved more than that. "I need to think about the job," I said, completely ignoring the rest of the proposition. "I can't make a decision right now. Thank you for offering it to me. It is very flattering."

Cole nodded. "I haven't made the official offer yet, but my lawyers are drawing everything up now. I'll let you know. Keep thinking about it. It's yours if you want it, Janie. There's no one I would trust more with that responsibility. You're the best."

I glanced across the room and saw Rocky staring at us. I wondered how much he had seen and what he could tell from his vantage point. "I need to leave now. You hosted a really nice event. Your mom would be very proud." I got off of the barstool and said again, "I have to go." I walked to the other end of the room towards Rocky and stood directly in front of him. "I think I'm in love with you," I said, and kissed him squarely on the mouth, after brushing the remaining tears off of my face. He grabbed my hands and said, "Let's go." We left the room, leaving Cole, at least for the moment, behind us.

15 - Labs and Lounges

WE SAT IN ROCKY'S CAR in front of the Cape Elizabeth house at eight-thirty in the morning on Monday. "What do you think we're going back to? I haven't talked to them at all since we've been gone other than to tell Alyssa that our flight was canceled and that we would be back later," I mused. Our remaining time had consisted of sleeping late in our gorgeous Ritz Carlton hotel room, meandering through the small towns on the north shore of Lake Tahoe via our rental car, indulging in a delicious lunch with Bloody Marys at Moody's Bar in the charming town of Truckee, and just as we began driving to Reno for our flight, receiving a notification that our flight was canceled. Extending our trip was an unexpected treat despite having to take a red eye home, but now we were faced with the reality of my home situation. Was it awful that I hadn't really checked in on Alyssa and Patrick?

My tired thoughts drifted back to our time on the West Coast. It had felt strange to relay my feelings for Rocky in such a forward way just before leaving the RoyalE reception, but at the same time, I knew that I didn't have anything to lose at that moment. Less than five minutes later as I was digging in my purse for the room key outside of our hotel room, Rocky blurted out, "Since I saw you walk towards me at the college fair, I've wanted to spend every single minute of every day with you. And luckily I almost have." I held up the key and looked at the incredibly kind, funny, smart, and patient person in front of me. The difference between him and Cole was staggering. It further cemented my intention to try to make this work with Rocky, but it also made the job opportunity that Cole had just offered to me even more complicated. I needed to discuss it with Rocky soon, but I wasn't ready yet. I hadn't wanted to ruin a moment alone with him.

"It looks quiet in there. They could be still sleeping, or maybe they went somewhere. Or maybe they all killed each other," Rocky said, looking up at the house from the driveway.

"That's terrible," I said with a yawn. "Or maybe they invited Yoga Dude and Slutty Waitress and they're all living here in a polyamorous relationship."

Rocky laughed. "And you thought what I said was bad. Although my theory was definitely worse. We're better off with yours. Okay, do we go in?"

"I guess so." We got out of the car and walked towards the house. I needed a shower and to find some decent clothes for the meeting early that afternoon with Kate Heathcliff and the Director of Development from Amville. There would have to be plenty of coffee first.

"Hi! Anyone here?" I called out, although the house seemed empty. Rocky brought our bags in and dropped them in the front hallway. There were breakfast dishes scattered around the kitchen and the coffee pot was half full. "I guess they left," I said to Rocky, just as I heard a door open and the sound of clunky footsteps. I poked my head out of the kitchen as a disheveled Alyssa appeared in the upstairs hallway, hanging over the railing to see us. She was wearing a t-shirt that appeared to be backwards and inside-out.

"Up here!" she yelled unnecessarily loud. "I guess I lost track, um, I didn't think you'd be home so soon."

"It's okay," I said. "Where are the girls?"

"Camp! I added early drop off to their program for the rest of the week." she replied, flustered. "Um, do you guys need anything?"

"Where's Patrick?" I asked. I really hoped that Yoga Dude wasn't in my parents' bedroom right now.

"Here!" I heard him yell from the bedroom. We had definitely interrupted *something*. Oh. My. Goodness. Alyssa looked sheepish and shrugged her shoulders. Rocky laughed.

"I'm giving you two one hour," I said. "We're going to Dunkin Donuts for a caffeine infusion. Remember that those Amville people are coming at one o'clock. I need time to shower and make myself look alive." We walked back out the same door that we had walked in three minutes earlier.

"Wow!" Rocky said, as we got back into his car. "Did you expect that?"

"Not really," I said. "I mean, from a truly selfish point of view, it's going to be a heck of a lot easier for me and for everyone else if they're back together. I just didn't quite think that they would jump back in the sack so soon."

"Old habits, perhaps? Everybody's getting busy in this house," he said, and I swatted at his shoulder, feeling myself blush as my mind momentarily flashed back to our hotel room at the Ritz. Everything about the past few days was so unexpected. "Okay, Dunks it is," he said. "We'll get the espresso shots that they pour directly into the drip coffee and stay awake for the next three days."

"Perfect. And then we can drink bourbon back at home to try to counter it. Hopefully right before our meeting with Kate Heathcliff. I'm sure that I'll be perfectly lucid and engaging." I laughed with the kind of giddiness that comes from a significant lack of sleep. And love. I was definitely feeling the early days of love.

Rocky started driving towards the promise of caffeine and sugar. "Lucid and engaging," he repeated. "Just like Kate Heathcliff herself."

AT A FEW MINUTES before one o'clock, a large sedan pulled into the driveway. I peered out the window just in time to see Kate Heathcliff almost trip over the stairs that led to the front walkway. Even with the door still closed, I could tell that she was practically falling over herself apologizing to the two people with her. There was a tall, thin, bald, pale, middle-aged man wearing a crisp suit with wire-rimmed glasses and carrying a briefcase, as well as an older, gray-haired African American woman holding a portfolio and wearing a dress and blazer. Despite Kate's presence, I sensed a tone of professionalism and formality. I hadn't been nervous about this meeting until now. What did they ultimately want from us?

Alyssa and Patrick were already sitting on the couch of the living room, thumbing through magazines as we waited for their arrival. Rocky was busying himself in the kitchen with making mint-lemon iced tea for our impending guests after I showed him what to do. He actually had no reason to be there as he was just my boyfriend—*yes, he really was my boyfriend now.* I was even considering reactivating my Facebook account to update my relationship status. I felt like I was sixteen—but I was very glad that he had agreed to stay—and I couldn't stop smiling when I looked at him. Things were good.

The doorbell rang, and Alyssa, not surprisingly, made no effort to answer it, so the honor was mine. I opened the door and said hi to Kate, attempted to shake her hand, and wasn't taken aback at all when it was an awkward and bumbled interchange. I didn't want to wait for her to clumsily attempt to introduce her colleagues to me, so I took the reins. "Hi, I'm Janie Whitman. Please come in."

The woman shook my hand, followed by the man. "I'm Veronica Zanders. I'm the Director of Development at Amville. This is Todd Brooks. He's the Vice President for Development. It's so nice to meet you. We are so sorry about the loss of your parents. They were such loyal members of the Amville family." Kate stood slightly behind them, nodding enthusiastically. I found myself vacillating between being baffled by her and feeling sorry for her. It was a tough call.

I led the guests into the house and to the living room. Alyssa and Patrick finally stood, and introductions were exchanged. Rocky was still in the kitchen, and I motioned for him to join us. "This is Rocky Macallen. He graduated from Amville two years ago. Kate knows him already." He nodded at everyone and began putting glasses of iced tea on the coasters that I had set on the coffee table.

Kate once again appeared to be completely shocked to see Rocky with me, this time in my living room. It was getting to be funny to see her reactions to us. "Oh yes, of course, yes, hello Rocky." I could only imagine the questions that she had swirling in her head.

Rocky smiled and sat on the arm of my chair. "Hi, Kate."

Once everyone was settled in their seats, Veronica took papers out of her portfolio. "I've brought some statements for you, and you might want to share these with your accountant and possibly your lawyer. These are records of the donations that your parents have made to Amville over the years. We have included the dates, amounts, and any designations that they have made for these contributions at specific times. As you can see, they have regularly contributed to a scholarship fund that benefits students with either an interest in flying or the creative home arts."

"Huh?" asked Patrick, looking up from leafing through the papers. "I know that Amville is a liberal arts school, but I have no idea what that means."

Todd cleared his throat. "My team researched this further, and it turns out that Mrs. Whitman clarified the creative home arts as including horticulture, esthetics, or the culinary arena."

Alyssa smiled wryly. "So, the things that she liked. That they both liked. Funny. Do you actually find students who fit into these categories?"

Veronica nodded. "It's a small applicant pool for this scholarship, but to be honest with you, it makes awarding it a lot easier. As noted in these statements, it's only six thousand dollars per year, but that can have a tremendous benefit for a student who might not be able to join us otherwise."

Todd continued, "You also can see that they contributed to various capital campaigns, which helps us to keep our campus buildings in great shape and to construct new facilities as necessary. Whenever they were asked, the Whitmans answered. These were not huge donations, but the College has always felt that they contributed appropriately to their means and other financial obligations. Their generosity was evident."

Patrick looked up from the statements at the professionals in front of him. "So, from what I am seeing here, there are no outstanding pledges or commitments. Nothing is owed to Amville at this time. Which leads us to this meeting right now. How can we—namely, Alyssa and Janie—help you today?" Despite everything that had happened, I was very glad to have Patrick with us at this meeting. It was helpful to have someone who understood these things at the table to help cut through the bullshit.

Kate looked down and started fidgeting in her seat more than usual, appearing uncomfortable. What *did* they want from this meeting? Veronica, obviously an expert in her field, put the portfolio that she had been holding onto the table and made direct eye contact with Patrick. "We want to discuss securing a living memorial for your in-laws." She shifted her gaze to Alyssa and then to me. "Your parents. We have many opportunities to make that happen. Todd, do you want to share with them some of the possibilities that we have prepared for their consideration?"

Alyssa cut Todd off before he could respond. "Living memorial? Like a plaque or something?" I was watching Kate for her reactions. Her face was reddening, and she was squirming. I saw her quickly glance up at Rocky and then look down again. Rocky had stood up and was starting to pace a few steps in one direction and then a few steps back behind the chair that I was sitting on. I turned and caught his eye, and he gave me a quick small smile. Why was everyone acting so strangely? I expected this from Kate, but Rocky was now being odd.

Todd cleared his throat. "There would definitely be a plaque of some sort with their names and graduation year, and likely we would include some other pertinent information. But that can be worked out later. What we are proposing is something that truly embodies their spirit and what Amville meant to them." He took three rolled-up large pieces of paper out of his bag and started spreading them out on the coffee table. "The first is a science lab. We understand that they met in a Geology class. This is a picture of a Geo lab in our Science building that is currently unnamed. It would officially be called the Michael and Corinne Olson Whitman '80 Geology Lab or something to that effect." The room had fallen silent at this point, as Alyssa, Patrick, and I just stared at Todd. *How did he know that they met in a Geology class?* Sensing that no one was ready to speak,

Todd forged ahead. "The second proposal is a lounge in the dorm that they both lived in during their senior year. Like the lab, it would carry their names and be prominently displayed and always referred to as their lounge. The Whitman Lounge. Same idea."

There was still no reaction from us, so Veronica continued with the sales pitch. "The third proposal is on a larger scale. We aren't exactly sure as to how much money there is in their estate for these plans, but our team has drawn up some potential models based on the probable sale price of the house in Massachusetts and what we judge to be their retirement savings, given their careers, both of your college tuition costs, etc. We are, of course, taking into consideration a certain amount of money that I am sure both of you ladies will need for property taxes and maintenance on this house, as well as your own general living expenses and potential trust funds for the granddaughters." For a school that hadn't even realized that my parents were deceased, they had worked quickly. "Anyway, if you would like to honor their memory in a truly unique and lasting way, and if it meets your family's philanthropic priorities, we are looking to name the new fitness center. We understand that Mike Whitman played squash at Amville?"

Alyssa mumbled under her breath, "For one season."

Todd pushed forward an upside-down piece of paper towards where Patrick and Alyssa were sitting. "These are the estimated costs of naming these facilities. These figures take into consideration similar naming projects on our campus and at competing institutions. Obviously, there is some room for negotiation here, but since the facilities are already built, we don't need to factor in variable construction costs, which makes this more straightforward."

Alyssa and Patrick looked at the figures and handed the paper over to me. The numbers were so huge that I was momentarily speechless. Alyssa and Patrick seemed to have no reaction whatsoever. I finally said, "This much? For a gym that's already there?"

Veronica seemed ready for this kind of response; I am sure this wasn't the first time that she had gotten a reaction like this from a potential donor.

"Of course, there are other options that we can draw up. There are study rooms in the library available, and there is a conference room in the Humanities building that hasn't been named yet."

I stood up. "A study room? Some windowless room that kids go to work on a group project? This *does nothing*. There is nothing transformative or inspirational about this. It will cost you about ten dollars to put their names over a door and maybe another fifty to put a plaque on the wall, and that's if you go with a really nice plaque. What are you going to do with the tens or hundreds of thousands that you have left?" Todd started to speak, but I interrupted him. "And you, this is the first I am hearing from you," I said directly to him, pointing my finger in his direction from across the table. "Where have you been, if you're so important? They died, and no one from your office fucking knew."

Alyssa tried to interject, "Janie, come on—"

I turned to her briefly. "No, you don't get to talk right now. You have done nothing with the funeral plans, the investigation, the sale of the house, the care of your children, the feeding of everyone. This is my turn to talk." I turned back to Todd and Veronica, but first caught the eye of Patrick and turned my direction back to him. "And I don't want to hear anything from you, either. What the fuck, Patrick? A waitress who served you and your wife *food*? Who the hell does that? You humiliated her. She has been acting like a totally different person ninety-five percent of the time this summer because of your bullshit. I didn't ask for this. *No one* asked for this. So don't speak." Patrick was biting his lip and staring at me with sad eyes. He wasn't going to say a word. Alyssa looked on the verge of tears. I did feel badly about that, but I had come this far. I couldn't go back now. Everything was bubbling over. I looked at Todd and Veronica. "How did you know that the house sold in Concord? How did you know that my parents met in a Geology class? Because if you knew those things but didn't know that they died in a hugely publicized plane crash, then you have your heads up your asses."

And then it dawned on me, and I didn't like what I was realizing. "Holy shit," I said to no one in particular. I turned to Rocky, who was now standing with his back against the wall of the living room and appeared to be lightly sweating and was watching me with a combination of nervousness and concern. "It was you. You told her." I gestured to Kate who was sitting on her hands and slightly rocking back and forth. She tried to speak, and I replied, "Shhh. Don't say anything. Whatever you say, it'll come out terribly anyway. Save us the time and energy of having to deal with *you* on top of everything else that's going down right here. You *always* have *your* head up your ass."

All eyes were on me, and I felt like the room was spinning. This was not who I typically was; I could be sarcastic, but I was never mean and nasty to people, and I probably hadn't had a temper tantrum like this since I turned sixteen and found out that I wasn't getting a car. It was silly and immature at the time, and perhaps it was at this moment as well, but everything was crashing all around me. I couldn't just sit in my living room and be taken advantage of by people who didn't seem to have my family's best interests in mind.

Amidst the newfound silence in the room, the doorbell rang, but no one dared to move. I was standing closest to the foyer at that point, so I walked over to answer it. Just before I opened the door, I said to no one in particular, "This better not be Lance Ashton." I'm sure that Todd and Veronica thought that I was a lunatic.

It wasn't Lance but instead a FedEx delivery man carrying a strange-looking package. "What's that?" I asked him, not even trying to be polite. Deep down, I felt sorry for the innocent people in my wake that day.

He seemed taken aback but tried to be pleasant despite my rough demeanor. "It's your lucky day. Someone shipped you three deep-dish pizzas from Chicago. They're in here on dry ice. Gino's East. I hear they're the best!"

I knew exactly who those were from. "Leave them on the porch," I said, going back inside briefly to grab my purse and car keys from the table in the foyer. I walked back out the front door, past the driver who was still holding the pizzas, got into my mother's car, and began driving towards Commercial Street in Portland.

135

16 - Peaks and Pizza

IT WAS ROUGHLY A FEW HOURS later by the time I got to where I felt like I needed to be, but I wasn't sure of the exact time because I had turned off my phone as soon as I had gotten into the car. I knew that I had overreacted to everything that had happened in the living room but staying in that situation just wasn't going to happen. I had to get out of there and drove to the only place that made sense.

The line to get onto the ferry to Peaks Island was luckily short, with most people coming back from spending the better part of their Monday on the pretty island three miles from Portland's docks on Commercial Street. I knew that once I got onto the island, I could rent a bicycle and burn off at least some of my frustration as I pedaled to my favorite spot. For once, with my phone tucked away and free of distractions, I focused solely on the beauty of the ferry crossing and all that surrounded me. Once I was on the island and on a bike, I found a rock that was comfortable enough and tried to relax. It was a partly cloudy day and not too hot for August, with a light breeze and waves big enough to kick up a fine sea mist. As I looked out at the ocean, I tried to tune out the thoughts that were crowding my head. *Maybe Alyssa is onto something with all of her mindfulness and meditation*, I thought. My head was full, and I couldn't let go of any of it.

"I've never been here before," said a familiar male voice from behind where I was sitting sometime later.

"How did you find me?" I asked Rocky, who was now standing in front of me on the sand, carrying a backpack. I looked behind me and saw a bike on the ground.

"As soon as you left, Alyssa asked our guests to leave and then spent the next few minutes talking to me. She told me all of your favorite places to go in the greater Portland area, but she guessed that this was the most likely spot."

I was impressed by both Alyssa and Rocky. "Is that your bike?" I asked, realizing that I had only been in Rocky's apartment once and didn't know much about what he owned and didn't own.

"It's Max's," he replied. "He wasn't home," he said with a laugh. "I'll get him some beer. I haven't ridden a bike in a very long time. You use very different muscles for this."

I couldn't help but smile. My favorite spot on Peaks Island was a bit of a pedal from the docks. "What's in the bag? You camping out here?" I asked.

Rocky sat down next to me. "Alyssa not only pointed me in the right direction, but she also helped me with a few other items. I realized that in the fabulous week that I have spent with you, there is much that I haven't learned. Your sister helped to fill in some blanks." He pulled out a brown bag from Whole Foods. "I promise you that there is a bag of ice in my backpack to keep this cold. Which weighs about eighty pounds. That's why I'm so exhausted. Yep, that's it. I'm definitely not out of shape right now or anything. Anyway, Alyssa said I had to keep all of this cold, because hot guacamole is disgusting."

I took the plastic container from him. "You brought me guacamole?" I was obsessed with Whole Foods' in-house guacamole, but that topic must not have come up over the last week.

"Chips, too," he said, handing me a small waxy bag. "These are the ones that they make in the store. I had to get something in a small enough bag to fit it in here. I hope these are okay."

"It's totally good," I replied, in a bit of a daze by what was going on. He was right; we hadn't really talked much about what *I* liked, beyond our silly music discussions.

"So, why chips and guac? I mean, they're totally good, but you're such an amazing cook. I'm sure you're great at making guacamole. Oh, and I have a cream cheese brownie for you from Standard Baking Company. I had to fight an old lady for the last one. I'm still recovering." He had been busy.

"Alyssa did well. Okay, I'll backtrack with these. Cream cheese brownies are the one dessert that I am terrible at making, and I absolutely love them. They always come out badly when I make them, but the ones at Standard are amazing. If we're going with full disclosure here, Cole and I used to go to a ton of Mexican restaurants in Chicago. We would find small hole-in-the-wall places where we wouldn't run into anyone that we knew, and these places made great guacamole. Mexican food in Chicago is out of this world. This stuff here isn't quite as good, but it's still pretty awesome. So thank you. That's the deal on these items. I love them. Anything else in your bag? I had no idea that Alyssa had been paying any attention to me this summer or even in recent years, but I guess I was wrong."

Rocky scrambled into the bag again. "I totally forgot. Not sure if you can drink and bike ride since you're such a lightweight, but I went into the craft beer store across from the docks. Alyssa told me to get Allagash White. Is there a story here, or do you just like it?" He had bought a cheap opener and popped the cap for me. I took a long swig. It tasted great.

"Wow, this is becoming the story of my life through food and drink. Okay, the story behind the beer is that I went with my ex-boyfriend Mark to Europe when he was interviewing for jobs at the end of business school. There was a possibility in Brussels, but he ended up in Hong Kong. Anyway, I loved the beer there, and this is the closest I've been able to find in an American brew. Thank you for all of this. It's so thoughtful." I looked out at the ocean and passed the beer bottle his way, not making eye contact with him. "So, are we going to talk about it?"

Rocky took a swig from the Allagash and sat down next to me. "The part where I was a stupid ass and told Kate way too much information before I realized what she was doing? Yeah, we need to talk about that. I'm really sorry."

I put my head on his shoulder, and he put his arm around me. "No, I'm the stupid ass. I behaved like a child in there. You did nothing wrong. If she hadn't learned those things from you, she could have talked to anyone else who knew my parents and would have learned the same things. Chris and Anne Manfried. ANY of their dozens of Amville friends. These weren't secrets. I know now how Kate operates, and she gets away with it because of the awkward giggling and clumsiness. It could have happened to anyone. And ultimately, who cares? I just have to deal with this now and figure out how to talk to these people rationally and reasonably again."

Rocky handed me the brownie from the bag. I broke it in half and gave part of it to him, which he gladly accepted. He was thinking and finally spoke. "Why do you think that whole situation bothered you so much? I'm sorry if I sound like a guidance counselor right now."

"You totally do." It was a fair question. "I think it was just the culmination of everything that has happened this summer. I didn't really think through why they wanted to talk to us prior to the meeting. I should have known that they had motivations, and it's truly not an unreasonable discussion to have. I just think that what they proposed is super lame and boring. Their names on the doorway of a fitness center? My mother never stepped on a treadmill or elliptical in her life. Her garden and her yoga mat were her gym. Nothing that they said today in that meeting captured the essence of who they were. The Geology Lab is cute in theory, but they only took one Geo class each from what I know. It wasn't like they were Geology majors or something." I looked at him. "As you saw tonight, I'm far from perfect. You and I have had this pretty blissful week together—I mean, there have been a few strange moments, like Lance's stupidity, Patrick's arrest, the reason behind our trip to Tahoe—but for the most part, we've had the kind of week that you get to have when you meet someone in college who you really like. Other than going to class, you pretty much get to see that person all the time. It's idyllic and if it's right, you fall really fast. I've loved every minute of this week with you. And I meant what I said the other night after the memorial. I really do think that I'm falling in love with you. You just haven't seen much of a bad side of me until this afternoon. It doesn't show up often, but it's there. I guess you need to figure out if you're okay with it."

Rocky leaned over and kissed me. "I'm more than okay with it. It shows me that you're a normal human being with typical emotional responses. More counselor speak. And I don't need to think about it. I know that I'm falling in love with you. Lance Ashton can punch me every single day, and as long as you want me with you, that's where I'll be." There was another kiss. I looked at his eye. All evidence of Lance was gone. Despite Rocky's chivalrous overture, I hoped that it would stay that way.

"So," I said. "You've had bad things happen in your life. Your dad walked out on you, your mom struggled, all of that. How have you dealt with it this well? You're pretty perfect yourself."

Rocky smiled and brushed the hair away from my eyes. "At some point I think that I decided not to let bad things define me." He started cleaning up our empty containers and putting them back in his backpack. "And I'm far from perfect. Wait until you see me next week when I have to go back to work. I'm going to be one miserable bastard. I'll get over it in a couple of weeks, but the transition is going to be tough. Especially when I can't spend almost every minute of the day with you."

"Fair enough." I had to tell him. "Rocky, there's something I haven't talked to you about yet, but I—we—need to deal with it. Cole offered me a job. It's a really big job. I mean, it's not definite; a pretty huge deal has to go through first. But if it does, it's mine."

Rocky looked back out at the water. "Tell me about it."

I took a deep breath. "I would be the editor of my old magazine. I would have his job. He would run the entire company, so I would be in charge of *Young Chicago*."

Rocky stood up. "That's why the fucker sent pizzas. Son-of-a-bitch." He didn't seem mad per se, but he didn't seem happy either. *This* was a side of him that I hadn't seen yet. "So, Chicago? You would be going back."

I didn't know whether to stand up with him, but he seemed to need space. I stayed seated. "Yes. I would need to live there."

He walked to the shoreline, and I finally rose and joined him. He didn't seem angry, but there was so much for him to think about. He looked at me and said, "It's a good career move for you, right? It seems like an amazing opportunity. I've known you for one week. I don't want to hold you back. But I don't want this to end, either. Do you want to go?"

I looked around me at the waves, the sand, the rocks, Portland in the distance, Rocky next to me. I thought about Alyssa and the girls, the Cape Elizabeth house, how much I loved being a part of their lives on a consistent basis. I whispered just loudly enough to be heard. "I don't think so."

Rocky turned towards me. "Really? You're twenty-four. Most people in your field don't get this opportunity at forty. Or ever. Look, I'm not trying to push you away. I want to be with you more than anything. But if you want to go, I'll figure it out. I love Maine, but I really have no roots here. I can come to Chicago. That is, if you would want me there. Maybe there's more to this." He paused, as if he was deciding whether or not to continue down the path of this conversation. "It's him, right? You have to decide whether or not you're getting back together with him."

I grabbed his hands. "No, no, no. I'm done with him. It's not happening. I don't know what I was thinking going out for that memorial. He asked, and I was trying to be nice. But no. I'm sure that I could have walked out of that room with him on Saturday if I had wanted to, but that's not what I wanted. I wanted to walk out of that room with you, and I did."

Rocky seemed more assured by my words, which was a relief. "So, what do you want now, Janie? It sounds like you're ready to turn down what used to be your dream job, and that you want to stay here in Maine. What happens now?" He was still holding my hands.

"I want to go home. I want you to come with me. I need to work some things out with Alyssa and Patrick based on my behavior this afternoon.

And then I'll start to figure out the rest. And I'll tell Cole that I'm not taking the job. How does that sound?"

He hugged me to him. "It sounds good to me. I really like it over here, by the way. I've never been to Peaks Island before. How long have you been coming over here?"

We started walking over to our bikes. "We used to come over here with our parents when we were kids. We would bring picnics and stuff like that. And then it became my go-to spot when I needed to clear my head. I came over here when I had to decide where to go to college, and I came over here when things got weird with Lance and after Mark went to Hong Kong. Sorry to bring up those guys, but that's the story behind my escapes to Peaks. It's a full disclosure day around here, I guess."

Rocky hopped onto Max's bike. "It's life. I've got a spot on Lake Union in Seattle that I like, too. I'll show you someday. Let's go home." And we did.

I FOLLOWED ROCKY back to his apartment so that he could drop off Max's bike, and then I drove both of us back to Cape Elizabeth. As we walked in the front door of the house, we were hit by the overwhelming smell of mozzarella and heated olive oil. I turned to Rocky and said, "They're eating the pizzas. Have they no shame? They were sent to me. By him."

Rocky shrugged his shoulders. "I guess not. But I've never had a real Chicago pizza before, so I'm willing to get past who sent them. There were three pizzas. There's got to be some left for us. Come on."

We walked into the kitchen and saw Susie and Trish happily gobbling the small bites of pizza that Alyssa or Patrick had cut up for them. The adults were drinking beer and indulging in the deep-dish pizza as well but put their forks down the second that they noticed us standing in the room. Alyssa looked slightly bashful. "Um, hi, Janie. We didn't think you would mind. No one had been to the store and there really wasn't anything for dinner so um—"

I shook my head. "It's totally fine. If there's any left, we're going to have some, too."

Patrick stood up and started getting out plates. "There's a ton of it, and we only put two of them in the oven. We stuck the third in the freezer. They're huge. I forgot how good this stuff is. Remember your graduation weekend? I kept going back for more of this. Let me get you guys beers, too." It was funny to see him scrambling around trying to serve us, and I gladly stood back and let him do it.

We ate and drank and didn't say much, beyond discussing the girls' camp adventures from that day. Alyssa had signed them up for another week, and they were more than happy to go each morning. When everyone was full, and our plates were empty, Alyssa said that she was going to give the girls a bath upstairs. Rocky knew that I wanted to talk to Patrick and Alyssa, so he announced that he was going out to the patio to deal with some school-related emails that were starting to trickle in as the fall approached. This left Patrick and me alone in the kitchen to deal with the small amount of dishes.

I started loading the dishwasher, while he put away some clean dishes that were sitting in the drain rack. "I'm sorry," I said simply, not knowing how else to begin.

Patrick kept going about his chores. "You have absolutely nothing to be sorry about. What I did was ridiculous. I never should have blindsided Alyssa like that, let alone do what I did. I've told her as much, but you need to hear it as well. I could blame what I did on a million different things, but they would just be excuses. I was awful, and I will never stop apologizing to her or to you for it."

He seemed sincere, and for once, he was speaking from a place without ego or arrogance. "You *are* lucky in one respect," I told him as I inserted the detergent tablet in the dishwasher and started a wash cycle.

"What's that, Janie? I feel pretty lucky that I'm even allowed in this house right now, if that's what you're getting at."

"You're lucky that my father isn't here. Mike Whitman would have killed you." I gestured across the kitchen to the family room, where the canvas portrait of my parents was hanging. I could feel them watching our conversation.

"I have no doubt. Like I said, I wasn't thinking clearly. If I had been, there is no way in hell that I ever would have taken that risk. There would have at least been castration involved if Mike was around. Ouch."

I grabbed us each another beer and opened them. We clinked bottles and took a swig, both leaning forward against opposite sides of the kitchen island counter, facing each other. So many conversations over the years between Patrick and I had looked like this, and I was glad that despite everything that had happened, we were still getting along. "So," I began. "What do you think about the meeting from this afternoon? I was obviously frustrated with it, but I was not in a rational state of mind when listening to their proposals. I want to know your perspective on it."

"Well," he said, easing back into his older brother-in-law role. "I was relieved to see that we don't owe Amville anything right now. That allows us to approach this from a place of a bit more power. Your parents were generous in the past, but none of what they did was over-the-top. I know that Amville's proposed figures seemed a bit high to you, but they might be appropriate. I'm not sure. I think we need to ask for more actual documentation of examples of what other families have done. There will be room for negotiating, I'm sure. But I see your underlying points. Beyond the Geology lab, none of these proposals really had much to do with your parents. It seems like there are some spaces on campus that they would like to affix names to, and they see this as an opportunity to do that. My guess is that there are other options, but we—really, you and Alyssa— will have to work with them to see what exactly is possible and for how much money. I bet that you can find something more fitting." He took another sip. "I'm not sure if I really just said anything that is helpful or if it's just a bunch of rationalizing bullshit."

He was making a tremendous amount of sense. "Thank you. On a day that I couldn't seem to be reasonable, you are being level-headed and rational. I like having you around here." I took another drink from my bottle before asking the question that was looming. "Are you and Alyssa okay now? I mean, not totally okay, of course, but getting there? It seems that way, but I have no idea what you've really been talking about. Besides that 'respectful coexistence' crap. Oh, and whatever it was that we interrupted this morning. I guess I'm just confused."

Patrick laughed and took a sip of beer. "I love your sister. I've always loved her, since I met her in that stupid icebreaker during freshman orientation. I didn't always tell her enough, and I certainly didn't show it. I'm changing that now, because I almost lost her. I think I still have her. We're starting to work with a therapist in Portland tomorrow, mostly because we have to figure out what we're going to do next, but also to make sure that nothing like this ever happens again. I know that she can't move back home to Concord. I've accepted that now. We both are just struggling as to where we should live and where I should be working. I mean, I know we have some money from the estate, but it's only so much. Especially if we give most of it to Amville to name a fitness center," he said with a wink. "What about you, Jae Jae? I'm guessing that there was more to these pizzas than just thanking you for coming to California. Especially considering what that card said."

"There's a card?" I hadn't even thought of that. "Did Rocky see it?"

Patrick handed it to me. "No, Alyssa read it and put it under all the Amville papers. Rocky is such a good dude. All he cared about was figuring out where you were and how he could make you happier. I guess that Cole is trying to make you happy, too, but shit, he's just so cheesy. No pun intended with the pizza and all. It *was* good, though. I forgot how good that Chicago pizza is. Did I tell you that my brother is applying to jobs out there? It might be worth him leaving Boston just so that I can visit him for pizza."

The card simply read: *Chicago is awaiting your return. And I love you just the way you are. Cole.* "This is pretty bad," I said to Patrick. "I'm glad no one else saw it." I sighed and ripped up the card, getting rid of the evidence. "I'm not going," I said, answering his earlier question. "He wants me to come back to work for him again, but in his old job. I haven't even told Alyssa about the offer yet. It's a great opportunity, but my life is here now. Wherever you and Alyssa and the girls are, I want to be close by. And I owe it to myself to see where things with Rocky will go."

Patrick nodded. "That's great news, Janie. You're such a great influence on all of our lives. And Rocky is a good dude," he said, thumping his chest for effect. Apparently, we had unleashed a bromance.

I could hear Alyssa saying goodnight to the girls upstairs, so I went to meet her in the hallway and issue another apology. "Hi," I said. "You're the last person on my list—at least in this house—who I need to apologize to."

She put her finger to her lips, and we walked down the hall to my parents' bedroom, where Alyssa had been sleeping that summer. Again, I apologized. "I'm really sorry for being an asshole today. You didn't deserve that."

"Please," she said, rolling her eyes and sitting on the bed. I sat on the comfortable chair in the corner of the room. I looked out the window and saw Rocky working on his laptop on the porch as the sun was setting. "I've been the asshole every day of this summer. You were allowed to have ten minutes of assholishness. I think I just created a word," she said.

"It's a good one," I replied, and I closed my eyes. It was good to rest and feel some peace in at least some of the situations that I was dealing with.

"Jae Jae," Alyssa said, and I opened my eyes. Alyssa's were sparkling with hopefulness that I hadn't seen in a long time. "I think that I have an idea."

17 - Changes in Attitudes

THERE WASN'T MUCH SLEEP that night. Once Alyssa told me some of the thoughts she had been having for the past few hours, I found a notebook in the nightstand drawer and started jotting down her initial ideas, plus adding my own suggestions as I came up with them. Patrick came upstairs at one point to check on us, but Alyssa kicked him out of the room and promised that we would come back downstairs to share everything with him and Rocky soon. Once he shut the door behind him, I broached the subject that Alyssa had been avoiding with me all summer. "I talked to him when you were putting the girls to bed," I said cautiously. "He said that you guys are starting therapy in the morning and that things are going okay right now. It sounds like he is really sincere about working things out with you."

Alyssa reclined back onto the pillows on the bed. "I think I am, too. We have talked more in the last few days than we've talked in the last few years. You'll see it for yourself when or if you have kids someday. You get so wrapped up in taking care of them. You don't sleep much. You don't really have meaningful or even coherent conversations with each other. At least, that was our experience. And we were so young when we had them, which I don't regret, but Patrick was just getting his career off the ground when Trish was born. And then there was Susie two years later. So much happened by the time we were only twenty-seven. Three years later, we realize now that we have to prioritize our relationship. We're going to work on that."

There was still one question that I didn't yet know the answer to. "What about Yoga Dude?" I couldn't for the life of me remember his real name. Was it Derek or something?

Alyssa sighed, for once not correcting my use of the nickname, but instead seemingly indicating her exhaustion with the situation. "I talked to Doug yesterday. I told Patrick beforehand that I was going to call him so that I could keep everything above board. Anyway, I apologized for how abruptly I left him at the inn, but I told him that it was definitely over. He didn't seem surprised at all and didn't fight me on it. I wonder how much he even cared that I was ending it," she mused, almost as if she was talking to herself, realizing this for the first time. "He was a victim in all of this in many ways, but I never once lied to him about my situation, either. He knew from the start what he was getting himself into, and it definitely wasn't his first rodeo. And I really did enjoy getting to know him. He came into my life at the right time, and he helped me to understand myself better. But he's not my husband. He's not Susie and Trish's daddy. It's time for me to move on. Or back, I guess. But not to Concord. Oh, and I think that I need to find a new yoga studio. That's also on my list of things to do this week."

"I look forward to reading all about it in his next novel," I said, and we both laughed. It was probably best for Patrick not to find out Yoga Dude's real name or when his books hit the shelves if we could help it.

We brainstormed for about another hour and then went downstairs to share our initial proposal with Patrick and Rocky. We found them sitting on the living room couches watching the Red Sox game on TV. Once we had their attention and disclosed our initial thoughts to them, it felt both overwhelming and exciting. Patrick began informally drawing up some different financial models, showing possibilities of funding and carrying out our plan. It looked plausible but would require some risk on the part of Amville, even with our family's significant contribution. Rocky didn't say much but seemed to sense my nervousness.

It was nine-thirty, but he didn't think it was too late to contact Professor Chris Manfried. "You're going to need a faculty liaison for this," he said as he began to text him. "He'll be able to work through many of the details with you before you formally present something to Development, and he can hopefully be a strong advocate for you moving forward. This is a pretty significant departure from what they initially proposed, so you're going to need some support." He looked down at his phone again as it buzzed. "Wow, someone has decided to fully embrace technology. Quick reply. All right, ladies, you have a noon appointment with the good professor in his office tomorrow. There's no turning back now." We made plans for the morning; Alyssa and Patrick would bring the girls to camp and then I would pick up Alyssa from their therapist appointment, after which we would drive up to Camden. This was really happening.

Alyssa and Patrick went upstairs—presumably to sleep in the same bed, which was still taking some getting used to for me—and I curled up with Rocky to watch the end of the baseball game. I had never been much of a professional sports fan, but if I was actually going to stay in New England, I probably would need to become more engaged in the things that the adults around me were interested in. I still couldn't get my mind off of what Alyssa and I had worked on though. "Do you think it's crazy?" I asked him drowsily after a yawn.

"Keeping Andrew Benintendi on the field after he got hit by the pitcher last inning? I'm not sure. Hopefully not," he said, giving me a kiss on my shoulder, which was against his chest.

"Silly," I replied. "Which one is Andrew Benintendi again?"

"Did you seriously grow up in Boston? We need to work on this. He's playing left field. No, I don't think it's crazy. It's big, and I'm not sure how the funding will exactly work, and it really depends on if they're willing to take a big risk in order to provide this kind of a place on campus. If they're smart, they're going to take into account not only the students, but the parents, the alumni, the community, the media, and I'm sure there are other constituencies that I'm not thinking of right at this moment. Your brother-in-law kept giving me beers, so I'm a little foggy. Anyway, it'll be a big decision for Amville, and you might have to wait a bit for your answer. But at this point in both your and Alyssa's lives, why not? Dive in. Neither one of you are big risk takers from what I've seen so far, but now is your chance. I think it's exciting."

He knew Amville a heck of a lot better than I did, and Chris Manfried knew its intricacies and politics, so I hoped that we were going about things in the right way. "I might have to move up there," I said. Curled up with Rocky, it was amazing to think that I had only known him for a week. He seemed so familiar, lying on my family's furniture, quickly becoming Patrick's BFF, dispensing wisdom about my life decisions. "At least for a while. That would be weird."

He was quiet for a moment. "One step at a time. It's not that far away, and the professors usually get to rent houses right near the main part of the campus, so maybe they would have a place for you, too. Somewhere big enough for Alyssa to grace you with her presence from time to time, as well. This is hers, too. She's great, Janie, and I really like her, but you need to keep her involved and engaged with this if it happens. She has to be an integral part of this."

He was right. "I need her to be a very significant part of this. She has a skill set that is critical for what we want to do. I'm not giving her a free pass this time. Plus, I really think that she needs this right now. She needs more of her own identity."

"Good. I totally agree," he said, sounding satisfied with my answer. "There's one more thing, and you might want to be prepared for it. You're offering them a lot more money than what they initially asked for. You're packaging it very differently, but it's still more cash. They might try to convince you to direct that towards something else."

"Like naming a laundry facility or something like that? I wouldn't be surprised."

Rocky laughed. "Or perhaps the equipment room for the ski team. Because your parents skied a few times every winter," he said, gesturing to a framed picture of them at Sunday River that was on a table across the room. "You get the idea. They might get really excited about the offer of more money and try to convince you to do something bigger but that doesn't require the efforts on their part that you are proposing. I'm sure Chris will have some ideas for countering that, but just keep that in mind when you're meeting with him tomorrow."

Alyssa and I had already talked about different reactions that we might get from the Development staff, but Rocky was absolutely right. This might go nowhere very quickly, and then we would have to decide what we were willing to do. "Are you sure that you can't come up to campus with us?" I asked. We had spent almost every moment together for the past week. This seemed like a big thing in my life for him to miss, especially since it was his alma mater and advisor we were seeing.

"I absolutely have to go to work tomorrow and hand out fall schedules to the kids. Shit's about to get real for me with the year about to start," he said jokingly. "But in all seriousness, you don't need me there. Look how badly it went when I was here for your last Amville meeting," he teased, which prompted me to lightly elbow his stomach.

"Are you concerned that I will go stark-raving bitch again on them tomorrow?" I asked. "They'll probably see me on campus and call security. No, seriously, I probably needed to melt down a bit to get to this point. Not that I'm proud of it, but I think that it helped Alyssa snap out of herself for long enough to at the very least get this process started with me. I also think that I had kept things bottled up for too long. It was going to come out at some point, but maybe a meeting with a college vice president wasn't the best time for it." *Or maybe it was.*

Rocky hugged me tighter. "It might give you an edge in negotiations. You know, if they think you might go apeshit in their office."

"True. Well, I'm glad you've now seen my true colors. I frighten people." It was late. The game was over, the Sox had won, and Rocky was tired. I was ridiculously wide-awake while being simultaneously exhausted.

"You're terrifying," he said with a yawn, and I sent him upstairs to sleep. After I kissed him goodnight, I curled back up on the couch, this time alone with my notebook, and began to scribble down new thoughts connected to our big plan. The ideas flowed more quickly than I could write them down, and it seemed like I was racing after them with my pen. I felt like a journalist again, but instead of chasing down a story about a new waxing technique or wedge sandal, I was creating a future.

THE NEXT MORNING was fairly straightforward, despite the fact that I had gotten approximately two-and-a-half hours of sleep, all of them on the couch with my notebook lying on my stomach and my pen creating an unfortunate ink stain on the rug where it had fallen. I woke to Susie and Tricia jumping on top of me while Patrick made coffee. He was singing Jimmy Buffett's "Changes in Latitude, Changes in Attitude" while measuring out the ground beans, which struck me as odd. Patrick's musical tastes typically revolved around fairly intense hip-hop which was also somewhat strange given his upbringing and career, but he said it motivated him. I never quite understood what he meant, but this was still a bizarre departure. I put the TV on for the girls and joined him in the kitchen.

"What's going on?" I asked. "Unusual song choice for you."

He grinned, getting out the half-and-half from the refrigerator. "But not for this house. I remember the first time that I came home with Alyssa. It was October break from Cornell, and we had only been together for less than two months. I still can't believe that she was brave enough to introduce me to your parents that early, and I can't believe that I was ballsy enough to go. Of course, they were both so nice and welcoming to me, but we had just started dating."

"Anyway, here I had been raised in this proper Upper East Side family, where my parents went to symphonies and operas and Broadway, and I come to Concord, Massachusetts and your dad is blasting Buffett. Imagine trying to make small talk with your mom while 'Why Don't We Get Drunk' is playing. Oh yeah, and you were twelve, and you didn't react at all. It was just what you were used to. Oh, and you made us our appetizers the first night that we were there. I still remember. They were the most incredible spinach and mushroom wontons. How on earth does a twelve-year-old know how to do that?"

I hadn't made those wontons in years. I would need to make them again soon. "I miss them," I said, getting a mug out of the cabinet. "It's too bad that it took all of this to bring us together. Or for me to meet Rocky. It's hard to make sense of it."

Patrick poured us each some coffee. "I miss them, too. Although I think they might have killed me, or at least inflicted some long-term harm on me if they were around. All of that calmness likely had a threshold. I mean, look at you yesterday. Whitmans can only take so much," he said with a wink.

"Come on," I said. "What I did was nothing compared to anything that you've done. You and I are cool, but I'm still going to keep giving you shit for it. That's my job as the sister."

"Which is why, my little Janie, I am going full-force into therapy with your sis. I'm looking forward to it. It's going to be great," he said, wringing his hands together, like he was eager to start working on something.

"You know it's going to be hard, right? You'll have to, like, talk about your feelings and shit." The coffee tasted great. I wondered how much of it I would be drinking over the course of the day. Likely a lot.

Patrick began unloading the dishwasher. It was strange seeing him being so helpful. "I am totally ready. I fucked up," he said quietly, knowing that his daughters were in the next room. "And I have to own up to all of it. I'm trying to fix it and work through the next steps of our life together. And I am so excited for your Amville plan. I think this will be great for both of you."

He sounded so upbeat, so optimistic, as "Boat Drinks" began playing on what was apparently a greatest hits compilation. I didn't want to be a downer when dealing with Patrick, but there was so much reality to at least admit.

"It might not happen. I want to be positive, but we are proposing something really big, and given what was presented to us, this is a major about-face." He was, luckily, nodding, which indicated to me that at least he wasn't in a total dream world. "But here's my other worry, and Rocky is concerned about this, too. I know that you are super supportive of this and us and especially of her right now, but if this ultimately happens, she needs to be a part of it. Not every single day, and I know that you both have a lot to figure out with logistics of your own family, but she needs to be involved. I don't have the expertise for some of the things that she's proposing, and I also think that she needs this." I quickly weighed out what I wanted to say, and finally decided to go ahead with it. "The only reason that she was hanging out with that Yoga Dude is because he listened to her. He made her feel interesting and important. If this all pans out, she will have something that will hopefully keep making her feel interesting and important. I want that for her so much." There. I had said it.

"I couldn't agree more," he said, gesturing at the stairs, as we heard Alyssa's footsteps walking towards us. I really wanted to believe him.

18 - Dive In

AFTER ROCKY HAD LEFT TO GO pass out fall schedules to students and Alyssa and Patrick had departed to drop the girls off at camp and then to begin their counseling at the therapist's office, I began to make my sister's favorite breakfast treat. I noticed that she only had coffee before they left, and I didn't want her going right from her appointment to Amville without at least something somewhat substantial in her system, mostly out of my own self-preservation during a significant drive; a hangry Alyssa was not for the weak.

Since we were much younger children, Alyssa had always loved doughnuts, but since she had had the girls and had become much more health-conscious, she rarely indulged anymore. My mother had recently bought some pans for baking homemade doughnuts, and the little girls had become big fans of these creations. I threw together a quick batter, baked them off, and whisked an easy glaze of powdered sugar and milk to drizzle over them as soon as they had slightly cooled on the wire rack. Making something helped me deal with my nervous energy and I knew that if I sat back on the couch, I would fall asleep and miss picking up Alyssa. From start to finish, my baking project took me less than an hour, and I packed up several doughnuts to take on our day trip north to Camden.

The plan was for me to pick up Alyssa and drive to Amville for our meeting, and Patrick would pick up the girls after camp ended for the day.

When Alyssa got in the car, she was wearing her sunglasses, didn't say a word, and plugged her iPhone into the input jack of the car. After fiddling with it for a few moments, we were listening to Howard Stern on the SiriusXM app. Prank calls to radio trading post shows were being featured. Alyssa cowered down into the passenger seat and did not seem to want to engage in any way, so I put the Rubbermaid container on her lap and began to drive towards I-295 North.

After about three minutes of us sitting in silence other than what was playing through the car's sound system, Alyssa opened the container and took a ravenous bite out of one of the doughnuts. "Jesus Christ, Janie. How do you make this shit? I mean, seriously. I could eat twenty of these right now. Fuck. I'm going to gain thirty pounds living with you. It's so goddamn good."

The Whitman girls had never shied away from a good curse word, but Alyssa was on fire a bit more than usual. "Are you okay?" I asked, merging onto the highway.

"Well, let's just throw this out there. I know that you talked to him this morning. So I know everything that you said. I'm not mad, but I know that you want me to be doing something other than just driving kids places and going to yoga. And he agrees with you. Hell, I agree with you, but this is a lot of pressure. I haven't done anything else since college. And even then, it was *college*. I went to classes and wrote papers and had intellectual conversations and got drunk and spent almost every night with Patrick."

"And then we got married. And we moved so many times in that first year while he did all of his training for his job that I really couldn't work, and then once we were in Concord, there I was. And there were a bunch of other women just like me who had babies and went to yoga and to Whole Foods and discussed the merits of which CSA to buy vegetables from that summer. Not that I *cooked* any of those vegetables. I mean, what was I supposed to do with a rutabaga? Come on."

"But it was totally fine and I didn't have any desire to do anything else. I wasn't miserable or depressed or anything. I know that everyone *expects* the little suburban mom to be a total hot mess inside and sure, some are, but I really was okay. And then HE went and fucked everything up. This wasn't me. But now I have to change everything because of what *he* did. How is that fair?"

As she was my sister, I knew that all of this was true. But she knew all of this going into the therapy session, so my best guess was that there was more to her unhappiness than what she had just told me. I broached it carefully. "It's not fair at all. He did some really stupid shit. Did you talk about anything else?"

Alyssa took another bite of doughnut followed a swig of the coffee that I had brought for her. "He wants to start a branch of his company in Portland. He wants to sell the house in Concord and live in Maine full-time."

I had privately really hoped for a scenario like this. "That's great!" No matter what came from the Amville proposal, I would be closer to her and the girls. I couldn't imagine being far from them anymore.

Alyssa sighed. "I don't think it's all that great."

This wasn't an easy conversation, and Alyssa wasn't making much sense. "Isn't this kind of what you want? You told me that you were too humiliated to move back to Concord."

"I am. For now, anyway. But to give all of it up and to live together again—whether it be in Cape Elizabeth or in another house nearby—I don't know." She pulled the hood from her sweatshirt over her head and sunk down a bit more. She didn't look like thirty-year-old Alyssa anymore, but rather seventeen-year-old Alyssa who had just found out that she hadn't gotten into Yale early decision. And if she was seventeen, then I was eleven, and I really didn't know how to help her.

I stayed silent for a bit, giving her space to process everything that she had just said and to give me time to contemplate it as well. She had been difficult to read throughout much of our time together that summer, but this reaction threw me for a significant loop. I continued to drive north, crossing small bridges and trying to focus on the beauty of another spectacular summer day in coastal Maine. The last time that I had made this trip had been with Rocky the previous week, and the tone and tenor had been much lighter.

Finally, I broke the ice and gently asked, "What are you most worried about? Do you think that you still love him?" I realized the enormous risk that I was taking asking these questions, especially the latter. I didn't want her to shut down and to stop confiding in me. But I really needed her to be one hundred percent a part of our Amville meeting, and if something was going to hold her back, I needed to know now right then and there.

Alyssa reclined the passenger seat and stretched her hands above her head. "What if he does it again? What if we're in Mom and Dad's house and I have to kick him out of there? Or if we're in another place and the girls and I have to move back again? What if it's the mother of some new friend of one of the girls? Or someone else that we know? If it happens in Maine, I have nowhere else to go. *This* is my safety net. He could fucking destroy my safety net."

Everything was starting to make sense; there was more risk to Alyssa than I had ever considered. I asked her the same question again. "Do you still love him?

She hit the ceiling of the car hard with her angry fist. "More than I can ever put into words."

CHRIS' OFFICE WAS IN the back of a building that was constructed in the 1800s, and getting there required navigating many twists and turns through hallways as well as walking up and down several half-flights of stairs. Rocky had warned us about this ahead of time, leaving Patrick to ask in his most older-responsible-adult tone, "How is that even ADA-compliant?" Rocky shrugged his shoulders. We ultimately turned one last corner and heard jazz music playing.

"I bet that's him," I said, and soon we were standing in Professor Chris Manfried's office doorway.

"Well, hello, ladies! Come in, please, come in." His office was a mess, with stacks of books and piles of papers everywhere, and he quickly moved several armfuls of materials aside to clear some space. "Dear Janie, so good to see you again. And this must be sister Alyssa. Welcome to the oldest and most decrepit building on the Amville campus! If it didn't have historic status, they would have mercifully torn it down many years ago." He shook Alyssa's hand, and gestured for us to sit in the two armchairs on the other side of the desk across from him. "So, my friend Rocky tells me that you have an idea to honor Mike and Corinne. Alyssa, Janie knows this, but they were both very dear to me. If I can help in any way, I certainly will, and gladly. So, please, tell me your thoughts."

I started to speak, "Well, we—" but Alyssa interrupted me.

"May I?" I couldn't believe that she wanted to talk first and make the initial pitch, but I was thrilled. I nodded, and Alyssa launched into a description of our meeting with the Amville officials the previous day and the brainstorming that she and I had subsequently done. After taking the lead with virtually everything in our collective lives for the past six weeks, it was both surprising and wonderful to hear Alyssa speak with such confidence and clarity. She was on board.

I felt my phone buzz in my purse, and I took it out subtly in an attempt to not be rude to either Alyssa or Chris. It was a text from Cole, with a link to a news story and the simple words "you in?" I clicked on the news story, which was from the *Chicago Tribune*. The headline stated, "Emerson Buys National Print and Digital; Promises Major Restructure and Chicago Jobs." I continued on to the first paragraph:

In a shocking financial move, former Editor-in-Chief of the now-shuttered *Young Chicago,* Cole Emerson has purchased the periodical powerhouse National Print and Digital for a currently undisclosed sum. The son of the recently deceased 1980s pop sensation Rayna Emerson—known commonly as RoyalE—has assured the public that he will move the headquarters of the company from New York to the

Windy City and will bring *Young Chicago* back into publication. Emerson states: "With the sudden and abrupt closure of *Young Chicago,* many talented employees unnecessarily lost their jobs. I am working to not only bring them back to their old positions, but to also expand job opportunities in journalism and publishing throughout the Chicagoland area."

Part of me never thought that it would happen; I thought that Cole might realize that leaving LA meant going back to cold, windy winters, working long hours, and most likely leaving Cari Connors behind. I had an unbelievable opportunity if I wanted it. I could hear Alyssa talking and Chris asking her clarifying questions, but I had no idea what they were actually saying. For someone who rarely got cold feet, I felt a chill go through my body.

"Wouldn't you agree, Janie?" Alyssa asked me, but I didn't know what she was referring to.

"Uh, I'm so sorry, I spaced out for a minute. What did you want to know?"

Chris smiled gently and looked up from his laptop. Alyssa had given him our written proposal on a flash drive, and he was vigorously making edits as they spoke. I had missed out on quite a bit. "Janie, here's what I suggest. I would like to serve as a faculty advocate or liaison for you both in this effort. I really like what we are all putting together here," he said, being quite kind to me despite my rude behavior. "I do think, though, that we need one more line or two at the conclusion of this proposal. I want to tie it up with a big red bow. As my students say, 'Go big or go home,'" he said with a hearty laugh. "Hmmm… how does this sound? 'This is a love letter to the liberal arts. When educating the young adults who will lead our world, care for our sick, teach our children, and protect our planet, we must also give them the tools to live enriched and nourished lives. We ask for your consideration of our proposal as a fitting tribute to the memory and generosity of Michael Whitman and Corinne Olson Whitman.' What do you think?"

Alyssa took a tissue from the box on his desk, wiping a tear off of her cheek. I imagined college students taking tissues from that same box in moments of frustration and struggle when writing their senior theses or figuring out the next steps in their soon-to-be adult lives. I had also seen Alyssa cry more in the past week than I think I had since she was thirteen years old and going through the hell of adolescent hormonal changes. She had changed so much that summer, or maybe I was just starting to see her in a different light.

"It's beautiful," she said. "Janie, what do you think?"

I thought that I should probably take the job in Chicago if I was only considering what my brain told me. It was by far the best journalism opportunity that I could ever hope to have in my twenties. But too much had changed that summer. I knew despite all logic and common sense, that what we were attempting to start that afternoon at Amville was right. I kept hearing Rocky's words from the previous night over and over in my head: *Dive in.* "There is a pretty good chance that they will say no, but at least we will know that we tried. We tried for Mom and Dad." My voice cracked a bit over those last words.

Chris' eyes were wet by now, too, and he nodded. "And yourselves. Don't forget yourselves here. The chance to carry your parents' legacy forward and to show your children this work is a stunning example of a life well-lived. I am happy to support you and to be a part of this. I never got to say goodbye to my friends either, and this helps to make that acceptable, at least for *my* soul. Maybe it's selfish on my behalf, but I also think that we can help so many students find more balance in their time here and to better prepare them for their adult lives. As someone who spends every day with them, I can tell you that we will all benefit from that. If we can make this happen, Mike and Corinne will continue to live through our collective energies." He was an exceptionally gifted communicator and such a kind man. I had no doubt as to why Rocky found him to be such a treasured mentor. I realized that I needed people like him and his sweet wife in my life then more than ever.

Alyssa cleared her throat, trying to keep her emotions in check. "So, what next?"

Chris typed a few more things and clicked his mouse a couple of times. A printer that was almost completely buried under loose papers on a small bookcase in the corner of the room began to hum. "I just printed four copies. One for each of us and one for the Development Office. We can go drop it off with them right now. I have saved everything on your flash drive as well," he said, handing it back to Alyssa.

She suddenly seemed a bit hesitant. "We're just going to walk over there and drop it on their desk?" she asked, a little sheepishly.

Chris mulled it over for a moment. "I'll call first. Hold on." He picked up the desk phone in front of him. "Oh, hello, Clara. Good morning. This is Chris Manfried... Yes, a beautiful day... Oh, you're too kind. I'll be sure to tell her that. I do need to ask you a favor. I need to get something to Todd... No, no, no emergency, all good things... Yes, I will be right over. Thank you, Clara." He hung up the phone and looked up. "Let's go take a walk over to Brady Hall. That's the administrative building. And then you ladies can be on your way back home."

We collected our things and followed Chris out of the maze that was his building. Alyssa fell back next to me and whispered, "What the hell has gotten into you? He's being so nice to us, and I feel like you're on Mars right now."

There was no use keeping it from her, but this wasn't the right time. I certainly didn't want Chris to hear any of it. "In the car. I'll tell you in the car. Don't worry about it."

"Hmmmm," she murmured. It was enough to hold her off for the moment. She walked forward next to Chris and began asking him friendly, benign questions about some of the buildings on campus. I reread Cole's text while walking behind them, trying to decide how I was going to eventually respond. There was no good way to handle any of this.

Brady Hall was a stately smaller building, filled with offices. Chris led us down the hall of the building's first floor, to an office with a placard on the door that read: "Todd Brooks, Vice President of Development." The woman who must be Clara sat at a desk when we first walked in, and there was another door to the left that was ajar, most likely leading into Todd Brooks' actual office. Clara looked up from her computer. "Well, hello, Chris. We don't get to see you much at this end of the hall. Todd said that you're welcome to stop in."

Chris gave her a tip of his nonexistent hat and said, "Thank you much, Clara. And Anne and I will need to have you and your wife over for dinner soon. We have discovered this new Bordeaux, and I think that you'll both enjoy it." I got the impression that Chris made friends wherever he went, and that people genuinely enjoyed him and Anne. I was so thankful that he had peeked into the tent at L.L. Bean the week before.

We walked with Chris into Todd Brooks' office, and he was sitting back in his chair reading what looked like the student newspaper. "Ahhh, Chris! What a nice treat. And Alyssa, Janie, I didn't expect to see you. Excuse my surprise; I didn't realize that you were acquainted with Professor Manfried."

Chris saved us the explanation. "I was close with their parents; we were classmates. Which is why we are here today, Todd. I understand that you and Veronica visited Janie and Alyssa yesterday afternoon, and that maybe there are other avenues to consider as you work to properly honor Mike and Corinne. The ladies have spent considerable time since your meeting drafting a proposal. I agreed to work with them as their faculty liaison, and I will continue to advocate for them through whatever arises. This is quite different from suggestions that you and Veronica offered, but I hope that you will take some time to read through this and to perhaps share it with some colleagues to collect their thoughts. That's all that we ask." He handed the papers to Todd Brooks.

"Well," he replied. "This is surprising, but I look forward to learning more. I can assure you that we will give it our consideration. It may take a while to gather responses and to get back to you; I do want you to know that. As Chris can likely tell you ladies, academia sometimes moves at a snail's pace. This can be frustrating, but please be assured that no matter what, your proposal will be part of a thoughtful process."

I didn't know much about higher education and how everything worked, and neither did Alyssa. We nodded our heads and listened. When Todd Brooks was done with his explanation, I piped up, "Thank you. We really appreciate it. And I want to formally apologize for my behavior yesterday. That isn't who I am, at least not most of the time. There was a lot that confused me and surprised me yesterday, and as you can imagine, this has been an emotional time. I hope that you can accept my apology so that we can work better together in the future." I had practiced these words in my head all morning. I still felt like an ass.

Todd Brooks kindly smiled. "If you think that Veronica and I have never been in a heated donor meeting, then you are mistaken. These things *can* be very emotional, especially since we are talking about honoring loved ones. Don't give it a second thought."

I did feel a bit better. "Thank you. If you don't mind conveying that to Veronica as well, I would appreciate it. I do want to try to catch one more person before I leave if you don't mind. Excuse me." I snuck out the door, leaving Alyssa and Chris to say goodbye to Todd Brooks.

Clara pointed me in the right direction, and soon I was down the hall in a cluster of small cubicles. Kate Heathcliff was dabbing white-out on a document, and when she looked up and saw me, she dumped it out all over her desk. I wasn't fazed by it at all given my previous interactions with her, and I helped to clean it up using tissues that were nearby.

"Oh my goodness, Janie. I wasn't expecting you on campus! Is everything okay?" She screwed the cap back onto the white-out bottle and awkwardly gestured for me to have a seat.

I shook my head. "Thank you, Kate. I can't stay. Alyssa and I need to get home. We had a very quick meeting with Todd Brooks, and I am sure you'll hear more about that soon. I just wanted to stop by for a moment and apologize. Even though I was uncomfortable with some things that happened when your staff was at my house, there was no excuse for how I treated you. Please accept my apology. You didn't deserve that. It's been an emotionally charged summer, and after holding it together the whole time, I had hit my limit. It won't happen again. I'm sorry."

Kate was flushed and was shaking her head rapidly. "Oh, no, Janie, please don't apologize. We don't always approach these things in the right way. Sometimes, we think we will be received well, and it turns out that we were totally wrong. I don't want to speak for Todd or Veronica, but maybe we should have reached out to your parents' friends before coming to talk to you with ideas. I only knew your mom a little from the volunteer work that she did. I think that I met your dad once at an event. I should have done my homework. But if you are fine, I am fine. I hope that you and I can continue to work together."

She was being lucid and reasonable. In some ways I felt better, and in other ways I felt terrible about being such an asshole to her in the first place. She was a bit of a mess of a person, but she was also a good person. "Thank you for being kind about this," I said. "I hope that things work out and that we can keep working together, too." Alyssa poked her head in the doorway, and I could hear Chris making small talk with some staff in the hallway. "We need to get going. Looking forward to talking to you soon, Kate."

"Yes, yes," she replied, nodding vigorously. "Oh, and say hi to Rocky for me? I assume you two are.... Sorry, I probably shouldn't be so nosy."

Despite my assumption that my mother had had some kind of intervention from beyond that had brought Rocky and me together, I realized that without Kate's carelessness yet persistence, we likely would have never crossed paths. "No, no, it's fine. Yes, we've been pretty inseparable since that college fair. I like him a lot. Thank you, Kate. Really." I walked out of her office with a clear conscience. *One thing dealt with, about a million more to go. Cole...*

We said goodbye to Chris and thanked him profusely for all of his assistance. "We should get some initial feedback from Development in the next week or two, I would imagine," he informed us. "The Board of Trustees doesn't meet for another month, so we likely won't know much for a while. My suggestion is to move forward with your lives, and let's hope for the best. You can always adjust things later to make this work if it goes in our favor." In actuality, it was a longshot, and even if it happened, it would take a while. There was way too much reality to deal with in the meantime.

19 - Spinach and Gold Coins

I TOLD ALYSSA ABOUT COLE'S TEXT and the *Tribune* article in the car on the way back to Cape Elizabeth.

"That's a lot to consider," she said, with her voice starting to shake and her eyes filling with tears. "Why am I crying? We don't cry. I never saw Mom *or* Dad cry ever. Stoic New Englanders. How come we're so emotional now?"

"No fucking clue. I've cried more this summer than I have in my whole life. I'm starting to accept it," I said, blowing my nose with the tissue she had handed me. "Anyway, I'm not going. The timing is awful. I want to be with Rocky. I want to help with the girls. I want to get this Amville project off the ground, if they'll let us."

"Thanks, Janie," Alyssa replied. "And I really like Rocky a lot. Patrick absolutely *loves* him. Especially now that his brother is interviewing for jobs away from Boston, I think he needs this kind of a friend that's not connected to work in any way. And I'm excited about this possibility of us working together on Amville. But of course, if you want to go to Chicago, we can figure it out…" Her voice trailed off at the end, and I could read between the lines. Life with Janie around was much easier than life without.

As we pulled into the driveway, we saw an unfamiliar car parked in it, and a tall, thin man pushing forty sitting on the step to the front porch.

"Someone's not letting go without a fight, huh?" asked Alyssa, as I shut off the ignition and got out of the car. We walked towards him and Alyssa gave a slight wave and nod before opening the front door and going inside.

I stood in front of Cole, not knowing how to act or what to say. "How are you here? You just texted me a few hours ago."

"I waited five minutes for you to respond. Those were five long minutes. After four minutes had passed, I ordered an Uber. When I got in the car, I bought an airline ticket with my phone. I'm thinking that a private plane is in my future. At least some kind of fractional ownership situation, you know?" I stared blankly at him. I couldn't believe that he was sitting on my front step. In the ten or so months we had been together, he had never once come to Maine. Alyssa only knew who he was because *she* had visited me in Chicago and had met him there. "Never mind that now," he continued. "Lots of things that we can figure out later. So, Janie, what did you think of the news? I can't believe that this is actually happening. It's crazy to be on the front page of the *Trib*."

"Congratulations, Cole. I mean it. I am really, truly happy for you." I was. It was probably the most mature decision that he had ever made.

He patted the space next to him on the step. It was theoretically harmless for me to sit next to him and it was stupid to keep standing, but in reality, it made me nervous. I did it anyway, perhaps so that I could prove to myself that I could handle the close proximity to him. We sat in silence for what seemed like an hour, but in actuality, it was probably less than a minute.

He knew me well enough to sense my uneasiness and tried to make a joke. "Where's Stone? Or did you kick him to the curb?" He chuckled. "Get it? Like kicking a rock? Sorry. You aren't laughing." I guess he only could be so mature for so long.

"Rocky is at work. Alyssa and I just got back from our parents' college. We're trying to start something there in their memory." I was trying to remain neutral and even keeled. The less emotion, the better.

"Oh cool. No, really, that's great. Let me know if you need a corporate donation. It might take a while to get all of that paperwork set, but I eventually need to start thinking of things like that. Community engagement, tax deductions, and all that shit."

"Yeah, all that do-gooder shit," I said somewhat icily. He didn't seem to notice my tone. "Anyway, we have no idea if it's going to fly, and we have huge hurdles ahead of us with the faculty and the Board of Trustees, but if it works out, it would be great for us and for the Amville students." I paused, trying to figure out how much I wanted to say. "This is something that I feel very passionately about. I want to stay in Maine with my sister and nieces. I want to see this through." Those weren't the only things that I wanted to see through. Half of me wanted Rocky to pull into the driveway at that moment, and the other half was nervous about the possibility of him showing up. I wasn't doing anything wrong, but I still felt pangs of guilt that Cole was even there.

Cole put his hand on my knee, and it felt like everything in my torso plummeted to the ground beneath me. I hated that he still had this effect on me. "Janie," he said softly, in a tone that he rarely used. The ego and attitude were gone, and he was just a normal person for the moment. It was not helpful. "I'll get Alyssa a job if she wants one. She can work remotely from here. Heck, if you want to divide your time and work part of the week from here, you can do that, too. I can fly you back and forth. I totally get it. My family is gone. Part of yours is, too. Hold onto what you can. What else can I do to make this happen? Just name it. We can work this out." His body was completely turned towards me, and his hand was still on my knee. I was trying to remain strong and stoic, but I felt myself starting to crumble. There was still too much between us.

I looked at him and immediately wished that I hadn't. "I just can't," I uttered. "I need to—"

His lips met mine, and I initially didn't pull away. This was so familiar but unlike Lance's attempted kiss the week before, it didn't repel me. Part of me could have brought Cole inside the house with me and led him into my bedroom and locked the door behind us. But luckily my better angels prevailed; I owed it to Rocky to back away. I was falling for him in a real, true way, and I couldn't toss that aside for retreating back into something that I knew was problematic and complicated despite its familiarity.

I moved back, not just with my face but literally with my whole body, scooting back on the step. "Cole, this isn't—" I noticed him looking over at the driveway. I followed his glance, and saw Meredith Ashton standing a few yards away. She was holding a covered ceramic dish, undoubtedly containing something absolutely awful.

"Um, hi, Meredith. This is Cole Emerson. We used to date when I lived in Chicago. He's about to head back there, uhh, in a few minutes. Cole, this is my neighbor, Meredith." Cole finally took his hand off of my knee to give her a small wave. This entire interaction was incredibly awkward. "Can I help you with something?" I asked, wishing I was anywhere else.

She walked towards us. "Oh, hello, dear. All of these nice-looking men coming and going at this house. I can't keep track of all of these boys. And a full range of ages!" Oh my God. Oh my God. This was mortifying on so many levels. "Anyway, my dear, I whipped up a lovely gold coin salad for you. It's a good thing, too, because you have so many people to feed in your house these days. That is, of course, if Patrick is still here. I'm assuming if he had been arrested again that we would have heard so that William could bail him out of jail again," she chuckled. I glanced at Cole. He looked completely bewildered. "Oh, and that other boy. The one who Lance doesn't seem to like. Although he probably wouldn't like *you* either, honey," she said to Cole. "My Lance has always been sweet on this lady here," she said, patting me on the head, like I was a puppy. "I used to dream of wedding bells for them when they were so young and innocent and sweet. But our Janie is a woman of the world now." I think she was calling me a slut.

Cole sat silently with wide eyes. There was really nothing that I could say except to ask again, "Can I help you with something, Meredith?"

"Oh yes, the salad! I'll just go put it in your fridge." She opened the front door as if it was her own, and I could hear her saying as it shut, "Oh, hello, dear Alyssa. I didn't realize that Patrick was still here." It was Alyssa's turn to deal with her now.

"So," I said, turning back to Cole, while scooting backwards again, being sure to keep my distance. "I appreciate you trying to convince me, and I am very flattered that you want me to be a part of what you are creating. But Cole, I really think that I am needed here. And if I'm here, I need to be able to devote myself one hundred percent to my family and this potential new endeavor with Amville College. I'm sorry."

He leaned over and kissed the top of my head before standing up. "The offer still stands. Take some time to think it over." He started walking towards his rental car and then turned around. "You're one of the good ones, Janie," he said, and then got into the car and drove away. As he drove out of the driveway, Rocky pulled in with his car.

I wasn't sure what to do at that moment, feeling paralyzed between two places. I could stand on the porch and wait until Rocky got out of the car and asked me who had just left, or I could go inside the house to avoid him for the time being but deal with Meredith Ashton. Regardless of what I chose, Rocky was likely going to have to interact with Meredith, less than five minutes after she saw me kissing Cole. Or Cole kissing me, to be more factual about the situation. Regardless, the whole thing just totally sucked.

I waited. "Hiya, Sunshine," Rocky said, closing the car door and heading up to the porch. "Who just left? I've never seen that car here before."

I stood up and grabbed his hand rather urgently. "I'm going to tell you in a second, but first I need to let you know that Meredith Ashton is inside of my house right now. And she might say some really strange and potentially awful things when she sees you. So please don't believe anything that she says on face value, okay? I'll be sure to set the record straight with you as soon as she's gone."

"Okay," he said, with some confusion. "She's a weird lady, from what I've seen so far. Super nosy. Why is she here?"

"Gold coin salad." There was really no other explanation.

"What the hell is a gold coin salad?"

"I have no idea. But she brought it over for us to eat." I was not at all surprised that Rocky shared my ignorance; Meredith Ashton's creations defied normalcy.

"So, who was that?" Back to his original question. *Shit.*

"Who?" I was only delaying the inevitable, but I really didn't know what to say.

"The guy I saw drive away in the car. Hold on, was that *Yoga Dude?* I can't believe I missed him. I'm a big fan of Patrick despite his faults but I'm so freaking curious about Yoga Dude. Did he confront Patrick? Shit, if I had only gotten here five minutes earlier." He seemed genuinely disappointed.

I had to tell him. "I wish it was Yoga Dude. No, I really don't, because that would suck, but it wasn't him. It was Cole. I had no idea he was going to show up. I talked to him for approximately six minutes. Maybe seven. Definitely fewer than ten. He's gone now, so you don't need to worry about him anymore."

Rocky looked both surprised and concerned, and I couldn't blame him one bit. "Why would he show up here? Why is he on the East Coast? What did he want?"

"Let's go inside, kick Meredith Ashton out of the house, and then I will tell you about it. You have nothing to worry about. I just need to deal with one thing at a time. Getting her out of here is my number one priority. I can't even imagine what she's saying to Alyssa and Patrick right now." I opened the front door, and Rocky followed me inside without saying a word.

"You can really use any kind of tomato soup. This is Campbell's," Meredith Ashton was explaining to Patrick, pointing at the contents of the dish that she was holding. "And it keeps in the refrigerator for days, so you can nibble on it whenever you need a snack." Once we came into the kitchen, Rocky craned his neck to look inside the dish with fascination. Alyssa was leaning against the kitchen island in utter boredom, drinking a very large glass of Chardonnay fairly quickly. Patrick tried to appear interested, but there was no denying the fact that no one in our house was going to eat a bite of this godforsaken conglomeration. "Oh, hello again," Meredith exclaimed to Rocky. "I swear I can't keep track of the comings and goings in this house. The Whitman girls sure are *busy*," she said, once again implying that I was easy, and this time dragging Alyssa into the gutter with me.

Alyssa stared at me, silently urging me to get rid of her. No one else was making a move, leaving me to awkwardly deal with the situation. "Thank you so much for the salad, Meredith," I said. "I need to work on dinner for everyone, but we will be sure to enjoy it as well. We'll get your bowl back to you later this week."

"Yes!" Patrick practically shouted, as if he had just made some kind of discovery. We all turned to look at him. Apparently, his enthusiasm for evicting Meredith Ashton from the house had gotten the best of him. He then became sheepish and lowered his voice. "It's a really beautiful bowl. I'm sure you'll want it back as soon as possible, and since we will surely eat this quickly because it looks so delicious, it'll be sooner rather than later," he said, steering her towards the front entryway as he spoke. "Okay, great to see you! Thanks again! Have a good day!" he said, opening the door.

"Bye!" we all said loudly, almost in unison. Meredith Ashton turned to us and nodded, looking a bit overwhelmed, and squeaked out a "bye" as Patrick shut the door.

"What the fuck is in that bowl? It looks absolutely vile. Why would you mix tomato soup with carrots? And Worcestershire sauce? Is this a Bloody Mary or a salad? I thought the cheeseball she sent over last time was bad enough," said Alyssa, pouring herself more Chardonnay. Rocky and I stared at her until the entirety of what had taken place over the past twenty minutes registered with her, and she finally recognized that we needed a few minutes of privacy. "Come on, Patrick. Come on," she said, gesturing for her confused husband to come upstairs with her.

Once we were finally alone, I opened the refrigerator. As I always did when I was stressed and overwhelmed, I felt the urge to cook something. Sitting prominently and purposely in front of me was a plastic clamshell container of baby spinach, a carton of mushrooms, a bunch of scallions, a package of wonton wrappers, and a bottle of Soy Vey. Patrick had gone shopping. I began taking the ingredients off of the shelf and putting them on the counter, and I took out a frying pan and the canola oil. I had everything to make the spinach and mushroom wontons that Patrick had enjoyed so much the very first time that he came to our house with Alyssa.

"What are you doing?" asked Rocky.

"I'm chopping up baby spinach and mushrooms and scallions to make these wontons that Patrick really likes. I think that you'll like them, too. They're really good."

"Why are you doing that?" he asked, watching intently as I began mincing scallions.

"Because we talked about them earlier and he said how much he liked them, and then he must have gone to the store today to buy the ingredients when Alyssa and I were at Amville."

"And he left them for you to make."

"Yeah," I replied, swirling the oil in the pan to begin sautéing the vegetables. I could see where he was going with this, but I wasn't sure what to say. I put the wonton wrappers on a large cutting board and retrieved a small bowl of water to seal the edges.

Rocky opened the refrigerator and took out two bottles of beer, popped the caps, and handed one to me. I continued to make the wontons, adding the chopped scallions to the spinach and mushrooms. "Why don't you want to take the job in Chicago?" he asked, shifting the subject for the moment. "I'm guessing that's why Cole was here today. I saw the news story this morning. It was all over Twitter. This is a pretty big deal. Much bigger than I realized when you first told me about it. It's a great opportunity for you."

"You want me to go?" I asked, drizzling a small amount of Soy Vey into the pan with the vegetables. It smelled amazing as it sizzled.

"Of course, I don't *want* you to go. But I want to know why *you* don't want to go. And for the moment, leave me out of it. I can come see you, you can come see me, and it wouldn't have to be forever, either. Or maybe it would be, and I could move out there. I'm only twenty-four. You know what they say about people our age; it's not like our parents' generation.

We don't stay in jobs for our whole careers. I have nothing really tying me to this place; it's just where I landed due to my life circumstances at the time. I think I'm pretty portable."

I began spooning very small amounts of the mixture into the center of the wonton wrappers, assembling them as I had been doing for years to prepare them to be pan-fried in more canola oil. "What about the Amville proposal? What's the point of everything that we just did if I'm not going to see it through? Alyssa can't do this without me. You see how she is," I whispered, just loudly enough for him to hear me but quietly enough that hopefully she couldn't hear me upstairs, even if she was likely eavesdropping from the hallway.

Rocky took a sip of his beer. "*She*," he said quietly. "is capable of much more than what she portrays. From everything that I've seen and everything that you and Patrick have told me, she was doing just fine raising those two girls mostly on her own. Not that their situation was ideal, but she seemed to think that things were going fine. She wasn't helpless or making your parents deal with the kids all the time, and they were just across town. But now that she's here, she doesn't have to do anything. She knows that you'll do it for her." He said this gently, but there was much harsh reality in his words. I knew that he was right, and I didn't have much of a response. "And Patrick knows it, too. He knows about Cole's offer. He ate the damn pizzas. Did he encourage you to go and pursue the job?"

"No," I answered, shaking my head. The wontons were done browning, and I was removing them with tongs to a wire rack on a foil-lined sheet pan as I listened to him.

"I didn't think so. Instead, he bought the ingredients so that you could cook something for him. Look, I really like him. I like them both. It's really fun to hang out with them and you. I didn't grow up with siblings and having everyone around like this is great. And the girls are awesome. This house is amazing. But Janie, please really think this through. The Amville thing is months away from being decided. I'm sure that Chris told you everything that he told me. Academia moves at a snail's pace. They have to go through so many steps, get it approved by so many groups. There are huge hurdles here, and likely a ton of resistance. I want to be really optimistic about this, and in many ways I am. But what are you going to do in the meantime? I'm going back to work, Patrick will have to be working again in some capacity, and the girls will start school. Do you just want to cook for them all day? Help Alyssa find a new yoga studio? If that's what you want to do, then own that. Of course, I'll support you in that and will love seeing you after work. Trust me, we'll all eat the food. And hopefully the Amville thing will work out. But what if it doesn't? What happens next? You have so many talents and are such a strong person. I love you for those things and so many more. But before all of this happened, you had dreams and goals and aspirations. Wouldn't it be great to just give those a fraction of a chance?"

"I need to make a sauce," I said, my voice shaking. "Can you look in the pantry to see if there is any pineapple juice?"

Rocky moved a bunch of cans and bottles around, and eventually he dug out a rather dusty-looking can of pineapple juice. "Wow, this is ancient. Do you think it's okay to use?"

"Has it expired?" I pulled out the soy sauce, rice vinegar, and ketchup from the refrigerator.

"No. It looks like you have another two years with this stuff. How is that possible? Here you go. I'll open it for you. Is anything that I'm saying making any sense to you?" He began digging through a drawer for an old-fashioned church key can opener.

"Of course, it is making sense. You're very perceptive and smart. But what about me working for Cole? Does that bother you? You've seemed concerned about his intentions in some of our conversations and you saw him in action firsthand in Tahoe, so I'm just a little surprised that you are encouraging me to go to Chicago."

He handed me the opened can. "Of course, it bothers me. I am absolutely sure that he's going to try to put the moves on you. I'm pretty sure that he tried to put the moves on you today and you're just not telling

176

me, and that's okay. I don't need details. But I have to be confident that since I'm standing in your kitchen right now opening jars of very old pineapple juice that you like being with me and that you've enjoyed our time together so far, and that you ultimately recognize that Cole is a bit of a narcissist and is also pretty immature. And he's like forty fucking years old. Cari Connors or someone like her is a great fit for him. I don't think that you are. I like to think that you're a great fit for me," he said, pulling me away from the counter where I was whisking cornstarch and water together. He wrapped his arms around my waist so that I was looking directly at him. "This is your decision. Only you can decide this. But someone needs to tell you that it's okay if you want to go."

I kissed him, and then pulled back slightly and looked into his eyes and said, "I highly recommend that you take some of these wontons before Patrick comes back downstairs. They'll be gone pretty quickly."

"We better finish that sauce then," he replied. "Can you show me how you make it?" I went back to the stove, and soon we were pouring ingredients into a saucepan. I showed him how to make a cornstarch slurry to thicken the sweet and sour sauce, and before long, we were enjoying my appetizers with our beers.

"Okay, I'm not mad at Patrick anymore," he said, gobbling his third wonton. "I understand why he wanted these again."

"When should we tell him that they're ready?" I asked, dipping one into the sauce.

"After we eat them all," Rocky said. I think that he was only half-joking.

20 - Football and Frappuccinos

"THE LAWN LOOKS GOOD," I said to Rocky as we pulled up to the Cape Elizabeth house. "I'm impressed that everything here hasn't gone to hell in a handbasket." It was early September, one year after I'd left Maine to return to the Midwest to work as the editor for the revitalized *Young Chicago*. I had returned briefly for short visits and holidays, but the reality of getting a shuttered magazine off the ground again proved to be intense and demanding, and Rocky ended up flying out to see me more than I had headed east. Knowing that I would be leaving my job at the end of the summer and would have to transition a new person to take over the position stranded me in the city, and I had missed the beautiful Maine summer that I loved so much. It was good to be back.

"I have to take credit for the landscaping," Rocky said. "Patrick asked me if I would deal with it, so I did. I'd much rather him spend his time up north with his family than down here managing a yard."

"You *did* all of this work?" I asked. "With my dad's piece-of-crap old lawnmower?"

"Hell no," replied Rocky, as we got out of the car. "Patrick wrote me a check. A big check. I hired a bunch of recent Amville grads who I met at a young alumni event. They're all living in the Old Port in an apartment that they can't afford because they haven't found real jobs yet. They were more than happy to use the piece-of-crap old lawnmower. One of them called it retro. I also sold them your dad's old gas grill for eighty dollars. Patrick told me to get rid of it because he wants to get a fancy new Weber one for here. I told the dudes that it was vintage, and they were psyched. Whatever. None of this is my money so I'm just playing along."

"You're family now, kiddo," I said, walking into the house. "We're basically going to be in a commune up there like we were here last summer, but this time it's more permanent. Unless we scare you and you run back here to Max," I said with a wink as we plunked down on the family room couch. "Why am I sitting? I was just sitting for eight hours. And eight hours the day before that. But this couch feels so good. I could fall asleep right now."

"I know," Rocky said, closing his eyes. "But we need to decide which stuff from here you want to bring to Camden and then go over to my apartment and get my shit. And then Scarlett and Jimmy's flight is coming in at seven. When do Blair and Bryan arrive? That sounds so weird. I can't believe they're together."

"Blair was working all day, and I know that Bryan had practice. They are landing really late and taking a cab here." It was only Blair's second day as the editor of the magazine, and he was nervous about taking any time off in his early days of being the boss. Turning the reins over to him was a no-brainer for both Cole and me, and we knew that he would do a great job. "Okay, let's start packing before I pass out." I had brought most of my clothes and other necessities to Chicago, and those were in a moving truck on their way to Camden now, but I wanted to gather some odds and ends for my new little house. *Our* house. Rocky was coming, too.

We worked for a couple of hours to collect what we wanted, being sure to leave enough behind to keep the Cape Elizabeth house stocked for the weekends that we or my sister's family wanted to use it. We then picked up the U-Haul trailer and went over to Rocky and Max's apartment to get everything that he was taking with him up north. He and Max had a faux tearful goodbye, and then we picked up Scarlett and Jimmy at the Portland airport before heading back to the Cape Elizabeth house. I had just left them two days earlier, but it was so fun to welcome them to my real home.

Rocky and I were exhausted, so we picked up pizzas and beer after the airport stop and headed back to the house. The four of us relaxed and enjoyed our dinner until Blair and Bryan arrived just after eleven. Anticipating their probable hunger, I took an extra-large pizza out of the refrigerator that I had saved for their arrival and brought it over to where everyone was sitting in the family room. "You guys want this?" I asked.

"I'll gladly take that," said Bryan, reaching for the pizza box. "Do you have anything for Blair to eat?" And we all laughed. Bryan played for the Chicago Bears on their practice squad, but he had tremendous potential and talent, and it looked like he would be brought up to the regular season roster soon.

"He's such a little shit," Blair joked, grabbing one of the slices and pretending to shield it from Bryan. "I'm still getting over the Frappuccino incident." They had met four months earlier when Bryan accidently dumped his Frappuccino into Blair's laptop keyboard in the Andersonville Starbucks. Leave it to Blair to find the one out professional football player in Chicago. "So, fill us in. Who is going to be there tomorrow afternoon?"

"Oh, it's going to be a cast of characters, that's for sure," I said. "Obviously, Alyssa, Patrick, Trish, and Susie. But don't get ahead of yourself. The primary reason that I invited all of you is to help Rocky and me move the contents of that U-Haul trailer that's sitting in the driveway out there into our new little house at Amville. Once Bryan came onto the scene, I knew that we would be all set. Your attendance at the ceremony in the afternoon is just secondary."

Blair rolled his eyes. "Gotcha, princess. Continue on with the guest list. I am here to witness any and all riveting drama after everything that you've told me about your volatile interactions with Amville."

I settled back into the couch next to Rocky. "You might be disappointed. Things with the College have been pretty smooth since my initial issues with Kate Heathcliff and the temper tantrum that I threw when the Development officers came to the house that afternoon. But they'll all be there. Watch out for Kate, though, as she has a tendency to spill things."

Blair rolled his eyes and pointed at Bryan, who then stole the rest of his pizza slice. It was so funny to see their relationship develop, or to even see Blair *in* an actual relationship.

I continued, "Chris Manfried, the professor who has served as our liaison through this process, will be there with his wife Anne. They're really fantastic. He was Rocky's advisor when he was a student there." Chris and I were in communication regularly, but I was excited to see him and Anne again. Alyssa's family had grown close to them since moving to campus, which definitely had helped to ease their transition to such new surroundings. "Oh! I know where there could be drama. Lance will be there."

Scarlett knew all about Lance and nodded her head enthusiastically. "That's right. How's he doing up there?"

"From everything that Alyssa has told me, he's doing a great job. She said that he has a renewed energy and seems like a much happier, healthier person. I'm glad that we were able to help him, and it seems like a good fit for him." Making Lance the Assistant Director of the Center was a great move for us, because we didn't have to go through extensive interviews and vetting, and it helped him in many ways, first and foremost by getting him out of his house. Amville was a place that he knew well, and a move there wasn't much of an adjustment for him.

Scarlett turned towards Rocky. "How's that going to be for you? Doesn't he, like, punch you whenever he sees you?"

Rocky laughed. "When my school offered self-defense training for the girls last spring, I volunteered to help out. I'm totally ready for him this time." He put up his hands in a defensive gesture.

I was hoping for the best. "Alyssa said that he seems much more grounded and stable now. He knows that Rocky is part of the deal and that he'll be moving up to Camden, too, so he's going to have to get used to having him around. Hopefully he can put everything that happened behind him." It was getting late, we'd had a long day, and we had an even bigger day ahead of us. Rocky began cleaning up bottles and glasses and plates. It was definitely time to get some sleep. "Oh yes, and his parents will be there. Lance's dad is totally harmless and benign. He's actually a very good guy. He's the lawyer who got Patrick out of jail last summer." I realized that Jimmy was sitting right there. "You knew about that, right?" With Patrick, I could see that going either way. I had no idea how much he told his younger brother.

"Yep," he said. "Our parents don't know though. Could you imagine our uptight Irish Catholic Kennedy-wannabee parents with that one? They don't even know the extent of what he did or what happened. I think that he just alluded to them about having problems and needing to make a life change to keep their marriage together. They're so proper and concerned about appearances and *New York Times* wedding announcements that they don't want any details, believe me. As long as they're still married, and Patrick has a reputable job and makes plenty of money, they're satisfied. So, no, they don't know about Patrick disturbing the peace at the White Barn Inn and getting arrested, but he told me. I'm just glad he never got ahold of the guy."

Rocky and I nodded and said almost in unison, "Yoga Dude." It seemed like a million years ago. So much had happened to my friends and me in the previous year, from Jimmy moving to Chicago and immediately losing his job when the company that had hired him went bankrupt, to Cole coming through and getting him a job as a lawyer for his company. The fact that he and Scarlett hit it off when he showed up at our apartment one night with a bottle of wine to thank me was an unexpected but welcome bonus.

"Isn't Lance's mom a pain in the ass or something?" asked Blair.

I yawned. "I'm too tired for Meredith Ashton. Rocky, how would you describe her for our guests who haven't met her yet?"

Rocky threw away the last of the trash and joined me at the base of the stairs. "Very nosy. Makes unnecessary, uncomfortable comments. Terrible cook. Enabler of Lance. Ultimately, I think that she means well and is not malicious, but that she just can't help herself. She can't stay out of her own way. How'd I do?" he asked me.

"Perfect. The terrible cook aspect cannot be emphasized enough. She has been bugging Alyssa about what she can bring for tomorrow. It's a brief ceremony in the late afternoon with a catered cocktail reception. Emphasis on the word *catered*. But she wants to bring meatloaf. She wants to drive for almost two hours to Amville with a meatloaf in the car for an event that she was invited to. But that's what we're dealing with here."

Bryan looked up from the pint of ice cream that he was enjoying. "I like meatloaf."

"Not this meatloaf, believe me. There shouldn't be *any* meatloaf there tomorrow. I was told that only *my* recipes were going to be served, and it's late summer, so trust me, there will be no meatloaf. If you see meatloaf, first of all, walk away. Her stuff sucks. And then please let me know. There should only be delectable little appetizers and treats there. Things like crostinis and little tarts and puff pastry cups with tiny grilled vegetables in them."

"It'll be great, Janie," said Scarlett. "You guys look tired. You've done enough entertaining all of us for tonight. Let's get some sleep. Tomorrow's an important day."

It was. Not only was it a celebration of the opening of the Center, but it was also a benchmark of how far my family had come since that terrible day the previous summer. Despite the crazy events of the last fourteen months, my family was working together and happy in its new mission, and as of the next day, would be permanently reunited. And it had grown by one person in that timespan. Rocky was starting a new job as the college counselor at the high school in Rockland, the town adjacent to Camden. We were excited to live together on the Amville campus, in a small but sweet house next door to my sister's.

As I crawled into bed next to Rocky, I felt the reality of the new situation hit me. I was both excited and incredibly nervous. "Are you feeling alright about your new job?" I asked. I had to keep reminding myself that this wasn't just about me leaving Chicago and plunging into a new life at Amville. Rocky had found a new job, resigned from his old job, and had worked up in Rockland for a week before coming out to Chicago to help me move. It was a huge change for both of us, along with the fact that we would finally be living together full-time. I had only seen the little house that we would be moving into once, but it really didn't matter. After a crazy start to our relationship and a disjointed year together, it was going to be great to be able to establish ourselves in Camden as a couple. I just hoped that Alyssa and Patrick remained functional.

"So far, so good. It's a small school, and there are only two other counselors. I have met a few of the kids so far, but they needed about ten different things from me. I think it's going to be a jack-of-all-trades kind of job, which will be a fun challenge. At least that's the attitude I'm going into it with."

Rocky was almost always positive and willing to give things a fair shot, which I admired so much. I felt very lucky to have met him, and I still couldn't believe that I had Kate Heathcliff to thank for that. "How are you feeling about tomorrow?" he asked.

"Every emotion sums it up," I said, yawning. I really needed to get some sleep. "The reason that this is even happening is tragic. And who would have thought that a Cornell grad and a Northwestern grad would be co-directors of a center at Amville College? And there with their families and boyfriend? And that I would hire Lance to be the Assistant Director, after all the shit that he pulled with you? And that Patrick would be back in the picture fully after what he did? And that I would have met you due to Kate Heathcliff's bizarre request? And that Scarlet would be seriously dating Patrick's brother and that they're both here? It's been a ridiculous year." I closed my eyes and tried to shut off my swirling thoughts.

"And Blair," Rocky said, laughing softly. "Don't forget Blair. Who would have ever thought that he would know the difference between a quarterback and a running back? I think that this is the biggest surprise of the year."

Life was unpredictable, which was the only thing that was *actually* predictable about it. Just when you thought you had it figured out, someone spills a Starbucks drink on you or asks you to work at a college fair on behalf of a school that you didn't attend. With that thought, I finally fell asleep.

21 - Headphones and Earplugs

"THERE'S A PROBLEM," SAID ALYSSA, as she greeted me at her front door with her arms crossed. The house that my sister was renting from Amville was on a pretty Camden side street only about one block's walk from the picturesque campus. It was an older but well-maintained white house with a matching picket fence surrounding a plush green yard. The girls were thundering across the floors and on the stairs, and I spotted Patrick scurrying past with his tie half-knotted. "Hiya, Jae!" he yelled breathlessly, with what looked like a little girl's sundress in his hand.

"What, Trish won't wear a dress for today?" I asked. I had left everyone else next door at my new place to begin unloading the U-Haul. Alyssa had sent a frantic text about an hour earlier, requesting that I come see her as soon as I could. I was used to Alyssa's dramatic behavior, so I was trying not to make too big a deal out of whatever this was.

"No, it's Susie. Trish picked out her own dress in Freeport last week, so that's not an issue luckily. Susie's the one driving us crazy. But that's not it. I have this weird feeling that something isn't right. Patrick says I'm overreacting and that everything will be fine. But I just know something is wrong. You know how that happens sometimes? I think that yoga has made me much more tuned-in to these sorts of things now."

I glanced next door and saw Bryan carrying a huge box into the house with ease. Blair was walking behind him carrying only a small tote bag. I suppressed a laugh and tried to refocus on Alyssa. "Yes, definitely. If the Psychic Friends Network was still a thing, you would put Miss Cleo out of business. How do you think that we can get to the bottom of whatever this thing is that's possibly wrong?"

Alyssa rolled her eyes. "You just remember my friends and I imitating Miss Cleo's commercials. Way before your time. Anyway, I decided that I should ask Lance. I figured if anyone would know what was going on today, it would be him. So, I texted him this morning but couldn't get in touch with him."

Considering it was only ten in the morning and I got the text an hour earlier, I could see where this could get problematic. Lance was historically not an early riser. "What time did you text him? He tends to be a late sleeper."

"At 6 AM," she said very matter-of-factly. "Look, he is the Assistant Director, and we are officially dedicating the center TODAY. It may be a weekend to the rest of the world, but this is one of the most important days in his career. A career, mind you, that he wouldn't have at all if it weren't for us. He needs to be responsive when big things are on the calendar. I think that our dedication qualifies as worthy."

"I thought you said that he was doing a great job," I said, attempting not to be annoyed with this conversation. The ceremony was starting in less than two hours. I wanted to change my clothes and have a few minutes to reread my remarks before heading over to campus. I hoped that this saga had at least some kind of ending soon.

"Yes, he's actually doing a totally fine job. Or he was doing a fine job until a few weeks ago. I started noticing some changes then, and at first, they were very positive. He was dressing up more for work, he was shaving regularly, got his hair cut, things like that. He seemed overall less, um, sweaty. Sorry, Janie, I know that you and him…" Her voice trailed off when she saw my annoyed expression. Perhaps someday Alyssa wouldn't remind me of my past entanglements with Lance. She continued her story. "But then he started looking for any excuse to go over to Brady Hall, even suggesting that we relocate our temporary office from our building to over there until our construction was totally done. That would have been a huge waste of time, so I got everyone headphones and earplugs to deal with the noise instead. No one else complained, but Lance seemed almost disappointed by my little gift. I brushed it off. Anyway, there were a few mornings this week that he was late to work, which I have no tolerance for, since his apartment is literally across the street from the Center. I mean, get your shit together. I know that he was used to living with Mommy and not having any responsibilities for years but come on. He wanted this job so badly."

I was losing patience. "Okay. I love you, but I need to go next door and make sure that everything is going alright. And I need to put on a dress and get some composure before we do this thing. So, is there any resolution to your hunch about something being wrong, or is whatever is wrong still a big mystery?" I needed some kind of conclusion.

Alyssa threw her hands up in frustration. "That's why I texted you. You're coming with me on a walk. I just know something isn't right. Come on." She walked out of the doorframe and down her front steps towards the rest of campus. "Come *on*."

I shut her front door and followed her. "Please make this brief."

"We'll walk quickly," Alyssa said, as I caught up with her and we walked towards the Center.

Amville was a small campus, and we reached the building in just under five minutes of speedwalking. Almost out of breath, I stopped next to Alyssa and looked up at the brand-new lettering that had been drilled into the brick the previous evening.

We were speechless for probably ten seconds, but it felt much longer. Finally, Alyssa let out a bellowing wail that caused the few people who were walking on the campus paths nearby to turn their heads. "I TOLD YOU!" she yelled, pointing at the building.

The letters were perfectly placed and looked very professional, fitting in well with the campus décor. They also read "Michael and Corinne Olson Whitman '80 Center for Integrated Students."

I started laughing. I couldn't help it. *What on earth was an integrated student?* It should have said *Integrated Studies.* I also was sort of in awe of Alyssa's intuition. She, on the other hand, was almost hyperventilating.

"What… on earth… am I… supposed to do… now?" She sat on the ground and shook her head before putting her head in her hands.

I sat down next to her, not knowing what to say or do. "It's not your fault, Alyssa. These things happen. We'll—I don't know—make a joke of it during the ceremony? Like in our speeches?"

"How am I going to make a speech? I can't make a speech!" she moaned.

I needed her to calm down and be able to function fairly soon. "What can I do to make any of this better?" I asked, not sure if there was an answer.

She stood up and pointed back towards the houses on the edge of campus. "We're going to Lance's. *He* was supposed to oversee this. He has some explaining to do."

After Alyssa pounded on the door several times, the knob turned and Lance peeked his head through the slight opening in the door. Alyssa pushed the door open, and Lance stood before us in his boxers. I turned away in slight embarrassment, but Alyssa didn't seem affected in the least. "What the hell is wrong with you?" she demanded.

Lance glanced around the room with a panic-stricken, nervous look on his face. "What do you mean?"

"The building, Lance! That was your one job for yesterday!" Alyssa grabbed a stack of programs for the Center's opening off of an end table. "See! You did it here, too!" she yelled. I picked one up to examine. Sure enough, Alyssa was right. And Lance was very, very wrong.

"Is everything okay out there?" I heard a vaguely familiar female voice call from the bedroom.

"Kate? Is that you?" I asked. I wanted it to be someone else. Oh God, how I wanted it to be someone else.

A sheepish Kate Heathcliff emerged in a bathrobe that was way too big for her. "Hi, Janie."

"I GUESS WE JUST ROLL with this until it can be changed, right?" I asked as Alyssa and I walked back to our houses. I would need to adjust my comments for the ceremony.

"No choice now," she said with a sigh. We had left Lance's apartment shortly after Kate awkwardly introduced herself to Alyssa, tripping over a pair of Lance's sneakers on the floor in the process.

"We'll adjust. At least we know ahead of time. I'll see you over there. Good luck getting everyone dressed," I said, seeing Patrick run by again chasing Susie, who yelled, "Hi Auntie! I'm naked!" I couldn't help but laugh as I walked next door.

The house that Rocky and I were renting from the College was a cute little three-bedroom house next to Alyssa's family. Chris and Anne Manfried lived on the other side of them in a bigger house that they had resided in for years. They had raised their two children there, who were now grown and living across the country. They were thrilled to have so much youthful energy next door to them, especially since our two houses had remained vacant for the past couple of years. It was nothing fancy and there were definitely some quirks to our house such as some doorways that were too short for Rocky to easily walk through, but it was a great segue into our life together.

There were bags and boxes lining the wall of the living room, and I knew that it was only going to be more chaotic when the small moving truck with the rest of my Chicago belongings arrived on Monday or Tuesday, but the fact that we had even gotten to this point—with everyone assembled in Camden and some of us staying beyond the weekend—felt miraculous. I could hear the rest of my crew laughing in the kitchen amidst the whirling sound of the Keurig being used; Rocky had luckily remembered to bring his coffeemaker with him from Portland. I grabbed the overnight bag that I had packed with everything that I would need for the ceremony. I spotted a stack of framed pictures in a small open box on the ground, and on the top of the pile was a photograph of my parents from two summers ago. They were on the deck at the Inn by the Sea, which was close to our house in Cape Elizabeth. We—Alyssa, Patrick, Trish, Susie, and I—had gone to dinner with them for their anniversary. I was visiting for the weekend; I had been working at *Young Chicago* for about a year and had just started seeing Cole. My parents were in their Tommy Bahama best, looking like an ad for Jimmy Buffet's new retirement community in Florida.

I brought the framed picture upstairs with me into the empty room that was now Rocky's and my bedroom. There was literally nothing except for a bagged air mattress in the corner that we would sleep on until the moving truck arrived with the furniture that had been in my Chicago apartment bedroom. I put my bag down on the floor and set the picture on the window ledge. I took my dress and heels out of the bag and laid them out on the floor, glad that I had had the good sense to pick out something that wouldn't wrinkle much. I then took out the leather portfolio that had my double-spaced typed remarks for the ceremony. I had worked on them for weeks, but I had never been satisfied with them. Now, breaking out of my exhausted haze and annoyance over Lance's missteps, I knew exactly what I wanted to say.

ABOUT THIRTY MINUTES before I was supposed to arrive at the Center, I felt so antsy and overwhelmed that I decided to show up early to acclimate to my surroundings. Unlike Alyssa, I hadn't spent any time in the building, so the thought of dedicating it without at least a few quiet moments in the space was unnerving.

Despite the incorrect lettering on the sign, the building that now housed the Michael and Corinne Olson Whitman '80 Center for Integrated Studies looked pretty wonderful. It was a small building on the edge of campus that had served many purposes over the past one hundred years since it was built, ranging from a women's gym back in the days when such things were segregated, to the campus radio station before it was moved to a different location, to most recently, classes and offices for the anthropology department before those were transferred into a larger social science building. Now, just outside of the building was a small plot with a few herbs and some tomatoes growing and a welcoming sign that simply said, "Corinne's Garden."

I walked through the double doors and saw college staff members setting up chairs and a podium in a large event room. Since the project was approved by the faculty and the Board of Trustees six months earlier, major transformations to the inside of the building had been completed. I walked into the kitchen, which was expanded and updated with modern equipment and was certified by commercial standards, ready for workshops on cooking and nutrition. I had given Alyssa my wishlist, and it was more amazing than I could have imagined. I moved into two connected meeting rooms that were ready for classes on finances and taxes, career development, journalism, self-care and esthetics, pilot certification, and whatever else we dreamed up with our work-study student staff. Alyssa, Lance, and I had an office space furnished for us from which to manage the center. We had gathered just about every aspect of our family's life and were ready to put it into practice for the students of Amville. Alyssa's idea was coming to life.

The last room that I explored was a gleaming yoga studio, outfitted with every prop imaginable and a top-notch lighting and sound system and shining wooden floors. Alyssa was sitting on a cushion cross-legged, with the ceremony program in her lap. When she caught my eye, she looked down at the program and she said quietly, "I tried, Janie. I wanted it to be perfect for you. I'm sorry."

I grabbed a cushion and sat facing her. "Because of the name? Come on, Alyssa. That's an easy fix. You've done so much here all these months. The kitchen, well, everything is perfect. I can't wait to get started. We're going to have so much fun."

She finally looked back up at me. "Really? Do you think it's all going to be okay? I mean, everything?"

I knew that she was talking about more than just the program or the sign. "I do. Come on. Let's start the ceremony." I stood up and took her hand, helping her up, even though she had been doing just fine without me.

AS ROCKY AND I APPROACHED the building with Scarlett, Jimmy, Blair, and Bryan walking behind us, Lance was waiting for us at the front door. Kate Heathcliff was standing right next to him, undoubtedly giving him some extra confidence that he probably needed given everything that had transpired. For once not cowering or making excuses for himself, he sheepishly said, "Hi, Janie." He gave me a hug, and I hugged him back. He looked directly at me and said, "I'm so sorry. I really fucked this up. And other things, too, of course. I won't make a mistake like this—or that—again, I promise." Before I could say anything, he turned to Rocky. "And I owe you an apology. Just because I wasn't happy that night at Amville or in Janie's kitchen last summer doesn't justify how I've treated you. I hope that you can accept my apology." He put his hand out to shake and Rocky gratefully extended his. It was finally time to move on.

"Hi, Kate," I said. "It's good to see you. Thanks for everything that you did to make this happen." I was about to introduce Lance and Kate to our friends when I heard a familiar voice heading towards us.

"Lance! Lance!" Meredith and William Ashton were heading up the walkway, luckily not holding anything resembling a meatloaf. Meredith walked right past my group and made a beeline to Lance, leaving William behind to exchange pleasantries with Rocky, since they already knew each other from Patrick's night of criminal behavior.

"Hi, Mom," he said, giving her an obligatory kiss on the cheek. "I have someone I want you to meet." I suppressed a chuckle, envisioning what poor Kate Heathcliff had in her future. I excused my little group from the others, and we walked into the Center and into the crowd of people that was waiting for us.

22 - Gorgonzola and Thanksgiving

THE LARGE EVENT ROOM IN THE Center was set up with rows of chairs and a simple podium with the Amville seal on it at the front of the space. Several catering tables lined the edges of the room, where uniformed staff were setting up appetizers from recipes that I had provided. There was a small bar with champagne, wine, and beer, and many guests were already enjoying a glass. Several people were slated to make brief remarks, with Alyssa and I speaking at the end. The atmosphere was light and filled with anticipation and a bit of excitement, which was the complete opposite of the tenor of the meeting that was the impetus for this project just over a year ago. Once everyone took their seats, the Amville College president—a man named Bill Knolls who I had spoken to once on the phone but had never met in person—went to the podium to welcome everyone to the ceremony.

"We are here today to honor the memories of two alumni who left us too soon," he began. "Mike and Corinne Whitman embodied the very essence of Amville College, and through the generosity of their children who wanted to ensure a meaningful legacy for their parents, they will never be forgotten." After a few more words, he introduced the Dean of Student Life, a woman named Courtney Gales who Alyssa and I had worked with quite a bit over the past year as the idea for the Center got fleshed out in more detail. She spoke of the importance of the Center for ensuring more well-balanced students who would be better able to handle the rigors and stresses of adult life, as well as the opportunity that it would provide for employment for work-study students on campus. Our collaboration with Courtney was a major selling point for the Board of Trustees in giving its final approval for the Center, and we couldn't have asked for a better partnership.

She next introduced Professor Chris Manfried, who spoke as the faculty liaison to the Center. He had been invaluable to us from the very first day of the life of this project, and there was no way that we could have proceeded without his guidance and advocacy. Moreover, he and Anne had become part of our family, and I was so grateful to Rocky for bringing them into our lives.

Chris approached the podium and adjusted his glasses as he peered out over the crowd. "Integrated students…" he said with a sly smile. "I see that Janie and Rocky are sitting between Alyssa and Lance as a buffer. Smart move." Those of us in the know chuckled softly, although I'm sure that most people in the crowd were perplexed by his aside. He shifted back to the purpose of his speech. "Mike and Corinne Whitman were my dear friends. I will talk about them more in a moment, but first I want to tell you a story. My wife Anne and I have had the good fortune of being welcomed into the Whitman family over the past year. How this happened is a rather odd but very Amville story that involves a tent at L.L. Bean and a glass of wine at the Harraseeket Inn firepit, but that's a tale for another time." The crowd laughed.

"Anyway, we were invited to enjoy Thanksgiving dinner with the Whitman family at their home in Cape Elizabeth this past November. If you don't know this already, Janie Whitman is a phenomenal cook. After we all finally stop yapping today from this podium, you will get the chance to sample some of her creations. I assure you that everything will be wonderful. So, to set the scene for you, we were assembled in Cape Elizabeth and just awaiting Janie's arrival from Chicago, as she was going to prepare the dinner for all of us. Alyssa and Patrick had bought everything already." He gestured to them, so that everyone would know who they were. "Our dear Janie, however, was massively delayed due to weather. Patrick and Rocky pulled it off, and Alyssa did an excellent job of pouring the wine!" More laughter. He told a great story. "They did a delicious job, but when I complimented their fine efforts at the end of dinner, they admitted to taking several shortcuts and omitting a few items. Patrick hung his head a bit and said quietly, 'If Janie had been here, this would have been the first course.'" Everyone laughed once again, and I felt my face redden. "We did save our dessert for when Janie did finally arrive around ten that night, and a fine recanting of the evening was enjoyed by all."

He continued, "Anne and I have had the honor of getting to know this lovely family for the past year. They are loyal to each other and take excellent care of their friends. Through the programming that will start to take place here, the students of Amville will grow in ways that we cannot easily reach them in our academic classrooms. The directors—Alyssa and Janie, along with Lance and countless others—will ensure that it is so. I have supported them from the beginning, and along with Anne, will continue to be there for them." He looked down at the podium and paused. "To lose a friend is tough, no matter how old you are and what the circumstances may have been. To lose two friends at once is doubly devastating. We can't bring Mike and Corinne back, but they will live here, at Amville, where they once met in their Geology class, many years ago. It is an honor to be a part of this." He stepped away and walked back to his seat, as enthusiastic applause erupted from the crowd.

It was a tough act to follow. Alyssa and I got up from our seats and walked to the podium. We had decided about a month earlier to stand at the front of the room together, as we knew that it would be a challenge to keep our strength and composure given the emotional nature of the event. We hadn't shared any of what we had planned to say with each other, probably because it had changed so many times. Given the amount of support that we were feeling from everyone in the room that day, even if our words came out wrong and weren't incredibly profound, it would be okay. We just needed to say something.

Alyssa had volunteered to go first, and I stood beside her as she spoke. "I'm the big sister, so I decided that I should speak before Janie. But if you have known the two of us at all, especially over the past year or so, you would know that Janie's often better at adulting than I am." There was light laughter in the crowd. I caught Rocky's eye, and he winked at me with a smile. "Although we are six years apart, now that we are at this stage of our lives, I could swear that we are either twins or she's the older one. The one difference is that I have two really fantastic little girls, and I am sad that they probably won't remember their amazing grandparents." She put her head down and shook it, pausing before she collected her emotions and looked out at the crowd again.

"I have not always been a great example for them of standing on my own two feet and being a good role model, but this has been my chance to show them otherwise. And now that they are getting older, I hope that this is what they will remember from their early childhood. They are lucky to have the opportunity to grow up on this beautiful college campus and to see their mom and their Auntie Janie as strong female role models." She cleared her throat and stood up a bit straighter. "This center offers Amville students the chance to develop new skills, to enhance their lives, and to actualize their inner potential. I am so happy that I can be a part of it. Thank you all for your support, and please come see me in the yoga studio soon." She smiled and stepped away from the microphone, and everyone clapped. I was so proud of her. I also realized that she said absolutely nothing about Patrick, and that was completely fine. This was her idea and despite his help, she had developed most of it entirely on her own. As Trish and Susie yelled, "Yay, Mommy," I felt like my heart was going to burst.

It was my turn, and I glanced down at my hand-scrawled words one last time. "I didn't want to go to school here. With both parents as alumni, there was always a bit of gentle pressure to at least apply to Amville. But like my sister before me, we resisted this path and went elsewhere. For me, the chance to be a Northwestern Wildcat was too great to pass up, especially because I was planning to pursue journalism. And I don't regret any of those decisions, because it gave me opportunities that I wouldn't have had otherwise.

"For the past three years, I have worked for a magazine in Chicago, helping the young adults of the city to live their best lives through telling them where to get a good drink, a great sandwich, a safe piercing, where to take a spin class, or where to try the latest spa treatment. These are all important things to many, but when our parents passed, I realized that I wanted to help people in other ways. My parents were remarkable people who had diverse interests but always came back together to enjoy a pina colada or go to a Jimmy Buffett concert. They loved to travel and to experience different places together. I think that my mom would love that an Amville student will now be able to learn how to grow basil, make their own exfoliating scrub, enroll in a seminar on how to file their taxes or pick the right healthcare plan, and take a yoga class, all in the same location. My dad would love that that same Amville student could instead choose to learn about pilot certification programs while also discovering how to make his or her own lasagna from our family's recipe or perhaps how to meditate. The possibilities for students through our Center will evolve and grow as different Amville community members get involved, and it will never be the same from year to year, much as we are never the same from year to year."

I glanced out into the crowd and saw Cole leaning against the far wall. I had no idea that he was coming; I had told him about it before I left my desk for the last time, but he never seemed to be fully listening. I tried my best to ignore him in order to finish my remarks. "Many things have changed in our family's lives over the past thirteen months. There has been heartache and there have been tough choices. But there has been so much joy and a lot of love. As we embark on this new adventure, I'm focusing on joy and love. Thank you for supporting our family and giving us this chance." I stepped away and hugged Alyssa, and the crowd cheered.

President Knolls returned to the podium and thanked everyone for their attendance, urging everyone to stay to enjoy my appetizers and a drink before departing. I squeezed Rocky's hand once I was sitting next to him again, relieved that it was over and that we had gotten through the event. I looked over at Alyssa and Patrick, who were in a tight embrace. He edged back slightly to kiss her forehead. I still was having a tough time figuring their relationship out, but somehow, they seemed to be moving forward and past much of what had plagued them. For now, it was good.

The crowd had shifted over to the catering tables, where there were platters and trays of fifteen different appetizers and small plates that I had provided recipes of to the catering staff. Although deciding on the options was not an easy decision, I hadn't had to cook any of it myself, and it looked as if the staff had done a great job. Rocky had already made a beeline to the infamous mushroom and spinach wontons, and Susie and Trish were thrilled to see their favorite chicken tenders. With everyone milling around eating and making conversation, I took the opportunity to walk over to where Cole was still leaning against the same wall. His hair now had more salt than pepper and at almost forty, he looked more like one of the College's senior staff members than someone who I would have dated. Our relationship seemed like a very long time ago, almost in the same category that I felt when I looked at Lance. It was very distant and removed from where I was at that moment.

"Hi," I said simply. "I wasn't expecting to see you here." We had seen each other in Chicago fairly regularly as he often paid visits to the magazine, but as things had gone well, he didn't need to provide much oversight. He had been more present recently as we worked to transition Blair to his new role, but everything had gone as well as could be expected.

He had stopped making overtures to me once he realized that despite the distance, Rocky wasn't going anywhere. They had even gone out for an impromptu beer one evening when I got stuck with a work issue and needed to get both of them out of my office. Although my romantic feelings for Cole were long over, I was glad that he was my friend. He was incredibly busy running a large company, and it was very nice that he had made his way all the way up to Camden. It wasn't an easy place to get to, and it meant a lot that he was there for such a big day in my life.

"Well, you know that you're family to me now. Ugh, that sounds kind of bad, because you and I... oh, never mind. I don't know what I'm trying to say." He looked almost bashful standing in front of me, shrugging his shoulders. It was not normal to see Cole at a loss for words. Rocky walked by us, handed Cole a beer bottle, and kept walking. I couldn't have adored him more at that moment. "That guy of yours, Janie, I can't help but love him. I didn't want to, but you found yourself a good one. I'm happy for you. And for all of this, too. I hate that you've left the magazine, but this is good. I'm really proud of you." He was sincere and sweet. We had come very far in all of this.

"Thank you. That means a lot to me. Really more than you could ever know." I opened my arms and gave him a hug, and it felt normal and good. "When are you heading back to, well, wherever you're going next?" Cole was dividing his time these days between New York and Chicago, with occasional trips to L.A.

"In the morning," he said. "Flying from Bangor to LaGuardia. I grabbed a room for tonight at the Samoset. Looks nice?"

"It's the best place up here," I replied. "You should come over to Alyssa's after this. Everyone is hanging out there for probably the rest of the day. It'll be—" I spotted Meredith Ashton carrying the platter of caprese salad away from the table and heading towards the kitchen. "Will you excuse me for a second?" I ran after Meredith and weaved my way around the small gatherings of guests and into the kitchen.

Once I was in there, I saw Meredith instructing the staff about the "proper" way to make the salad. She had already taken all of the mozzarella off of the platter and was taking a small container out of her purse. She began sprinkling what appeared to be gorgonzola cheese on the tomatoes and basil. "And this way you get a very nice mix of flavors, much bolder than with that silly bland mozzarella," she said.

"What the hell are you doing, Meredith? This is my recipe and my salad." I was done being polite. And a container of cheese *from her purse*? She had driven up from Cape Elizabeth hours earlier. I shuddered at the thought of the effects of a late summer day in a leather purse on a perishable foodstuff.

"Oh dear, I was just trying to help. Your staff is just learning how cook and can really benefit from an experienced chef," she said. Her opinion of herself was really remarkable. *Experienced chef?*

"This is not my staff," I replied. "These are college employees who work at these kinds of events many times every week. They're fine." I took the tainted platter and dumped the contents into the nearby trashcan. Meredith gasped. "We're done in here," I said. "Let's go find Lance and Kate. I think things are getting serious between them. Maybe she'll be your daughter-in-law someday soon." I said, leading a bug-eyed Meredith out of the kitchen and back out into the event room. "Kate!" I said when I saw her. "Do you know how to cook?" She shook her head. "Meredith *loves* to cook. Maybe she can teach you." I left them to themselves, as Meredith began launching into her perspective on salmon pot pie. I laughed to myself as I walked towards Rocky, who was chatting with Jimmy and Scarlett.

I pulled him away from them, took his beer out of his grasp and set it on a nearby table, and grabbed both of his hands.

"Hi," he said. "What's up? You look like you have something to say."

"I've never been so happy in my entire life." I felt my eyes filling up with tears but tried to ignore them.

Rocky squeezed both of my hands. "Even though the reason that we're here is kinda, you know, awful?"

"Despite all of that, yes. I've got everyone here in one room. You, my sister, the girls, Patrick with all of his faults, Scarlett and Jimmy and Blair and Bryan and Cole and even Lance and Kate Heathcliff. Chris and Anne. Even ridiculous Meredith and that saint William who is married to her. My whole life is in one room. I guess that's what people always say about their weddings, and now I understand it. You look around and everyone you care about is in one place." I looked around and it was both surreal and wonderful.

Rocky smiled. "So, we'll have to recreate this again sometime soon then," he said, holding up my left hand and pretending to inspect it. I laughed. Despite the day's spelling mishaps and rancid gorgonzola, I was going to focus on love and joy.

Alyssa came up next to us. "I hate to interrupt whatever is going on here, but the caterers are clearing everything away. I think we are supposed to vacate soon. Let's get everyone to head over to my place. I told Cole that he can be the DJ. All Billy Joel all the time, I'm guessing? I figured that would make him feel less out of place."

"That's very charitable of you, Alyssa. We'll be right there." I looked at Rocky. "You ready for a rousing sing-along of 'We Didn't Start the Fire?'"

"Always," he said. "But I'm putting in my request for 'Vienna.' I really like that one."

"Seriously? That's Cole's favorite song," I said as we walked out of the Center and out into a sunny Maine late summer afternoon. I knew that there wouldn't be many more days like this with fall quickly approaching, but autumn was Maine at its best. There was so much to look forward to.

"Well, then we have more in common than I realized. I thought it was just our mutual admiration of you," he said, taking my hand and walking by my side across the street towards our family's houses. Susie and Trish were already darting across our two lawns, and Cole was blowing bubbles for them to run through. The rest of our friends and family were sitting on Adirondack chairs on the grass or on the porch of Alyssa's house, and Patrick was handing out drinks. As Rocky and I approached them, we were walking into our new life, and nothing had ever felt better.

Acknowledgements

Writing a debut novel is a big leap of faith, and I absolutely could not have done this without the tremendous support of so many wonderful people.

To Sheri Williams and Ashley Carlson at TouchPoint Press, I cannot thank you enough for making this a reality. Jenn Haskin, you are an incredible editor and delightful person to know. Thank you for understanding this book and helping me take it where it needed to go.

To Ursula DeYoung and everyone at Grub Street in Boston, thank you for your support and encouragement. To everyone in the Women's Fiction Writers Association, you are such fabulous motivators and friends. To the 2021 Debuts group, I'm so glad we all found each other!

I am surrounded by the best people imaginable in my life. To the women of the NHS Social Studies Department, you get me through most days. To the Bedford Mom Squad, I don't think I could have done this—or gotten through the past year—without you. And to the lifelong friends—Nick Davis, Kristin Vander Els, Lara Clark, Betsy Campbell, Rob Ayres, Lee Stoll, Page Hall 1995-1996, my SHS ladies past and present, Bates Thursday Night Crew… I love you all and am so lucky.

Stephanie Galvani is the first person to read anything I write, and I am beyond grateful for her discerning edits and friendship since we were in high school. Thank you for your support!